STALKED BY THE OTHERS

Claws skittered across linoleum. I kept one gun in front of me, aimed low, the other held at my shoulder with the business end pointed at the ceiling. The clicking and scraping sounds grew louder as I approached. Turning the corner, I barely registered what I was seeing before the gun popped again, impossibly loud in the enclosed space.

A wolf—silvery gray fur, not big enough to be Chaz—let loose with a howl, charging at me, its paws slipping on the slick tile as it shot around the table that still burned with the remains of a shattered Molotov. There was blood on its shoulder, but clearly the silver bullet wasn't enough to stop an enraged dominant Were. Jesus, the thing was *huge*—teeth as long as my fingers and a body that would put a St. Bernard to shame—and it looked like it was intent on latching onto my throat. . . .

Books by Jess Haines

HUNTED BY THE OTHERS

TAKEN BY THE OTHERS

DECEIVED BY THE OTHERS

STALKING THE OTHERS

Collections

NOCTURNAL
(with Jacquelyn Frank,
Kate Douglas, and Clare Willis)

THE REAL WEREWIVES
OF VAMPIRE COUNTY
(with Alexandra Ivy, Angie Fox, and Tami Dane)

Published by Kensington Publishing Corporation

STALKING THE OTHERS

AN H&W INVESTIGATIONS NOVEL

JESS HAINES

ZEBRA BOOKS
KENSINGTON PUBLISHING CORP.
http://www.kensingtonbooks.com

ZEBRA BOOKS are published by

Kensington Publishing Corp.
119 West 40th Street
New York, NY 10018

All Kensington titles, imprints, and distributed lines are available at special quantity discounts for bulk purchases for sales promotion, premiums, fund-raising, educational, or institutional use.

Special book excerpts or customized printings can also be created to fit specific needs. For details, write or phone the office of the Kensington Special Sales Manager: Attn.: Special Sales Department. Kensington Publishing Corp., 119 West 40th Street, New York, NY 10018. Phone: 1-800-221-2647.

Zebra and the Z logo Reg. U.S. Pat. & TM Off.

ISBN-13: 978-1-4201-2402-6
ISBN-10: 1-4201-2402-1

First Printing: July 2012

10 9 8 7 6 5 4 3 2 1

Printed in the United States of America

ACKNOWLEDGMENTS

Of course, I need to thank my eagle-eyed beta readers. Binah, for putting up with my squeamishness. Kristin, for her pep talks about strippers and for listening to my whining. Allison, for being an amazing cheerleader. Eve, for being Eve, and once again loaning me the use of Christoph. KB, for believing in my ability to write smut from the very beginning (I'm saving Devon for you, I promise). Tori, for telling me to hurry the heck up and get on with things already, and sending me cookies. And my Chocolate Thunder for riding in on her white stallion to save my ass at the last minute like Lady Godiva. You guys rock my socks.

As always, I also need to thank my agent, Ellen, for being amazing at all things.

John, I'm totally framing your acceptance letter for this book. Thank you for your kind, and very flattering words, as well as putting up with my endless questions. Oh, and trust me, you don't want to know where I learned to write that stuff. . . .

Last, but not least, I need to thank the guy who jumpstarted all this writing business. I'll never forget what I owe you for that.

Chapter 1

My fingertips pressed against the cool stone of the ledge, helping me balance as I crouched on the balls of my feet. The heavy winds choked with smog and tainted with the stink of the Hudson threatened to push me off the edge of the apartment building's roof if I wasn't careful.

People bundled against the cold moved five stories below me, oblivious, never thinking to look up. Hours had passed since I'd fled Alec Royce's apartment building with nothing but murder on my mind. It had taken me a while to find my current perch. I'd been waiting up here for nearly an hour after first checking inside the apartment, and my mark had not yet shown. Strain burned in my calves, but I remained as I was, held in check despite my desire to rampage through the city, destroying everything in my path until I found my targets.

'You are so impatient,' a voice, tinged with an edge of laughter, whispered in the back of my skull. *'Just wait. He has to come home sometime.'*

I growled, the sound reverberating deep in my chest.

'Touchy.'

"Shut up," I snapped, running my fingers through my hair to shove the errant curls out of my eyes. "If he doesn't come soon, I won't have enough time to do anything. The sun will be up in less than an hour." I'd been counting on Dillon's being home so I could destroy the bastard before he hurt someone else. Or at least beat him into new and interesting shapes to make him think twice before infecting another uncontracted human.

'Maybe he spent the night with someone. Or left for work before we arrived.'

I didn't say anything, a pang of doubt giving me pause. The belt wrapped around my waist was the source of the voice in my head, a voice that would be banished once the sun rose. Aside from getting rid of my moral support and snarky commentary, the first rays of morning light creeping over the horizon would also take with them all of my enhanced skills and senses, leaving me frail and human again. Though most of the time I hated what the belt did to me, I couldn't afford to be without its help while facing down an angry werewolf.

'Then wait until tomorrow night to face him. Use the

day wisely; get some rest and food to build up your strength, and use those P.I. skills of yours to track him down.'

I nodded, turning away from the street and huddling into my trench coat against the cold. Now that I'd had a few hours for my ire to cool, I found that I was suffering from a wintry, calculating hatred instead of the heated, unthinking rage that had driven me here to begin with. Despite the wait's really weighing on my nerves, it had given me plenty of time to think about what I was going to do once Dillon showed his face, and what I would do about the other Sunstrikers who had driven me to hunt them like the cowardly dogs they were.

In the space of a few days, my entire life had turned upside down. It hadn't been particularly normal to begin with, but my now very ex-boyfriend Chaz had been cheating on me. He'd also been running some kind of werewolf mafia ring right under my nose. Though I had no solid proof, I was sure his pack had something to do with the murder of Jim Pradiz. Not that I'd liked the sleazy reporter, but it was terrifying to know that the werewolves were willing to stoop so low to silence him.

To top things off, one of the Sunstrikers had scratched and quite possibly infected me with the lycanthropy virus. It would be weeks before I'd know for sure if I was going to join the ranks of the terminally furry come the next full moon. Clearly, thanks to the murder of Jim Pradiz— which the Sunstrikers were somehow connected to, I just knew it—I would never be one of that pack, whether or not they accepted me. It was entirely possible that they were out to kill me, too.

Thanks to Chaz's pack, I was on the run from a bunch of murderous werewolves, the police, and half the media in the state. The last straw had been my father's telling me point-blank that I wasn't his little girl anymore. Being disowned by my family for my involvement with the Others had been a gut blow I wasn't prepared for. Recalling the raspy, accusing tones of my dad as he forbade me from ever coming home to him and Mom again made my eyes burn, but I'd cried my last tear over his pronouncement hours ago. I had work to do to make sure that the people involved with bringing this load of misery down on me and my family paid for everything they'd done. My resolve only firmed as I paused at the edge of the roof, looking down at the rusting metal framework of the fire escape that would lead me back to the filthy alleyways and webwork of New York City streets below.

Considering it was Chaz and the rest of his pack's fault that everything—my life, my livelihood, my family, and possibly my humanity—had been taken from me, I was not in a forgiving mood.

'*That's an understatement.*'

The droll tone of the belt had me grinning, though it was more a feral baring of my teeth than an expression of agreement. Stone chipped under my fingers as they tightened on the cornice mold-ing on the edge of the roof. I absently flicked blood from my fingertips before dropping lightly down to the fire escape. It clanged dully at the impact, the sound rattling through the framework. I barely gave it time to finish shuddering before I leapt over the side, my already-healed fingers catching on the rail as I propelled myself down to the level below. Ladders and startled faces in windows passed in a blur, my body moving with the grace and surety of an Olympic gymnast and my stomach edging up into my lungs as I gained speed. Soon, much too soon, I was airborne.

Before I knew it, I was in a feral crouch on the alley floor, hair in my eyes and trench coat billowing around me like one of those clichéd action movie heroes, and the last echoes of my landing ricocheting off the alley walls. An inhuman feat I wouldn't have been able to accomplish a few weeks ago without breaking my legs, even with the belt's help. Something about giving in and letting the belt take over had changed how we worked together; it augmented my strength, speed, agility, and stamina to a far greater degree than the first time I had worn it. Not to mention, it helped me heal my minor injuries nearly as quickly as a vampire. I wondered if this was what it felt like to be an Other.

Adrenaline burned in my veins, but I didn't give in to the belt's siren song or halfhearted pleas for violence. Instead, I shoved my hands in my pockets and edged out of the shadows, past the

Dumpsters, and into the trickle of pedestrian traffic in the city street.

Clenching my fingers around one of the vials of Amber Kiss perfume and the box of ammo I'd shoved in my pockets didn't hurt, though flakes of dried blood and scar tissue from cuts received and healed on my way down from the rooftop rubbed off in the process. I didn't want to think about what I had become, or what I would be once I saw my quest for revenge to its end.

'*If not for the vampire, you wouldn't be in this mess,*' the belt whispered. '*You should plan to remove him, too.*'

"Aside from the fact that he'd kill me if I tried it, Royce didn't do this to me," I muttered under my breath. "Don't push me."

A woman walking next to me glanced over, arching a silver-studded brow before ignoring me. That was the most attention I'd received from any of the sea of pedestrians all night. Not that I was complaining.

'*He might not have infected you, but he's the one who brought you back into Chaz's sights, and he's also the one who keeps involving you in supernatural business. You wouldn't have been bitten by vampires—*'

"Enough!"

I nearly shouted the word, and this time I did merit a few stares from early morning strollers, late night revelers sloshing their way home, and a handful of people in power suits on their way to the office. Ducking my head and popping up the collar of my trench coat, I sped up the pace, growling under my breath. I would've snarled something nasty back at the belt, especially since it was laughing at me again, but I was attracting too much attention as it was.

In fact, only yards away from me, a black-and-white was cruising past. I couldn't help but watch over my shoulder as it went by before realizing how conspicuous that must look. I drew out of the press of foot traffic to pretend to consider buying a magazine at a nearby newsstand. My stomach did a turn at the headline on one of the local rags: "NEW YORK'S HOTTEST VAMPIRE-SPONSORING CHARITY CONCERT!" There was a picture of him on the cover of the latest issue of some financial news magazine, too. I twisted away, scowling. No matter how far I ran, it seemed Alec Royce would follow me everywhere.

Oh, great. When I looked back, the cops had pulled into the alley I had just come from, flicking on their searchlight as they parked.

That was my cue to hightail it. I needed to be less conspicuous if I was going to carry out my plans without ending up dead or in jail before the month was out. Abandoning my feeble ruse, I turned and took to a brisk walk in the opposite direction from Dillon's apartment building.

I needed to figure out where to go once the sun came up. After the stunt I'd pulled, there was no way I was putting myself back under Royce's watchful eye. Knowing the vampire, he'd chain me up in the basement or something to keep me from escaping again. Going home was out of the question, as was Sara's house and my parents'. Arnold might let me crash, but he'd tell Sara, which meant the vampire would know where to find me. I didn't want that.

Not to mention that I didn't have any money to get myself to my theoretical daytime hiding spot. In my headlong rush to escape Royce's building, I hadn't taken any necessities with me but my hunting equipment. My duffel with my clothes and my purse had been left behind.

Assuming I survived long enough, I needed to work on my ability to plan ahead.

Chapter 2

My options for transportation were not quite as slim as the pickings for places to safely hide until the next full moon.

Fingering the vials of Amber Kiss perfume in my pockets and absently dodging pedestrians, I scanned the streets for some inspiration. I could utilize the belt's benefits for another half an hour or so and make good time getting across town—but I didn't like the idea of being caught somewhere in the city without money, food, or shelter, not to mention tired enough to fall over. From experience, I knew all of the "little hurts" that didn't hurt so much now would make themselves known as soon as the spirit inside the rune-branded leather was banished for the day.

Flickering neon lights dragged my attention to a tattoo parlor across the street. Aside from a regret-filled pang—I'd never again hear my mom telling me not to even think about getting inked—it sparked an idea. Jack the White Hat had an illegal weapons emporium under a tattoo parlor not far from here.

As much as I disliked Jack, he had a decent hideout, weapons, and a safe place to avoid authorities. We hadn't parted on the best of terms the last time I'd seen him, but I was willing to bet he'd set aside his personal dislike of me if I let him use me the way he'd so obviously intended to from the beginning. While willingly going along with his plans wasn't a fantastic idea, I felt certain that he would welcome me if he knew I wanted to use his hunters and their resources to track and kill werewolves.

Imbued with a new sense of purpose, I picked up my pace, intending to hoof it the rest of the way.

The cops waiting for me when I rounded the corner had a different plan in mind.

Two boys in blue had double-parked and waited in that I'm-doing-my-best-to-look-casual-and-failing-miserably stance just to one side of a newspaper stand. The one on the left spoke up, his voice smooth and deep, nonthreatening.

"Ms. Waynest? We need to talk."

I turned and ran.

"Hey! Halt!"

I kept going and didn't look back. The belt was elated by this sudden action, flooding my limbs with enough energy to make my speed kick up a notch, leaving the cops far behind. Jumping over or darting around obstacles was a breeze, and most everyone moved out of my way, but I was attracting too much attention.

Stairs leading down to the subway appeared on my left. I cut across the street, dodging honking, swerving cars with ease. Strangely, I didn't feel in the least frightened of being hit by one of those cars—they were zooming by fast enough to send my hair flying and to clip the trailing hem of my jacket—but I was worried about being caught by one of the cops. Priorities, eh?

As soon as I hit the sidewalk on the other side, I bolted down into the darkened stairwell, sending people flat against the rails as I shouldered aside the ones who didn't immediately get out of my way. Ignoring the curses and threats and even the switchblade one of them pulled on me, I took the stairs two and three at a time until I hit the bottom, jumping over the turnstiles and launching myself down the platform.

There were shouts, but I dismissed them and went to the edge. Some of the people milling around waiting for the next train were staring at me, but most of them didn't seem to care that I'd drawn the ire of one of the few security guards on the premises. Probably because the majority of them were not pleased to be awake at this hour.

The guard was headed my way with a glare and her hand settled firmly on the butt of a canister of mace attached to her belt. Just my luck to be spotted by a rent-a-cop on the one day I decide to jump the turnstiles instead of paying my fare.

With a surge from the belt, I ignored the shouting security guard and jumped onto the tracks—

taking care to avoid the electrified third rail—hightailing it into the tunnel. It was dark and disgustingly grimy, infested with rats and roaches, but there was no rumble of an approaching train or sounds of pursuit that I could detect. My eyes watered from the combined stink of hot metal, grease, and old piss no doubt left behind by the homeless who roamed these tunnels. Once I was sure I was in the clear, I slowed down just enough to take a look around, searching for any doors or stairwells to maintenance rooms that might have street access.

'*Why don't you just head to the next platform? You were trying to get across town, remember?*'

"Security is probably waiting for me. Can't risk it. Jack's place isn't far, maybe a mile or two from where the cop stopped me." I rolled my shoulders, groaning as the first hints of strain bit into my muscles. The spirit was fading. Daylight must be creeping over the horizon. "I've got to get out of here before you go. How much longer?"

'*Not long.*'

Crap. With that helpful tidbit in mind, I sped up my pace, eyes searching. It wasn't my imagination either—the tracks had started vibrating, warning of an approaching train. Using some of my remaining energy, I leapt with a distinct lack of grace onto the narrow service walkway, digging my nails into the thick crust of dirt coating the walls to find purchase as I slid in an oily puddle.

A roach the size of a VW Bus crawled over my fingers in its haste to scuttle into a crevice I hadn't seen.

I shrieked and danced back. The sound echoed dimly, lost in the eerie screech of a distantly braking train.

That, and the laughter of the belt.

Scowling, I stomped down the walkway, rubbing my grimy hand on my jacket to rid myself of that skin-crawly feeling. Though I'd felt its approach, I gasped and flattened myself against the wall as the train coming from behind me lit up the tunnel. I watched with wide eyes as it raced by only inches away, lights flickering and blinding me as it passed.

Heart pounding, I resumed my trek down the tunnel once the train was gone and I was no longer blinded by bright spots. The belt had almost completely faded when I found a recessed door. Locked. Using what little extra strength it could give me, I kicked it just to one side of the knob, splintering the wood around the handle. It jarred the lock, but didn't force the door open as I'd hoped. Five minutes earlier, I could have blown it off its hinges.

Aches and pains worked their way from my feet up my legs, reminding me that I'd been sitting in an uncomfortable crouch for most of the night when I wasn't playing at being a marathon runner. I got the door open with one more kick and, with a wince, hobbled inside.

It wasn't much to look at. There were a few old electric panels and some lockers looming in the shadows, and the only light drifted in on dust-laden beams through the broken door. It was cooler and less humid in here. The floor was cleaner than the tunnel, and someone had left an empty bottle of soda on a bench, but otherwise it didn't look like anyone had been by in a while. I wasn't too worried about the tracks I was leaving—walking was too painful for me to focus on much else.

Limping, I made my way to the lockers. All locked or empty. Though I was tempted to settle down and rest on the bench for a few minutes, I knew I wouldn't get up again if I gave in to temptation.

Exhaustion was settling in right next to the pain, dual sensations guaranteed to haunt me the entire way to the tattoo parlor. If only I'd thought to bring some money with me before I ran out of Royce's home, I could have caught a cab and saved myself the pain.

Muttering under my breath, I searched for a light switch, running my hand along the wall next to the lockers. It wasn't necessary to flick it once I found it; it was right next to a door that clearly led outside, since I could hear sounds of traffic and voices behind it. The knob turned easily under my hand, and I was greeted by a set of litter-strewn steps leading up to a narrow, street-level alley. A gated fence topped with barbed wire kept out any intruders.

Every step burned like hot knives being shoved into my heels and calves. Holy mother, I'd have to remember to tone it down next time I used the belt. Even my fingers ached when I gripped the railing.

By the time I reached the top, I had to stop for

a breather, my eyes watering with pain. I had no idea how I was going to make it to the tattoo parlor like this, but I couldn't sit down to rest yet.

I shuffled across the alley like an old woman with arthritic knees. The gate didn't give me any trouble, opening silently on oiled hinges. No one paid me much mind as I crept out into the pedestrian traffic. This part of midtown wasn't far from where I needed to be. My run had taken me closer than I'd thought. Thank goodness.

Huddling into my trench coat, I popped the collar and ducked my head. Though every step was torture, I doggedly kept my speed to a decent clip, nearly matching that of the people around me. Every time I passed a deli or bakery, my mouth watered at the scent of fresh coffee and pastries. At this point, I wouldn't be above begging Jack for food, either.

As intent as I was on reaching my destination, my body was equally intent on slowing the hell down and curling up for a nap. Despite my need to hurry, I had to stop a few times to rest. People looked at me askance when I paused to lean heavily against cars or walls or telephone poles to catch my breath. These breaks came more and more frequently, and my eyes were starting to feel like they had bricks tied to the lids.

By the time I reached the store, it must have been past eight. Some kid with a Mohawk and a faded T-shirt with a logo for some band I'd never heard of was bustling around in the back, moving some stuff around. He looked up from behind the counter, his mouth falling open as he took in my hair flying in a frizzy red halo around my head, my no doubt haggard expression, and the three silver stakes lined up in a neat row on the belt around my waist. I lightly tapped them with my free hand, and his expression shifted from shock to unease.

"I need to see Jack," I said. Well, I meant to. What came out was more like a raspy smoker's growl.

"Excuse me?"

I cleared my throat, trying again. "Jack. Is he here?"

"Jack who?"

I gave him a look. The kid blanched, rubbing the back of his neck. "No. He's not around, but Nikki is." His shifty eyes and nervous behavior could be put down to nerves due to my appearance, but I was willing to bet he was lying to me. "Do you want me to get her for you?"

My pain-addled brain fumbled with this mystery for the ages. Nikki was one of the hunters, I recalled. A blonde with a penchant for sharp weapons and guns who'd only made an impression on me because she was the lone female hunter I'd met in Jack's cadre of White Hats. Her attitude toward me didn't make me inclined to think she'd be willing to play nice, but if Jack wasn't around, I'd take what I could get.

"Yes," I managed, gesturing weakly for the guy to find Nikki for me. There were a couple of plastic chairs set up around a table with books of tattoos. I sank into a seat and buried my face in my hands before remembering all the gross stuff I'd touched. Ugh, my face and hair were probably caked with grime.

A few minutes later, Nikki came striding out of the back, her hips swaying in low-slung jeans. A small jewel glinted at her navel, framed by the cropped T-shirt she was wearing. She wiped sweat from her brow with one arm, her free hand resting ever so nonchalantly on the handle of a hunting knife as long as my arm. The kid didn't come with her; he was probably hiding in the back. Wise move.

"I thought you were done with us, corpse-bait. What are you doing here?"

Well, nice to know I'm still loved by some people.

"Nice to see you, too, Nikki," I said, putting in an extra effort to keep my words from slurring. "Listen, I need a favor—"

"That's a laugh. How will you repay us this time? Walk out again as soon as you get what you want?"

I scowled, flushing.

She stalked closer, resting one hand flat on the glass display case holding an array of silver studs and plugs. The other circled the hilt of the blade in a clear threat. "Listen, bitch. My brother didn't have to help you. He risked everything to—"

"That's enough, Nikki."

Jack was in the doorway, his icy blue eyes rimmed in red, his cheeks a little more sunken than I remembered. His face had always been made of sharp angles and planes, but those cheekbones were now razor sharp. His frame was thinner than I recalled, too. Almost corpse-like. An illness? Nikki dropped the attitude and immediately went to his side, placing a concerned hand on his shoulder.

Then it hit me.

The two of them were related? I hadn't picked up on it before, but the family resemblance was obvious seeing them next to each other now. Using violence and threats to solve all of their problems must run in the family. Jack's expression was decidedly unamused. He didn't appear happy to see me at all. Not that I was much surprised by this.

"Shiarra, I didn't think I'd ever see you again. Not in daylight."

I forced a thin smile. "No need to worry about that. I'm not planning on turning into a walking corpse anytime soon." No, I just might turn into something else. Something worse.

"Why are you here?"

What an excellent question. I wasn't about to tell him it was because I could no longer afford to hide with Royce. The vampire most likely would have tried to prevent me from carrying out the plan I had formed to get rid of Chaz and his pack, and I didn't have enough time to risk being detained. The White Hats were my best shot at ensuring the Sunstrikers were destroyed before the next full moon.

The werewolves needed to be stopped before any other innocent bystanders got hurt or killed because of a connection to the werewolves. If I turned into a monster at the end of the month, I'd be one of them. It was imperative that I found and stopped Chaz, Dillon, and any of the other

Sunstrikers who were responsible for the deaths of a number of people who had been infected outside of a legally binding contract with an Other and then killed before they could press charges. Even if not for myself or those other victims, I owed it to Jim Pradiz, also murdered—most likely due to his last big story that leaked the names of the victims and the local Were packs involved—to do my best to stop them.

I met Jack's expectant gaze with a steady look of my own, praying he would consider my request. After how I'd walked out on him and the rest of the White Hats some months ago, declaring them too extremist for my tastes, to join forces with Royce against Max Carlyle, it wouldn't be out of line for him to flip me off and send me on my merry way.

"I'm here to ask for your help. There isn't an easy way for me to say this, and I'm too tired for tact. There's a chance I might become a Were at the next full moon."

Nikki stared. Jack said nothing, a tic starting in his cheek.

"I came here because someone from my ex's pack might have infected me. I want to find him. I want to make him and the rest of the Sunstrikers pay." I left out the part about what Chaz had done. He might have been the alpha of the Sunstriker pack, but he was a poor decision maker, and I wanted cheating on me to be the last mistake he ever made. "There are people after me, including police. If I do turn into one of . . . into an Other at the end of the month, I know I can trust you to end it. Until then, I need a place to stay, and some-one to work with me to find where the Weres are hiding. Will you help me?"

Nikki's wide-eyed stare grew into a rather unbe-coming gawp that made me want to walk over to shut her mouth, if only my feet didn't hurt so much.

For his part, Jack wasn't showing any emotion. His only reaction was to lift one hand to rub at the pale stubble on his jaw. I think it's the first time I'd ever seen him anything but clean-shaven.

He edged around Nikki and rested both palms flat on the display case as he loomed over it. The intensity of his gaze was a bit much, and I found I couldn't meet his eyes directly as he examined me.

"You realize what you're asking? You know what we'll do if you turn?"

That question gave me enough courage to meet his eyes again. "Yes, I know. I'm counting on it."

His smile, white and shark-like, sent a shiver down my spine. "Welcome to the White Hats."

Chapter 3

"Not that I'm not pleased that you came to us first, but what changed your mind? As I recall, you were more interested in siding with the monsters last time we spoke."

The smell of the place—cigarette smoke and stale beer—was getting under my skin. Though I was bordering on too-tired-to-care territory, I used the back of my hand to rub at my eyes, hoping I wasn't grinding dirt under the lids. "Yeah, I know."

Nikki gave a growl that would have done a Were proud. "That's it? Just 'I know'? No apology?"

It took a great deal of effort to muster the energy to give Nikki a glare, but once I did, her already pale skin whitened, and she couldn't meet my gaze. There was something eminently satisfying about her reaction, but it also gave me the feeling I was turning into something I didn't want. Forcing my eyes away, staring at some of the pithy T-shirts and posters plastering the walls behind the counter, I mustered up the apology she and Jack so obviously wanted.

"I'm sorry. You were right when you warned me not to trust them. Blind, stupid luck is all that's kept me alive this far. I'm surprised I survived that vacation, to be honest. Though I'm wondering how you knew something bad would happen to me there, Jack. You tried to warn me ahead of time. How did you know something was up?"

Jack had folded his arms over the counter and was using it to support most of his weight. He shifted, his boots squeaking on the cheap tile, not answering me right away. He coughed and mumbled something, so I dragged my attention back to him to see what was wrong.

So help me, the man was blushing.

"Come on, Jack," I said, smiling despite myself. "You can tell me."

The big bad hunter covered his eyes with one hand. "We never stopped watching you. Didn't have a choice."

Didn't have a choice? That sounded ominous. Odd to think the hunter was embarrassed about spying on me. Or maybe it was due to his failure to recruit me?

"I kept hoping you'd change your mind. Leave the leeches and the dogs alone. There was some word on the local OtherNet message board that the Sunstrikers were planning a trip, and that you'd be going with them. There was a group of people calling themselves the Nightstrikers who were making threats and saying they were going to cause some kind of trouble."

"Oh," I said, unable to think of something more coherent to give in response. This was not the first time I'd heard of the OtherNet, but things were becoming clearer to me now. I'd have to investigate it further, once I had access to a computer again.

"I should have stopped it somehow. Should have known there would be trouble like this."

Nikki lightly punched his shoulder. "Don't start that shit again. . . ."

"Jack, please don't beat yourself up over it. Nobody could have foreseen the trouble I ran into out there. The Nightstrikers weren't after me, they were after Chaz. They're decent guys, and they wouldn't have hurt me."

I hated to think that Jack was looking like hell because he had been worried about me, but I was starting to suspect it. He took his work far too seriously.

His icy response made me blink and wonder whether I'd really seen that chink in his emotional armor at all.

"You don't understand, do you? Don't you know why I wanted you to join us?"

I blinked at this sudden turn in topic. This conversation was giving me whiplash. "Uh, no. Not really." I couldn't say I had cared before now, either.

Jack rose to his full height, which would have

been more impressive if he wasn't skinny as a rail. He came around the counter and pulled out a chair across from me, studying me intently. I shifted uncomfortably under that probing look, finding both the topic and his scrutiny to be out of place. Though I'd known in advance that this conversation was coming, I had hoped he wouldn't want to hash all this out right from the start.

"You really don't," he said, something like wonder tingeing his voice.

"Just tell her," Nikki said, using her foot to nudge a box aside from the counter so she could lean her hip against it and watch us from across the room. Her blue eyes, so like Jack's, blazed with some emotion I couldn't place. With the two of them staring at me like that, I was starting to feel a bit like a kid caught with her hand in a cookie jar.

"I was hoping Devon would replace me," Jack said, and I started at the mention of the other hunter's name. Devon, too, had unsuccessfully tried to reach me before I left on my vacation to the Catskills. He'd also abandoned the White Hats to come play with me on the side of the good vampires about a month ago. I hadn't seen him since the morning after the fight against Max Carlyle in Royce's basement. "He seemed like a good choice. He was smart, capable, a fine leader, and an experienced hunter. It's unfortunate he decided to leave."

"Why do you need a replacement?" I thought the question was safe, but the sound Nikki made clued me in that it was an uncomfortable topic. "And what does that have to do with me?"

Jack laughed, though there wasn't any humor to the sound. He reached into his shirt pocket and plucked out a pack of cigarettes and a lighter. I shook my head when he offered me one. He didn't speak again until after he'd plucked out a cig with his thin lips and lit up, taking a deep drag.

"I'm dying."

Though I wanted to be sorry for him, knew it was the right thing to be feeling, I couldn't find it in me to react. Maybe I was out of emotional room for surprise with all my own baggage taking up the space in my mind. He took another drag before continuing, meeting my gaze frankly and without any sign of fear or self-pity I could detect.

He was brave. I'd give him that.

"Cancer. Both lungs." He held up the cigarette. "Always knew these would be the death of me, if hunting didn't take me first."

"Don't say that, you asshole," Nikki said quietly, her voice hitching. I didn't dare look at her. She didn't need me to see her tears. "You won't die, damn it. Don't say it again."

Jack glanced at her, then back at me. His lips quirked in a sardonic smile. Gallows humor. "I've known for a long time it was coming. Nobody here was smart enough or ruthless enough to take my place. We tried to groove Devon in, but he just wasn't a fit. Nobody here could stomach the idea of it. Then I heard about a P.I. Some new girl who hated vampires, but was working with them anyway. Someone trying to save a kid from a leech."

I stared at him blankly. Though I knew he was talking about me, David Borowsky had been anything but a victim of the vampires. Instead, he'd forced Alec Royce under his thumb. In the end, I'd saved the vamp—and destroyed the kid.

Jack knew that. So why had he pursued me?

"That's not how it really played out, I know. But I was grasping at straws. And I was being told to recruit you by someone I couldn't say no to." He grinned, again without humor, just a baring of gleaming white teeth. He must be religious about brushing, considering his smoking habit. "I do hope Tiny and I didn't scare you too badly. At first I was just trying to fuck up recruiting you to our cause. It was necessary at the time. I thought you were a pawn—and you were, no mistake—but not in the way I'd feared. It took me a while to realize that you could be useful."

Now that was surprising. As far as I knew, White Hats didn't answer to anyone but their own, and I'd thought Jack was the leader of this branch. "Who was telling you to recruit me? I'm afraid I can see where this is going, but I can't say I understand it yet."

"I'd thought you might have guessed by now. Alec Royce told me to do it."

I stared. Jack stared back.

I tried not to. I really did. But despite my best

efforts, I unleashed an explosive laugh right in Jack's face.

He frowned at me.

"Sorry," I said, once I got the worst of my giggles under control. "Really, sorry."

His frown deepened, and some of the red crept back into his cheeks. His discomfiture was due to his connection to the vampire then, not on my account. I should have known.

"I'm not joking, Shiarra. I made a deal when I was first diagnosed. His blood is all that's kept me alive this long. I'm bound to him, just like you were."

A loud noise from behind startled me. Nikki had kicked a nearby box into a wall and stalked into the back rooms. I turned back to Jack, wiping any lingering mirth off my face. "I'm sorry. I had no idea."

"Neither do most of the other White Hats," Jack confessed. "It would tear the organization apart. Only a select few know. Once I told Devon, he didn't want to take over. Nikki is too hot-tempered to lead, even if she wanted to, and Royce won't abide Tiny's taking my place. He wanted someone he could control to take over for me. It's why he thought you might be a good fit. I'm running out of time, and we need someone sympathetic to his cause who will still hunt vampires or other dangerous Others under his direction."

I considered this. The White Hats were supposedly against all things with fangs or fur, the more active of the bunch going so far as to actively hunt them down, so if it got out that one of their leaders was bound to a vampire, the whole situation would turn into a clusterfuck of epic proportions. Jack either trusted me more than I had guessed, or he was so far gone in his illness that he no longer cared about the potential consequences of telling me his secrets.

Royce always had a million and one plans roiling in that devious mind of his. It wasn't unlikely that my becoming a member of the White Hats was some kind of backup plan, or maybe something he'd been considering using me for all along. My potentially turning Other must have thrown some kind of wrench into his plans. Who knew what he wanted to use me for now. Or how he would have broken the news to me if he really had wanted me to take over the White Hats' New York chapter.

That the vampire had his fingers in so many pies was unsurprising. What worried me was the possibility that he might use his connection with the White Hats to keep tabs on me. Or maybe force me back to his side.

The possibilities and second-guessing were making my already aching head hurt worse than ever.

Maybe the belt was right. I should consider getting Royce out of the way before he dragged me into something even worse than what the Sunstrikers had started.

Or maybe this little hunting trip of mine had been part of the vampire's plan all along.

"Listen, Jack, I'm sorry—very sorry—that you're ill. But I'm not leader material. Even if I don't turn, I'm not the person you need to run this kind of outfit. And I'll never answer to Royce. Being bound to him once was enough. If you tell him I'm here, I'll leave and find some other way to deal with this problem. But if you'll have me and keep my involvement secret, I could use your help. And I'll do what I can to help you, too—at least until I know what's going to happen to me."

Jack regarded me steadily, stubbing out the cigarette on the table. "I wouldn't expect any less from you. And don't worry. He doesn't know. He won't be able to drag it out of me unless he asks me directly. I've figured out how to play some of his games."

I started to relax, but he leaned forward, holding up a single digit.

"But—here's the deal. You owe me. Us. You owe the White Hats a favor. One we can call in at any time. In return, I'll give you a safe place to stay. I'll make the others help you hunt. It's something we might have done anyway, but at least we'll have good reason now."

Despite my worries, this was the best shot I had at bringing down the Sunstriker pack. I reached across the table to take his cool, dry hand and shake on it. A compact with the devil wasn't new to me, but I had the feeling I wouldn't live long enough to pay Jack and his White Hat buddies their favor back. If I did, I'd just have to bite the bullet and pay the price, because there was no way I could get my revenge working alone.

"Yes. We have a deal."

Chapter 4

Jack and Nikki had work to do, but there were some cots set up in the basement. They offered to let me catch up on sleep for a few hours until it was time for them to go back to their headquarters. I gratefully accepted.

After taking an age to get back on my feet and an exceedingly painful millennia to limp down the stairs, I collapsed into one of the cots in the storage area and slept for a while.

Nikki woke me with a rough shake some time later. All that kept me from punching her was the protesting ache in my muscles. Even so, I felt better, not quite so sore, and followed the two hunters to a black SUV parked a couple blocks away from the shop. The sun was still out, but the end of the workday was approaching and the streets were quickly becoming packed with traffic. I dozed again on the ride, the sounds of a low, droning announcer on the radio lulling me into a groggy stupor.

By the time we reached Jack's hideout, a spacious house in the exclusive community that made up City Island, I was too hungry to sleep and desperately hoping they would let me raid the fridge once we got inside.

"I need to make some calls," Jack said as he pulled into the garage next to another car, a beaten up Jeep that looked out of place next to the sleek lines of the Suburban. "Nikki will show you to a room and find you some clothes. After you shower, you remember where the kitchen is? Come down and we'll discuss who it is you're looking for over dinner."

I followed Nikki up the stairs (God, not more of those!) to a guest room that was warm, furnished, and showed signs of prior habitation. Somebody had left a stack of magazines touting the joys of hunting, big guns, and barely clothed biker babes on an end table next to a window with a fabulous view of the bay.

"Sorry," Nikki said, not sounding sorry at all. "Bo must have left these up here. Make yourself at home. I'll see if I have anything in my closet that would fit you, but there should be some men's sweats in the drawers that you can wear until we can get you some of your own clothes. Towels are in the cabinet across from the sink. See you in a few."

She shut the door behind her without bothering to wait for me to respond. From the looks of things, the upcoming month spent in close quarters with Nikki was going to be full of sunshine and rainbows.

With a great deal of groaning and pain, I shed

my jacket, my weapons, and the body armor that clung in a way reminiscent of leather to bare skin. Once I managed the contortionist acts necessary to get the clingy material off, I gingerly settled the pile of dirty clothing on the dresser and tucked the weapons, extra ammo, and Amber Kiss perfume into an empty dresser drawer.

The shower was one of the most heavenly experiences of my life. The pipes rattled a bit, and the water took an age to get hot, but it was a *real* shower. The warmth of the water sucked the aches right out of my muscles, and I used the crappy bar soap to scour the filth that had collected from my hands and face. I didn't stop scrubbing until the water spiraling down the drain was clear instead of a dingy gray.

By the time I finished, I was feeling relatively human again. With my hair lying in a damp tail down my back and the grossly oversized sweats rolled up over my wrists and ankles, I plodded downstairs to join Jack and Nikki again. The scent of steaks and veggies wafting out of the kitchen made me feel a little less awkward about wandering around a strange house in someone else's borrowed clothes.

I wasn't expecting the grumpy siblings to have invited company, and paused with a hand on the door as a few voices drifted out into the hall.

". . . and I don't see how you can assume the leech didn't plant her. You have an obsession with this woman, an unhealthy one, and I guarantee you she'll bring trouble to our door just like she did last time."

I didn't recognize the voice, which was male and edged with aggression. Another unfamiliar voice chimed in.

"I agree. We cannot trust that she is what she says. Why don't we kill her now and get it out of the way?"

I backed up a step, pressing a hand to my mouth. Jack spoke up next, and I wasn't quite certain if I was thankful that it was in my defense.

"We don't know for sure that she's been infected, and we have literally dozens of better uses we can put her to while she's still alive. I never said we should trust her, only that we should go along with her little scheme for now, because it might present a better opportunity for us later."

A yelp was forced out of me as someone shoved me through the swinging door, sending me stumbling into the room to meet the startled, distrustful eyes of half a dozen hunters. Nikki strolled in behind me, dusting her hands off, and I shot her a dirty look she soon returned in kind.

Then I had to face the hunters.

"Uh," I said.

Jack kicked out a chair beside him at the table, his eyes narrowed and jaw clenched. I shuffled over to it with as much dignity as I could muster, mumbling something that I hoped passed for a greeting so I wouldn't have to meet their probing gazes. Nobody said a thing as I gingerly lowered myself into the chair, or as I cast surreptitious, longing looks at the piles of steaks, veggies, and other trimmings placed around the table. No one had filled their plates yet, so I didn't dare reach for anything, and I wondered what the heck they were waiting for.

Nikki brought a couple of bottles of red wine to the table, popping the corks and pouring. At this point, I was too hungry to care about the awkward silence; I just wanted the wait to be over so I could dig into those heavenly-looking steaks. Once everyone had a full glass, she took a seat, and then we all started filling our plates.

"Shiarra," Jack said, startling me so badly I almost dropped the salad bowl on my lap, "I believe you remember Dr. Morrow and Bo, yes? If you haven't been introduced, I'd like you to meet Jason, Patrick, Adam, and Keith."

The other hunters gave me sparse nods as Jack said their names. Patrick, Adam, and Jason were watching me with mixtures of speculation and dislike. They looked vaguely familiar, and they all had the bodies of men who pumped iron and probably hid tattoos of things like barbed wire cuffs and flying hearts with "Mom" banners on them under their long-sleeved shirts. Keith, a skinny kid who reminded me of Arnold the mage, gave me a disinterested once-over before digging into his steak.

Dr. Morrow and Bo seemed to be the only people who didn't loathe me on sight. Dr. Morrow had treated me a few times when I'd been in scrapes before. I hadn't known until I was suffering from severe blood loss after a vampire bite that he was working for the White Hats.

A group of them, including Bo, had saved me from the clutches of a vampire bent on revenge. Why Max Carlyle had thought Royce cared enough about me to think that I would be useful as bait was still beyond me. Though I was grateful to the White Hats for saving me, I'd never considered becoming a member of their crazy organization. Bo had badly injured his leg in some fight or another (maybe in the process of saving me from Max?), and we'd spent some time together in the infirmary. Judging by the wink he gave me, he didn't begrudge my walking out on the White Hats to go back to Royce's side the way Jack and Nikki did.

"Still waiting for that movie night, chica," Bo said, giving me a flash of white teeth against dark skin. "Got any plans after dinner?"

"Sure, I owe you one," I replied, returning his smile in kind.

Patrick kicked Bo under the table, not so subtly that I missed it. Bo shot him a look before returning his attention to his meal. Jack sipped at his wine, not touching the small portions of food Nikki had put on his plate, earning a frown from her.

It was probably the most awkward dinner I've ever attended, even counting the time Chaz and Arnold came to my parents' house for my younger brother's birthday. Every time Bo would try to strike up a conversation with me, someone else would cut him off. Dr. Morrow was as disinterested as could be in anything but his food. Jack, Nikki, Patrick, Jason, and Adam seemed as if they couldn't care less whether I lived or died.

Keith surprised me by being the first to show interest. He finished his second helping before anybody else, and swirled the wine in his glass while he stared at me from across the table. He had to lean slightly to one side to peer around a vase of flowers Nikki must have put there as a centerpiece.

"So, you're looking for somebody, right? Is that why you're here?"

I glanced up, fork halfway to my mouth, uncertain if he really was talking to me. Everyone else but Bo feigned disinterest in the conversation.

"To hunt, right? Some Weres?"

"Yeah. Yes, I guess Jack must have told you. I had a run-in with the Sunstrikers. There are a few of them I need to find."

"Good," Keith said. He was surprisingly eager, leaning forward and setting his glass aside. "I'm the resident computer nerd, so it'll be my job to track them down. You have their full names? Addresses, places of work, anything like that?"

Though I knew my face was burning red, both from embarrassment and anger, I didn't hesitate. "Yes. The pack leader was my boyfriend. I can give you everything you need."

That earned another round of awkward silence. So, Jack hadn't told them everything. I was quick to cut into the quiet before they could start jumping to the wrong conclusions.

"I know where to find him. Plus, I'm a private investigator, so I can probably help you search. I'm not after the whole pack, just a few specific people."

"Oh," Keith said, his eyes aglow with excitement. "Oh, this is good. This is very good. Lady, forget your after-dinner movie. I'm going to need to pick your brain."

"Hey," Bo protested. "That's not fair."

Jack pushed his chair back, leaving his food untouched. "Fair? Who said anything about fair? We've got a month before we might have a new shifter on our hands, gentlemen. We move fast on this, or not at all."

Though his words turned my blood cold and killed what was left of my appetite, I nodded and firmed my resolve. With Keith's skills, and my knowledge of Chaz's haunts and my talent for skip tracing, it shouldn't take long at all to find the Sunstrikers.

I hoped.

Chapter 5

(Days left to full moon: 19)

"Stop that."

For the umpteenth time, I did my best to put a cap on my nervous fidgeting, but even Patrick's growled command couldn't scare me into being still for long. Soon the grip of one of my stakes was squeaking again as my fingers tightened on the leather.

We were waiting in a van parked outside of some skeezy-looking place called The Tease in northern Jersey. Nikki was in the bar wearing clothes that made her look like she might be one of the featured strippers taking a night off. How she expected to fight a werewolf in those heels and with that much skin showing was beyond me, but I had problems of my own.

Sitting in the van doing nothing was torture. The belt kept yammering about its violent urges and sending surges of adrenaline through me. If not for my worry about hitting innocent—okay, maybe not innocent, but *human*—bystanders, I might have charged in with guns blazing.

Keith hadn't been paying me much mind. His attention was focused on the panels in the back, and on listening in on Nikki's conversations through headphones that must have led a former life in a sound studio. Their equipment had drawn my interest for a while. Any P.I. worth their salt would have been drooling over the high-resolution video feeds, listening devices, and GPS tracking systems. Judging by the quality, I had to guess that some of the stuff was military grade.

If the belt hadn't been a constant earache—and if I weren't feeling so paranoid about whether or not I'd survive to return to my job as a private investigator once the month was out—I would've been far more interested. As it was, the van was too overcrowded and I was too irritated to do more than fidget.

We hadn't had any luck until yesterday digging up any information on where the Weres had gone to ground. Visiting Chaz's, Dillon's, and a few other Sunstrikers' homes a few times a day hadn't yielded anything of use, other than noting cops staking them out, too. Somehow the Weres had known, and found, places to hide where even I couldn't find them.

Finding out about Vic had been a stroke of luck. I'd been so frazzled by Chaz's disappearing act that I hadn't thought to search for one of the lower ranking Weres to interrogate until after two fruitless days of hunting for my ex. Jack didn't want to waste time and had used his network of contacts to find one of the thirty or so werewolves high enough in the pack who might know where Chaz and Dillon and the rest of the dominant wolves were hiding. Even then, it took some time to dig up the info.

Somehow, through whatever connections the White Hats had and some legwork on Keith's part, they'd tracked Vic Thomasian to this crappy neighborhood just a few miles southeast of the Newark airport. Nikki was supposed to lure him out. The stink of a nearby wharf and the surrounding industrial buildings only added to the charm of the sagging brick shithole. The place was cradled between two abandoned warehouses, centered in a cramped parking lot that had long since had the lights burned or shot out. The only illumination came from above the entrance in the form of a flickering neon sign depicting a dancing naked woman, and one other sign advertising Budweiser dimly seen through a dirty window.

The Were was in there, somewhere. His car, a rust bucket that might once have been a blue Geo, was parked at the far end of the lot. According to whomever it was Jack had contacted, Vic spent a good portion of his paycheck here on his nights off. So far, Nikki hadn't had any luck. Unless you counted nearly breaking the hand of the guy who tried to feel her up. It raised my respect of her a notch. She'd since settled at the bar, facing out so the tiny video camera hidden in the big gem in her necklace would pick up whatever was going on in the room. As much as it might have engrossed the boys in the van, I wasn't interested in the floor show.

"There he is."

I glanced up at Keith's announcement. He was pointing at a figure on the screen who was coming out of a back room toward the bar. The Sunstriker pack tattoo—a stylized sun pierced by a spear—was visible on his upper arm. Vic's stringy black hair looked greasier in the video than it had in the picture we'd found on the Internet. He slicked it back when he spotted Nikki, giving her a toothy smile. She must have returned it, because he took it as invitation enough to make a beeline to the empty seat beside her.

After Keith adjusted some dials and flipped a switch, obnoxious boom-boom music flooded out of some speakers, and Keith hung the headphones around his neck while we listened in on Nikki's conversation.

"Looking for a job, pretty girl? Or a good time?"

Nikki handled his proposition with more aplomb than I would have managed. "A little of both, baby. You think you can handle this?"

I missed whatever they said next. Between Keith and Bo's laughing so hard, Jason's making some kind of lewd comment, and Jack's shouting from the driver's seat for everybody to can it, it was impossible to hear anything. Everything simmered down once Nikki got up from her bar stool and took Vic's arm. They were headed for the exit.

Showtime.

Bo, Patrick, Jason, and Adam reached for their weapons. Mine were already on me, and it took effort to keep from surging to my feet and shoving my way past the men to the rear of the van. Jack eased his door open, not wanting to startle the target. We kept an eye on the video feed to make sure Nikki was leading Vic to the darker side of the building where we were hoping to pin him and force him to tell us where Chaz and the other Sunstrikers were hiding.

Everything was going according to plan. She tugged him away when he was making as if to go to his car, gesturing to the alley. Judging by the sudden leer and eagerness on his face, she must have given him one hell of a suggestive look. He practically shoved her toward the shadows.

That was our cue. Bo was the first out the door, and I was the last. I wasn't expecting it when Patrick grabbed me by the throat and yanked me back against the side of the van. The man had *huge* hands. He leaned right into me, his nose nearly touching mine, as he opened his mouth to speak.

I socked him in the solar plexus, and he staggered back with a groan, releasing me to clutch his stomach. With the belt's help, that little tap would have been nearly as painful as being punched by a shifted Were. Jogging to catch up with the others, I didn't look back. Jason and Adam paused when I passed, looking over their shoulders.

Moving to Jack's side, I reached for one of my handguns, now loaded with silver bullets courtesy of the Highly Illegal White Hat Weapons Emporium. They didn't trust me to be on the front line yet. Jack was supposed to move in to hit Vic with a stun gun as soon as he was distracted. Bo, Patrick, and Adam were going to wrap him in silver-plated chains. Jason and I were backup, meant to shoot to wound the Were if things got too hairy or he broke out of the chains. We needed to question, not kill, Vic Thomasian.

Once Patrick stalked over to us, he wouldn't look at me. I returned the favor, though he did growl something at me under his breath.

"Same to you, buddy," I muttered.

Jack shook his head, then gestured for us to follow. He whipped around the corner and dashed forward. I couldn't see Vic around the linebacker shoulders of Bo, Patrick, and Adam, but judging by the sounds of things, he wasn't going down easy.

"What the fuck?" Vic's voice. Followed by a meaty thump. There was no telltale crackle of the stun gun going off. Had Jack dropped it? "Shit! Ow!"

I still couldn't see clearly around the men, but they weren't using the chains effectively. The Were was using his fists, pummeling them, shoving them off, hissing every time one of the chains brushed and burned his bare skin. The smell of cooked meat and charred hair was contributing to the already considerable stink of the area.

Vic was a good fighter for a beta wolf. He'd gone deadly silent save for small sounds of pain from the silver, backhanding Nikki out of the way when she shoved a butterfly knife between his ribs. Even wounded, he was a formidable opponent. The guys were getting their asses kicked.

With a heave, Vic threw Jack into Bo with inhuman strength, sending the two men sprawling. Nikki hadn't gotten back to her feet, and Adam and Patrick weren't doing so hot, either. Adam tried to get the chain he was holding around Vic's throat while he was distracted, but the Were tore it out of his hands and flung it aside, leaving Adam weaponless. They were too close for me or Jason to get off a shot without potentially hurting one of the hunters.

Patrick managed to get the silver around one of Vic's wrists, which brought the Were to his knees with a harsh cry of pain. Before Patrick or Adam could grab his other wrist, the Were used Patrick's grip to jerk him off his feet and slam him bodily into Adam. Stunned, the two men collapsed as Vic leapt to his feet—straight at Jason.

The hunter kept his cool. I'll give him that. Before he was tackled, he got off a single shot that clipped Vic's shoulder and chipped the dirty brick wall. The bullet ricocheted and whined off to disappear somewhere in the dark. Tucking my own gun away, I sprinted forward as Vic tackled

Jason to the ground, fighting for the gun with the hand that wasn't wrapped in silver chain.

I kicked the Were in his wounded side where Nikki's knife still protruded. He voiced a coughing snarl and rolled away, getting to his feet in a fluid movement that I might have admired if I hadn't been so busy trying to take his ass down.

Though I was intending to shoot out one of his knees, the belt overrode my plan and sent me rocketing after the fleeing Were instead.

"What the hell!"

'*Go, get it, get it, now,*' it demanded. '*Faster, move, just* move*!*'

Though I stumbled, trying to wrest control of my body back from the belt, I couldn't stop running. "Stop it! Don't do this!"

'*Shut up and let me drive,*' it demanded.

I had no control over my movements. We left the other hunters far behind, the Were running in smooth strides that would have prevented a normal human from ever keeping up. The stench of Dumpsters and cheap beer was soon left behind, replaced by the salt stink of the wharf and the heavily panic-laced musk of Were.

He was fleeing. Running. From me.

He couldn't get away. I wouldn't let him.

Something inside me clicked into place, and with a hunger I had never before experienced eating at my insides, I gave in to the chase. Every step brought me nearer to closing the distance between us.

We ran between buildings. People. Cars. I didn't get any of it except as blurred impressions as I passed. My entire focus was on the beast running from me. I could almost see it. The fur and the fangs and the madness under that human skinsuit. The monster hiding below the surface. The thing I had to rid this world of, because there was nothing more important than making sure there was one less moon-chaser on the prowl tonight.

Chapter 6

Once I gave in to the belt's urging, keeping up with Vic wasn't difficult. He sensed he was being chased, obviously, but he didn't make any effort to check who was after him until he'd run perhaps a mile from the strip joint. There was a flash of mixed puzzlement and recognition in his expression as he glanced at me over his shoulder.

Two blocks from the gas station we'd blasted past, he turned a hard left into the dark between a body shop and a boarded-up building.

He was waiting for me, though I wasn't far behind, once I rushed into the shadows after him. I don't know if it was because I was a girl or because he recognized me that he decided to stop. It wasn't a bad place for a confrontation.

I managed to skid to a halt before plowing into him. He made a grab for me that I avoided, hopping back a few steps to keep out of what would no doubt be a bone-crushing grip. The armor I wore was meant to stop claws or fangs, not that kind of pressure.

His eyes glowed with an eerie, yellowish luminescence in the dark, and he was baring his teeth, which were flat and fangless. Even with all the pain he'd endured, he wasn't able to force a partial shift outside the full moon. That meant he was weak—for a werewolf—though he could still tear me apart with his bare hands if I got too close.

How funny to think of a werewolf as weak. No wonder Devon had once commented that I was crazy for being willing to approach Chaz on my own while he was in his half-man, half-wolf form. What the hell had I been thinking?

"Aren't you the alpha's pet human? What the fuck are you people doing?"

I snarled and darted forward, landing a punch that did a satisfactory job of wiping the disgust off his face, replacing it with pain and surprise. As he staggered back, I closed my fingers around his windpipe, shoving him flat against the wall.

"Where is he, you son of a bitch?"

Vic gasped, clawing weakly at my arm. The pain barely registered.

'*Easy*,' the belt said, the sound of it echoing in my skull with its excitement. '*Too easy. Must find the alpha*. Must.' I got the idea that it wanted to find Chaz for the challenge—the kill—not because I wanted to find him to prevent him from hurting someone else while handing him a nice helping of revenge in the process.

Vic was struggling to speak. My fingers eased up just enough for him to take a breath. ". . . not . . . you can't . . ."

With a shake that thumped the back of his head against the graffiti-stained concrete of the body shop, I hefted him higher until his feet left the ground. He choked, his eyes bulging. The belt was radiating a fierce desire to squeeze the life out of him by collapsing his windpipe, which I only barely managed to suppress.

'Kill it. It doesn't deserve to live.'

"I need him, you fucker. Shut up and let me do this."

Vic was already looking at me like I was off by a few degrees on the crazy meter. I'm sure by now I had notched over from "a little nuts" to "totally batshit" in his eyes. Maybe I was. Gritting my teeth, I ground out a few more words, all the while battling the belt's urging to crush his windpipe.

"I need to know where Chaz is hiding. Tell me. *Now.*"

With a little more effort, I eased my grip on his throat just enough for him to speak.

"Not . . . not telling . . . you!"

"Talk, you mangy excuse for a moon-chaser! Or do I need to use some silver to cut it out of you?"

"Never!" he choked. By then he'd regained the urge to fight, and started struggling. He kicked me, hard, using the leverage of the building behind him to shove me off him. We both landed on our asses, me sprawled a few feet away.

He made the mistake of trying to jump me instead of running.

Already hyped up from the earlier chase, burning with the need to hunt, the belt rose up in me like some leviathan from the deep, sliding into my limbs and directing my actions like I was no more than a marionette. With a detached sense of dull horror and panic, I could only watch and take in the sensations like a bystander in my own head as I whipped out one of the silver stakes, using the momentum as Vic yanked me toward him to embed it deep in his shoulder. He let out a howl of pure agony, his grip loosening, and I forced the stake in deeper as I rolled him to his back to straddle his waist.

His irises still burned that strange yellowish color as he gaped up at me, the hand from his uninjured side weakly clawing at my shoulder. The silver was paralyzing him. Even through the gore and the rip in his shirt, black corruption was visibly creeping over the edges of the wound and into his blood as it spread through his veins like poison. Unlike Chaz, Vic's body wasn't strong enough to handle the taint for any length of time. If the weapon stayed in his body too long, he'd die, even if the wound alone wasn't a fatal one.

This was too much. While I was caught up in the chase, the thought of killing Vic hadn't seemed so bad—but this wasn't what I'd signed on for. He wasn't who I was after. This wasn't how I'd pictured this hunt ending. Maybe beating him up, hurting him a little, yeah. But I'd had every intention of sending him on his way and moving on to Chaz as soon as Vic told me where to find the bastard. The threat of using silver on him had only been that—a threat. I had never intended for things to go this far.

I silently told the belt to stop hurting the lesser Were and to pull the stake out. It ignored me. My muscles wouldn't respond no matter how hard I concentrated on shifting my position.

For the first time, it used my mouth to speak, one of my hands cupping Vic's jaw to force him to look at me while the other still held the stake firmly in place just below his collarbone.

"Where is your pack leader? Where are the rest of the Sunstrikers hiding? Tell me now and I'll make it quick."

The Were stared up, his eyes now bloodshot and dilated with panic and pain. His voice was weak, every breath a gasp. "Can't . . . won't . . ."

My facial muscles twisted in a frown. It wasn't me making it happen. Inwardly, I was screaming, searching for the key to get out of this prison in my mind and stop this before the belt went too far.

". . . kill you . . . Every Other in Tri-State Region will kill you for this. . . ."

That set my heart to skipping a beat, even though I doubted the truth of the statement. No doubt, the local shifters in the community wouldn't be happy to find out one of their own had been hurt by a silver-wielding vigilante hunter. Thanks to the pictures of me in full hunting regalia that had made it into the news after the fight against a crazed sorcerer in Royce's restaurant, *La Petite*

Boisson, no one would have difficulty figuring out that Vic's wound came from one of my stakes.

I hadn't wanted to do anything more than rough him up. What if he died from silver poisoning before I could regain control of myself? I stepped up my efforts. A shiver traced down my spine, and the belt backed off, letting me withdraw the stake from Vic's shoulder.

It left a dark hole that instantly filled with blood and pus threaded with black flakes of rot as his body fought to repair the damage. The smell of putrefaction that wafted up made me gag, but I managed to keep from tossing my cookies and concentrated on the task at hand.

"You can still walk away from this," I said, hoping it was true. That wound made me worry. Had the stake been in too long? Was he going to die anyway? "Just tell me where to find Chaz. I'll let you go."

Though his eyes were glazed with pain and he'd gone frightfully pale, he pulled his lips back in a rictus grin. Blood flecked his lips when he answered in a gurgling whisper. The stake must have clipped his lung. That, or the internal silver taint had spread faster than I'd thought. ". . . die . . . You'll die for this . . . hunter. . . ."

Chilled, I rose on unsteady feet. This wasn't what I'd meant to do at all. The White Hats were supposed to help me interrogate and then release him. Killing him wasn't in the plan. Wasn't part of the deal.

My preoccupation gave the belt an opening. Once again, my limbs moved of their own accord.

Before I could stop myself, the belt had me draw one of my guns and fire point-blank into Vic's forehead in one smooth motion.

The gunshot echoing between the two buildings was extraordinarily loud.

I screamed and staggered back, dropping the pistol as the belt released me just as fast as it had taken possession. Vic's feet and arms jerked, his body moving in small spastic fits as if denying the last spark of his life had been stolen away. Something oatmealish splattered the concrete below his head in a growing pool of blood, and his eyes stared up and up into nothing.

"Oh, fuck. Oh, fuck, *no.*"

'*What? He would have died anyway. That just sped it along.*'

"You . . . What the fuck *are* you? How could you say that! Oh, fuck, he's *dead,* I *shot* him—"

'*No one who matters will ever know it was you. Stop worrying.*'

I staggered back, reaching for the edge of the nearest building. I leaned over, and my chest heaved in an effort to take breaths to calm down, but they were coming so fast, too fast, I couldn't stop seeing those eyes staring up—

"Hey! Hey, look—over here! You okay?"

I whirled at the sound of Jack's voice. He was leaning out the driver's side of his van and waving to get my attention, stopped at a light across the street. I gestured weakly for him to pull into the alleyway.

The headlights washed over the dirty concrete, the Dumpsters, piles of trash, the spill of blood, and the body. Jack didn't move right away. I'm sure he must have realized what I'd done. The rest of the White Hats spilled out of the back of the van, looking around.

Bo came over to clap me on the shoulder. "You ran out of there like a speeding bullet! Watch out, or I'm gonna have to start calling you Wonder Woman. That wolf get away?"

I shook my head and pointed. Bo squinted at the shadows, then walked over to the body. Patrick and Jason soon joined him, giving low whistles.

"Did a number on that poor bastard," Jason said. Though I was expecting disgust or horror, his tone was completely matter-of-fact. "Better get the water, bleach, and a tarp."

"Got it." Jack walked past me with some folded-up cloth and rope under one arm, and a couple jugs in the other hand.

I watched, mute and dull with shock, as Patrick and Jason rapidly rolled Vic's body into the tarp and tied it shut, and then carried it to the back of the van. Bo leaned down to pick up the gun I'd dropped, handing it back to me. He didn't say anything about the way my hand shook when I took it from him. He then proceeded to take one of the jugs from Jack, and the two of them tore the seals off and used the water to rinse away some of the blood and bits of bone and brain matter from the cement. They followed up with some bleach, I guess to keep anybody from finding any DNA evidence to connect us to the scene.

My stomach did a queasy flip at this, watching as they did a quick, practiced job of clearing away at a casual glance any signs of the murder I'd just committed. Jack finished off the job by pulling a Swiss army knife from his back pocket and using the pliers to pry the bullet out of the concrete. Bo urged me to follow him back into the van.

Nikki was in the passenger seat. Adam was slumped in the back. Both were looking the worse for wear, but neither surprised nor impressed with the body. Or me, for that matter. Everyone else was quiet as we sat down on the benches opposite Keith's equipment, squished together, as Jack pulled out and headed for home. For my part, I could only sit and watch in a numb haze, occasionally picking at the flakes of dried blood on my hands.

I'd just killed a man. It hadn't been out of self-defense. It hadn't even been because he was a real threat to me. The belt was controlling me more than I'd ever guessed. Even if it had forced me to move, I'd knowingly put it on and let it take me over. Known that it wanted to do more than hurt. That it was made to hunt and kill.

Who had Vic Thomasian really been? Did he have a wife I'd just widowed? Kids? Parents still alive? Someone waiting at home, someone who cared about him, wondering where he was?

That man was dead tonight, and it was all my fault.

With the plastic-covered lump at my feet, I could think of nothing else as we drove in silence back to City Island.

Chapter 7

(Days left to full moon: 18)

Unlike the others in the van, I couldn't find it in me to catnap on the way back. The belt, usually busy making cracks and bothering me all night with observations or requests, had gone silent. The only sound breaking the hiss of tires on asphalt and Jason's snoring was the occasional wet cough from Jack. My elbows rested on my knees, and I bent over to stare down at the tarp-covered lump at my feet. There was a touch of dark, rusty red spattered on the outside of the treated blue fabric that kept drawing my eye again and again.

The time on the dash read 1:42 AM. I had eighteen days left until the full moon, and the only hope I'd had of finding Chaz had been dashed along with Vic's brains in the shadows of that stinking alley back in Jersey.

And I'd just made myself even more of a monster than I might already be turning into.

If I didn't need the belt so badly, the minute the sun rose, I would have burned the damned thing.

Bo had put his arm around me at some point. I hadn't noticed until his fingers tightened on my shoulder, squeezing to get my attention. I pushed a few red curls out of my eyes and tilted my head to peer up at him, noting his somber expression.

"It's your first time killing one, isn't it?"

I frowned before resuming staring down at the body, avoiding the concern in his gaze.

"You don't have to beat yourself up over it. The first time is always rough."

That prompted a surprised, bitter laugh out of me. I kept my voice low, acutely aware of Jack's sudden scrutiny through the rearview. "Are you kidding? Is that supposed to make me feel better? This guy is *dead*, Bo, and I did it. Me. What did he do to deserve it, other than be different from us?"

Bo's brows knitted, and he hunkered down over his knees, answering me as quietly as I had him. "Do you really think he was innocent? He was a Sunstriker, Shia. He must have known what he was signing on for."

I thought about Scott, the Were who had accidentally become infected in a bar fight and been taken in by the Sunstrikers because no one else would have him. Though I hadn't met him, I'd heard his story when I went up to the Catskills with the rest of the pack—less than a month ago, back when I'd been scratched by the talons of a shifted werewolf. Like me, Scott hadn't asked for the infection, and I was certain he hadn't signed on with the Sunstrikers knowing what they were really up to. Would he be press-ganged into the fight against me? Was he one of the Weres working to kill me?

'*Being a victim doesn't make him innocent.*'

A low sound escaped my throat, helpless anger rising at the belt's attitude and my own inability to decide upon a direction for my moral compass. And what if I didn't turn into a monster? What if Arnold found a cure? He'd promised he would try. Maybe there was still some hope for me to remain human, even if I was damned for my actions.

'*The mage can't help you. There is no such spell.*'

That made me flinch.

'*You were consumed with thoughts of murder when you left the vampire's building. You're suppressing them, but they're still there, hiding in the darkest parts of your mind. You're committed to this, aren't you? Stopping the moon-chasers. They hurt you, and they killed that reporter. Or have you forgotten?*'

I shook my head and looked at Bo, torn between rage and anguish. "What if Vic was like me? What if he'd been infected by accident, and was just trying to get by? I'll never know for sure, and now I don't even know what we're going to do with his body. What if he has kids, or a family somewhere? They wouldn't want to see him like this."

"They won't," Jack said, jerking my attention to the front of the van. Bo sat back as I did, withdrawing his arm. Somehow the loss of his touch made Jack's words colder, harder to bear. "We'll be taking him out on the boat and dropping him somewhere offshore. Someone will report him missing, eventually. We took care of the security feeds and cleaned up signs of the fight from the parking lot at The Tease. They'll find his car, and someone might remember he walked out with some blonde, but there's very little chance it will ever be connected to the White Hats. Or to you, Shiarra."

Though there had been a bit of worry about that in the back of my mind, I hadn't been concerned about being caught so much as I was about the moral implications of my actions. If Vic had left behind a family, I'd find a way to make it up to them. Somehow.

'I don't understand you.'

I don't get you either, I thought back to the belt as I closed my eyes. *You're on my shit list right now, buddy.*

It had the gall to laugh at me. *'Is that so?'*

The rising fury burning in my breast was answer enough.

'Let me tell you a little story, hunter. Haven't you ever wondered who I was before I became this hunk of leather and metal?'

My lip curled in response.

'This isn't about you, much as you'd like to think you're such a special snowflake and that it's all your fault so you can wallow in guilt for the rest of the night. You're serving a greater purpose by letting me help you rid the world of these things. I used to be a mage. I lived on the outskirts of Andover. My coven was small, and most of the members were family. We served the local villages as blacksmiths, tanners, and fur-trappers, mostly.

'Some vampire had already established himself in Boston, but we had little contact with him. We kept to ourselves until he drove a pack of Weres out of Cam-

bridge and into our area. I'm not sure you understand just how much Weres hate magi. They slaughtered most of my family. The few of us who escaped went to petition Max Carlyle—'

That nearly jerked me to my feet. The belt must have been expecting it, because I only managed a slight twitch and a faint sound in my throat before my muscles went rigid against my will.

'*Don't act so surprised,*' the belt admonished.

I should throw you into the fireplace when I get back to the White Hat hideout, I thought as hard as I could at it. *What connection do you have to Max? Why would you want to have anything to do with him?*

'*Enough with the dramatics. You've met him. You know what he's like and what he's capable of. It was custom in those days, and most likely still is today, to petition to the most powerful Other in your region if you wished to seek shelter from or vengeance against another Other. Vampires have never been known for their sense of justice or mercy. Instead of doing something to leash the monsters he had loosed onto my family's land, he trapped my sister and nearly had me in his hands before the rest of us escaped. With our circle broken, we had little power, no protection, no homes to return to, and no hope of vengeance.*'

That confused me. Max worked out of Chicago, not Boston, as far as I knew. And what would he want with a mage?

'*He was driven out of Boston some time ago by Alec Royce. Some other vampire—Ian Taft—runs the northern New England territories now.*'

This was all news to me. I couldn't recall Royce or any of his people ever mentioning this.

Shifting impatiently in my seat, I was careful to keep from speaking aloud and drawing Jack or Bo's attention again, keeping the conversation internal. Somehow, against my better judgment, the belt's motivations were starting to make a twisted kind of sense, and I was gradually losing my desire to destroy it. *Why didn't you tell me this before? Why didn't you try harder to kill Max when I was fighting in Royce's home?*

'*You know as well as I do that you wouldn't have survived the fight.*'

Okay. Good point.

'*I've waited this long. I knew you'd have a reason to use me eventually, running in the circles you do. That you'd give me a chance to really work through you. You had to be in a certain mindset and use me to kill—which you did—for me to influence you as much as I do now. It's made you stronger. Better. A more efficient killer. And once you've had enough practice, we can take down the one I really want.*'

Well. You had to admire the thing's work ethic.

'*Your mission hasn't changed, and neither has mine. If you truly want vengeance, then you won't deviate from this path, and you'll let me help you do what needs to be done. It won't be easy, and it won't be pretty—but in the end you'll get what you want, and so will I.*'

This put things into a different perspective for me. As angry as I'd been at the belt, it did have a point. I'd never expected this hunt for Chaz and Dillon to be easy, or that there wouldn't be bloodshed along the way. It didn't make Vic's death right, but it did make me less inclined to destroy the belt the minute I could take it off.

It also put some of my other dealings into a new light. Maybe Arnold and Chaz had never gotten along for deeper reasons than I previously had understood. There seemed to be a whole different world of politics and history that they'd kept from me. My ire against the Others was rising again.

Maybe it was time I stopped just using the belt, and took some time to listen to it instead.

'That would be wise. We'll be much more effective if we're not working at odds.'

I considered it. Then, another thought struck me.

What was your name? Is any of your family still alive?

The belt didn't answer me right away. There were some strange emotions roiling around in my mind, deep down in that place where the belt often took up residence, tickling in the back of my skull. Like me, but not, an alien presence that somehow felt right at home. Once it answered, its voice was the most quiet and subdued I'd ever heard it be.

'No one has asked me that in a very long time.'

That gave me pause. *I'm sorry. Do you remember?*

'Isaac. My name was Isaac Tanner. Three of us died to fuel the spell that made me into . . . this. My father, Abijah, used me to seek vengeance and try to save my sister, Cornelia. He failed, but managed to pass me to another mage before he died. They're all gone. Dead. All I've known is sleep when I am not in use, then the minds of those who wear me, the weapons they wield and the language they use, and the need to fulfill my purpose. There are no dreams for me, no body, no real rest. I am alone now.'

The overwhelming grief it radiated brought the

sting of tears to my eyes. I pressed my fingertips to the leather, though I knew the belt itself couldn't feel my touch—only feel the sensation through my skin.

I'm sorry. You have me now.

I already hated Max Carlyle, but I now knew that, like the belt, I couldn't rest until I'd found vengeance for Isaac and his family.

Those thoughts stayed with me when we arrived at Jack's house, as we carried the body in the dead of night to a small boat moored on the docks behind the house. Though I still felt a faint pang of regret when we dropped Vic in the water a couple miles offshore, still tied up in his tarp trappings and now weighted with rocks, I no longer felt that I'd made the wrong decision.

The hunters knew what they were doing. They felt no qualms or regrets about the death of another Other.

From this point forward, neither would I.

Chapter 8

When we pulled into the dock, almost everyone went straight inside to go to bed or they went to their cars to head to their respective homes. Jack went to the front porch to have a smoke, and no one commented when I eased away from the others to join him.

He offered me a cig when I sat down on the rail of the fencing surrounding the porch directly across from the bench he'd taken a seat on. I shook my head, picking at a splinter in the wood and avoiding his gaze.

"I need to make a phone call."

Jack ignored me until he'd finished lighting up and took the first deep drag, making the tip of his cigarette glow brightly enough to cast eerie shadows on the valleys and depressions of his face. "Not a good idea. Modern technology can be traced, given the right skills, time, and budget. This mess with the werewolves has the Feds interested, and I'm not interested in leading them here."

I bit back my first reaction, which was to curse and break something. After taking a few deep breaths and counting to ten, I was composed enough to continue. "I'm not asking permission. We're short on time and leads. I know some people who might be able to help."

Jack gestured with his cigarette for me to continue.

"There were two police officers who wanted me—"

"Are you crazy? Bad enough to make a call, but to the cops? I thought you were smarter than that."

Scowling, I kicked at his foot. He winced at the contact, and I instantly felt bad, but at least he was glaring and listening instead of brushing me off. "Let me finish! They can help. These two, they wanted me to hide, not come to the station. They're investigating werewolves connected to Jim Pradiz's murder, so they might have some leads. If they have any info we could use, they could help end this mess now."

Jack ashed his cigarette and rose, the scent of death and smoke heavy on his breath as he leaned in to me to whisper a few words before retreating inside the house. "Don't think even for a moment that they're on your side. Not after what you did tonight."

I recoiled as if he'd slapped me. Jack was every bit as much of a killer as I was, but he had a point. Talking to the cops immediately after committing a murder was not the smartest thing to do, but I was out of other options. With two weeks between now and my potential change, I had to act fast.

I hopped off the fence and grabbed Jack's shoulder. He didn't turn, but he did stop and glance back at me, one pale brow rising as he flicked his cigarette into the barrel of sand nearby.

"Listen, Jack. I know you don't like it, but I think they can help. I don't believe for a second that you've cut yourself off from all technology out here. You had to be able to reach those other hunters somehow."

Jack's eyes narrowed, but he jerked his head at the door. "Talk to Keith."

Looked like that was all the help I was going to get from him. I brushed past him and entered the house, taking the stairs two at a time to reach Keith's room on the second floor. Like me, he had taken up residence with Jack and Nikki, relying on their hospitality and bankroll to stay hidden from—well, come to think of it, I'd never asked him who he was on the run from. I was most likely better off not knowing.

Keith answered on the third knock, wearing nothing but socks and boxer shorts. The bright red and blue stripes seemed especially garish against his pallor. There was a video game paused on the screen of one of the computers lined up against the wall.

He blinked, rubbing the back of his neck, when he saw me standing there. "Hey, Shia, what's up?"

"I, uh . . ." . . . forgot what I was going to say at the sight of his skinny frame. For a second the belt had a twinge of reaction like I was confronting a vampire. That boy was *pale*.

"Look, I'm kind of busy here. Do you need something or what?"

I cleared my throat. "Sorry. Yes. I need to make a phone call. A secure phone call. Jack said I should talk to you."

"Oh. Sure. One sec."

He turned away and went to a closet. He pulled out a moving box that was literally full of cell phones. A couple fell out when he dragged the box closer. He kicked one of them toward me that I stopped with my foot, then knelt down to pick up.

"We have these for emergencies. The signal here sucks, but if you walk a few blocks north you should get a couple bars. Don't turn it on until you're ready to use it. I reprogrammed it to scramble the signal, but it can still be traced if the equipment is sophisticated enough. Keep your convo short, and make sure you pop out the battery as soon as you end your call. Bring it back to me and let me know if you need another one."

"Thanks." He returned my smile and turned away. I glanced down at the phone in my hand, then back at him. "Hey, Keith?"

"Yeah?"

"You know anything about the OtherNet?"

He scowled, then turned away to shove the box back into place. He didn't bother to pick up the phones that had fallen to the floor or shut his closet before stalking to the rolling chair in front of his computer and plopping into it. "That place is full of flamers and posers. Hardly any Others use it anymore since some asshat on the West

Coast hacked it and blew some other hunters' cover. Goddamn wannabe black hats don't know when to quit. The few legit Others who do still use the forum aren't in our territory or aren't one of our targets, and most of them are treading far more carefully about posting their plans and whereabouts these days."

"Oh," I said, though I wasn't totally sure what he meant. Black hats? I wondered if there was any relation to the White Hats. "I don't suppose you could pull it up on one of those computers for me, could you?"

"I guess. We have a sock puppet account. You can browse, but don't post anything."

I nodded, but he wasn't looking, already sliding his chair over to another keyboard. He pulled up a browser and typed in a cryptic URL that made no sense to me, but it pulled up a Web forum with the heading "The OtherNet—Where Others Come Together." Huh.

He moved aside so I could hunch over the keyboard and mouse. There were sub-forums broken down by territories. I clicked open the New York sub-forum, and was somehow unsurprised by the number of repeat postings that A.D. Royce Industries and The Circle were both hiring. I hardly noticed when Keith went back to his game, abruptly riveted by the sight of a recent topic—*Sunstrikers*.

My elation at finding a clue was short-lived. The topic was a few pages long, but the most recent posts were about the newspaper article Jim Pradiz had written—and a follow-up by another reporter that I opened in a new tab. Skimming the story chilled my blood. According to that article, I was the last surviving witness. The most recent posters were speculating whether or not I was dead since I'd gone missing after the last sighting by police a few days ago.

The last few posts were made by "NytStryke289," "MadeofWIN42," and "BooksBabesBeer"—and the signatures at the bottom of each post told me they were Hawk, Spike, and Doc. The number of "LOL," "STFU," and "newbsauce" comments removed any doubts as to whether it truly was the misfit pack of Weres who called themselves the Nightstrikers. Maybe this wasn't such a bust after all.

"Can I make my own account here?"

Keith shook his head, not looking away from his screen. "No. You have to get a special invitation from an admin to make an account. That's part of how they keep anyone who isn't Other out. We had to steal the account info from someone else in order to get in, and I don't have the time to find another dead Other to impersonate for you."

Shit. My tracks wouldn't be covered, but that didn't mean I couldn't use this as a resource. "I'm going to send someone a private message here. Let me know if he replies, okay?"

That caught his attention. He glanced over at me, frowning, and red splashed across his screen. Cursing, he nodded, then turned his attention back to his game.

I typed a message to NytStryke289—Hawk—with my lips pressed into a thin line of displeasure as I concentrated on wording it in such a way that

he'd know who I was and what I wanted without
naming names.

> Hey Hawk, it's the knuckle-dragger's girlfriend.
> You met me upstate last month. I could use your
> help tracking down the asshole—he's gone into
> hiding. Think you could lend me a hand? Watch
> your reply; don't know who is looking for me.

I wasn't expecting him to get back to me right
away, but a reply popped up on the screen while I
was scanning over some of the other topics. I was
a little too afraid to click on the thread about me,
but the ones discussing the White Hats and the
"friendly agents"—people sympathetic to Others—
might be useful to peruse later. The message from
Hawk was short and sweet, but gave me hope.

> ZOMG! Thought you were dead! Lots of people
> looking for you, including popo and the big
> fanged kahuna in NYC. You sure know how to
> piss people off. I'll see what we can dig up. Might
> take a couple days if he's hiding, but we've found
> him before. We can do it again.

That was more than I expected. I sent him a
thank-you note in reply and breathed a quiet sigh
of relief. The Nightstrikers might not be compe-
tent hunters, but they had connections to Others
that I was lacking as long as I avoided Royce.

'*You don't need the vampire*,' the belt snapped.

I rolled my eyes and didn't bother with a response.

With some regret—for as much as I wanted to, it would be dangerous to send e-mails to my mother or Arnold or anyone else who might be missing me—I pushed away from the desk, thanking Keith, who gave me a brief wave without looking away from his monitor. There was maybe an hour left before sunrise, and the belt was radiating an antsy need to work off some residual energy. Detective Smith was probably asleep, but it couldn't hurt to leave him a voice mail directing him to leave a message for me with Sara if he'd come across any info. I needed to check on her anyway. I hadn't had any contact with her since I had fled Royce's apartment building.

Leaving Sara behind hadn't been an easy decision, but I couldn't afford to bring her any deeper into my mess. She didn't have the benefit of the belt or magic or training as a fighter, so I couldn't risk bringing her along with me when I left. Hiding her among Royce's people seemed like a good idea at the time, but I had no idea how he was treating her or what he had done with her since then. It had been a worry in the back of my mind for days, but I hadn't wanted to contact Royce in case he might trace my whereabouts or somehow figure out where I was hiding.

Running briskly through the neighborhood was peaceful, surrounded by the scent of the ocean and the whispery rattle of autumn leaves. It had the added benefit of taking the edge off the belt's need for an adrenaline rush. The trench coat hid my weapons, and the armor was sufficient for keeping me out of harm's way, but it wasn't a great substitute for a turtleneck and some sweatpants. I stopped when I reached the Pelham Cemetery on King Avenue, glancing around to make sure I wasn't being watched.

No one was awake at this hour to see my intrusion into the domain of the dead, and it seemed a fitting place to make my call. Ignoring the PRIVATE PROPERTY, NO TRESPASSING sign, I slid over the black wrought iron fence. The headstones loomed in the darkness, lit by little more than moonlight and a few distant lights from a nearby marina.

Passing a tall, blue-white spire dedicated to someone named Jennings, I crouched in the dead grass by a thick shrub to minimize my visibility to anyone who might happen to drive by or look out his or her window. No one to see me here but any lingering ghosts. The salt sea breeze laced with smells of gasoline and old fish stung my nose, and the biting cold seemed worse here, this close to the water. Shivering, I dialed the cell phone number I had committed to memory that had been scrawled on the back of the cop's card, figuring I'd leave a message. The detective surprised me by picking up after a couple rings.

"Hello?"

"Detective Smith? It's Shiarra Waynest."

There was a very lengthy pause before he answered. "It's good to know you're alive. I'm surprised you called."

"Yeah, well, I wouldn't have if I could have avoided it. I don't suppose you know why some of your fellow boys in blue tried to pull me in for questioning, do you?"

"Someone very high up wants to get their hands on you. First it was just for questioning as a witness in the disappearances and murders. Running made you a suspect." That sent a thrill of fear down my spine. My grip tightened on the phone, and I had to lean against a nearby tree for balance while he continued talking. "Wherever you're hiding, you're doing a good job. Stay there, and keep your head down. We've managed arrests on a couple of the Weres who were involved, but most of them are still at large, and you and your friend are still in danger. Plus, you're the only witness in our case against the Sunstrikers who's still alive. I know you didn't do it, and I need you to close this damned case, so stay out of downtown as much as you can."

"Okay. Shit."

"Yeah. By the way, your ex and his cronies are doing a better job of hiding than you are. I don't suppose you might have given him some tips on where to hide? So far we haven't been able to track down any of the men you indicated were involved. Have you and Ms. Halloway had any run-ins?"

I wasn't about to tell him I'd been searching for Chaz and Dillon, too. Disappointing, since he'd already essentially answered the question I'd been intending to ask him. Then his last question registered. "Sorry, what? I haven't, but—hasn't Sara been keeping in touch with you?"

"Not since the phone call a couple weeks ago. I assumed she was with you since both of you fell off the radar after one of our officers jumped the gun and tried to take you in. Are you saying she isn't with you?"

I cursed softly. "No. No, she's not with me, but she's safe." I really, really hoped that wasn't a lie. God *damn* Royce. Whatever the vampire had done to Sara, I'd make him repay a thousandfold.

Unfortunately, there wasn't enough time to pay him a visit before sunrise. Without the belt, during the day I'd be at a bigger disadvantage than he would.

"Wherever it is, it better be safer than Fort Knox. The vampires in the city have been withdrawing their assistance from any programs that support Weres since that girl was killed—Trish Booker, the CEO of that genetics research corporation—and there have been a few skirmishes. Killing someone who was contracted to Alec Royce wasn't smart. I just hope we get to the person responsible before the vampire does."

And I hoped I would get to him before the police *or* the vampire did.

"Anyway, check in with me again in a couple days if you can. Stay low and keep out of trouble, and I'll keep you posted on how the investigation is coming along."

As soon as I hung up, I dialed Royce's cell phone, also from memory. I was startled when it was answered by a woman. Using a very throaty, just-had-sex voice. A voice I had zero patience for dealing with at the moment.

None of my business. None whatsoever. I silently repeated that to myself a few times while I asked, "Is Royce there?"

"He's occupied at the moment. Who is this?"

I gritted my teeth when I recognized her. Miss Sunshine herself. "Jessica, please don't play games with me. This is Shiarra. I need to talk to him. Now."

"Oh! Oh, yes. Hold on one sec."

It seemed "one sec" meant, as usual, an age and a half for Royce to deign to talk to me. Staring over the water, listening to the monotone lapping of the surf didn't sooth my nerves at all. Once he finally got around to it, the vampire sounded about as thrilled to talk to me as I was to call him.

"Ms. Waynest. What a surprise."

"What have you done with Sara?"

"That's it? No hello? No 'terribly sorry for throwing your hospitality back in your face and all the inconvenience I've caused you despite your generosity'? Not even a 'I have a really good explanation for my actions, I swear'?" I could almost visualize him doing talky hands at the phone while he assumed a higher tone to mimic my voice. He did a rather scarily accurate imitation, actually. If I hadn't been so red from embarrassment at his statements, I might have laughed at the sheer incongruity of the thought of him doing something so absurd. It didn't help that I could hear Jessica giggling in the background. Damn it.

'*Don't fall for his tricks,*' the belt hissed, startling me. '*You know as well as I do that it's a monster. It doesn't deserve an apology. Not from you.*'

Common sense warred with the belt's warning.

Royce had been devious and underhanded, yes, but he hadn't done anything to do me direct harm. Still, he'd never been fully forthcoming with me, and offering him any kind of apology now might lead to my giving him more information he could use against me. I'd have to remember to be careful about that in all my dealings with him from now on.

"No," I managed to say aloud, responding to Royce in a much more subdued tone. "Not now. Not yet."

He made a sound that might have been a snort. It was hard to tell over the crappy cell connection. "Forgive me if I don't have the patience to deal with your insufferable attitude this evening. Good day."

And the bastard hung up on me.

I had to look at the screen to be certain. But it was true.

That fucker.

He probably would have said as much if Sara was hurt (or, God forbid, worse). Surely she was fine. But now I wouldn't know until the next time I confronted the vampire in person.

And apologized.

That. Fucker.

I'd make the time to see him and check on Sara. Somehow. Meanwhile, with both the Nightstrikers and a couple of NYPD detectives on my side, I should be able to track Chaz down in no time. The sooner I put an end to this mess, the better.

Chapter 9

I returned to the house much subdued. There wasn't a lot of time until sunrise, and despite my confidence that I could find Chaz, I was consumed with a sense of quiet desperation about what to do about Sara or what would happen if I turned. No matter if I turned or not, I was certain there would be consequences for killing Vic, too. The belt wasn't helping with its alternately radiating senses of smug superiority and irritation. When the sun rose and the belt went inanimate, the soreness and aches of the night settled in to take their places as my companions for the day.

Muscles burning, I settled into a bath, tears from a combination of pain, frustration, and helplessness mixing with the steam.

I had to concentrate on the one thing I thought I could do something about. There had to be some clues to where Chaz was hiding. He wasn't clever enough to conceal himself from me or the cops forever—but that was just it. I didn't have forever. I had eighteen days left. If I didn't step up my efforts, and I turned before I found him, Jack and the other White Hats would kill me before I could see this thing through to the end.

I would visit Chaz's brownstone after I got some rest. Even with the heat soaking into my muscles, it didn't help me relax. Without the belt there to shield me from myself, guilt was gnawing at the edges of my consciousness, teasing at my brain, my inner voice telling me what a fantastically shitty person I was.

That I would even briefly consider justifying murdering a man who had done me no wrong was sounding a lot less plausible now that I didn't have the belt telling me why it was so right. The more I tried not to think about it, the more it ate away at me, consuming my thoughts.

Even after I got out of the bath and lay down on the bed, I couldn't sleep. Every time I closed my eyes, Vic's surprised eyes stared up at me from below the hole blasted in his forehead, while a phantom gunshot echoed in my ears. Tossing and turning for what felt like hours, I eventually gave up and threw on a robe, padding downstairs to the kitchen.

Most of the people in the house had drifted into nocturnal schedules, save for Jack and Nikki. They ran the shop during the day, and would only pull all-nighters when a hunt was on. The house was quiet and dark with all the shades pulled down. No one stopped me when I rummaged through the cabinets in search of something to drink that had a little more bite to it than the milk, OJ, and soda in the fridge.

"Looking for something, pretty lady?"

I jerked, banging my head against the top of the counter cabinet as I pulled back, scowling at Bo as I rubbed the newly forming bruise. He smiled sheepishly, tugging absently at a loose thread on his Looney Tunes T-shirt before holding his hand out.

"Sorry, didn't mean to startle you. Can't sleep?"

I accepted the offering, and he tugged me to my feet. "No. I just . . . No."

He nodded, then ambled over to the freezer, pulling out a bottle of vodka hidden under a bag of ice. Of course. The one place I hadn't looked. That perpetual smile of his briefly waned when he looked at me again, maybe put off by my expression. Desperation is never flattering.

"We'll find him. Maybe not today or tomorrow, but we will. Soon."

I only nodded, pulling out a couple of glasses while he brought the vodka and orange juice to the table, pouring a liberal helping of each into the glasses. We settled into our seats, cradling our drinks, sipping in companionable silence. It took a little time for me to build up the courage to say what was on my mind.

"It's his face, Bo. I can't stop seeing it. Can't stop feeling my finger tightening on the trigger. Over and over again." Taking a big gulp of the drink, I prayed it would hit me hard enough that I'd manage to pass out and get some rest today. Even if it meant the hangover from hell later, all

I wanted now was a little slice of oblivion. "How do you live with that? Knowing you took somebody's life away?"

"You don't," he said, avoiding my eyes as he spun his glass between his palms. "You just keep going, and remind yourself every step of the way that you've got a bigger purpose in mind. If you're looking for peace, you won't find it with us. If you're looking for forgiveness, the only one who can give you that is you. Justice, now, that we can help you find—but you'll have to accept that there will be some collateral damage in the process. No one can help you accept that but you. If you can't carry the weight of that knowledge, you're not in the right place."

Well. Good to know. Though the serious words were a bit incongruous coming out of the mouth of a man wearing a Daffy Duck T-shirt, I wasn't about to point out the inconsistencies.

Bo nudged the vodka and juice closer to me and then got up, taking his glass with him. He clapped me lightly on the shoulder before heading back to bed, saying nothing more as I pondered the mysteries of the contents of my glass.

Bo hadn't used a bad analogy when he compared the burden of knowing what I'd done with a heavy weight. My shoulders were stooped with the burden of knowledge, and I felt as if I was carrying around about a thousand extra mental pounds. Nothing wanted to line up like it had in my formerly simple life. It might not have been perfect, but it all made *sense* before, and my worries, though they had seemed huge and occasionally insurmountable at the time, had become laughably minuscule in the face of the need to kill-or-be-killed.

Though I was a private investigator, I had been reluctant to use old-fashioned, reliable methods to gather what I needed and end this as rapidly as possible. I was thinking too much like a law-abiding citizen. Early on, using my key to get into and search Chaz's home and sending one of the White Hats to question some of the people at the gym where he worked hadn't led to any clues, but I had done a very haphazard job in my haste.

Now that I was thinking about it more rationally, I couldn't imagine Chaz hadn't called and said something about where he was going to the guys at work. At the very least, he must have contacted them to let them know he wouldn't be in to teach his regular cardio and body-conditioning classes. I'd been expecting him to hide somewhere off the radar, and I was acting under the assumption that the only way to find him would be to use supernatural connections.

Though I was still counting on those supernatural connections being my best bet, there had to be some other, more mundane means of finding him, too.

The police were hindered by procedure. I doubted they had solid proof of Chaz's connection to the murders of those people who had been suspected of being infected with lycanthropy outside of contracts, other than what Jim Pradiz had provided only a few weeks before. Since the cops might not yet have thought to use banking or credit card activity to track him down, or even bothered getting started on looking for him when he wasn't necessarily implicated as a suspect, the wait to get a search warrant approved for credit card records could take a while. Not only that, but the credit card company had up to ten days once they were served to supply the records. Theoretically, that could drag out beyond the end of the month, if the cops even thought to go that route to find him.

Chaz received his bank statements via e-mail. I'd seen him check one, once, using his computer at home. He'd set up his system to automatically download his e-mails without a password. If his computer was still there, there might be an e-mail trail or something in his bank statements that would lead me to him.

I did some mental calculations, picking up the bottle of vodka as I rose and headed back to my room. From my recollection, he wouldn't be getting that e-mail from his bank for another few days. Painful to wait, but I could manage. In the meantime, I'd return to Chaz's gym and do a search for the next best thing.

It was about time Kimberly and I had a reckoning.

Chapter 10

There is nothing quite like going on a bender when your life is on the line.

I woke up with a taste in my mouth like something had crawled in there to die, my joints still burning with the fire of a thousand suns, and a jackhammer pounding its way out of my skull. Not to mention a queasiness that rivaled the one time Sara and I had bought one of those big box taco deals from some fast food joint after a night of beer and karaoke—which I'm never doing again, thanks—coupled with a fierce craving for something sweet and full of carbs. Pancakes smothered in syrup and butter sounded like both an awesome and disgusting idea right about now. Belgian waffles would be even better.

Odd. Breakfast for me usually meant coffee and some eggs or yogurt and granola.

Putting my cravings down to a side effect from

the drinking, I rubbed my temples and sat up with a groan. The shade over the window was pulled, and it seemed too dark in the room. Turning on the lamp at my bedside was a horrible idea. Pain instantly shot from my retinas all the way to the back of my skull, making the pounding worse.

Getting up to shamble over to the bathroom seemed like a good idea until I stood up. The swaying and the dizziness wasn't fun, but it passed after I gave myself a moment to adjust.

Splashing my face at the tap helped marginally. Rinsing away the taste of roadkill and drinking a little cold water helped more. Though I still squinted against the lights, I felt much better, more refreshed.

Throwing on some clothes, I gave the belt a passing glance, curled as it was on top of the dresser like a snake poised to strike. Putting it on could wait until tonight.

My muscles protested the stairs, but I made it to the kitchen in good time considering I was walking like someone had wound barbed wire through all the joints in my legs. The pain and soreness eased away by the time I got to the bottom.

Strangely, the scent of Italian food—tomatoes and oregano, garlic and parmesan—drifted my way long before I opened the door. Jack and Nikki were puttering around, doing dishes, and clearing things off the table, counters, and stove. Bo and Keith were at the table, picking at bowls of ice cream, Keith's nose buried in a book. Clearly I'd just missed a big meal.

Nikki smirked at me over her shoulder before shoving a container into the fridge. "Sleeping beauty's awake."

Jack glanced my way, then went back to rinsing out a big pot. Bo and Keith waved me over, and I edged past Nikki and Jack to sit with them. Bo pushed a bowl and a container of cookie dough ice cream my way. It wasn't waffles, but it would do.

"What the hell time is it? How long was I out?"

Keith shrugged. "It's a little past 8:30. Nikki said she found the empty bottle of Grey Goose on the dresser. We all thought it'd be better to let you sleep it off."

I turned about six shades of red, covering my face with my hands. Bo and Nikki laughed at me. All I could think of was the day lost to me. The hours that could have been spent hunting. The ticking time bomb I was becoming.

"Don't worry about it," Bo said, elbowing me lightly to get me to stop hiding my face.

Still feeling like an ass, I kept my head down, pushing my hair back just enough so the curls wouldn't fall into my bowl or stick to my spoon when I shoveled a bit into my mouth.

Speaking around the bite of sugary bliss, I shook my spoon at Jack. "I know you wanted to wait for news from your contacts in the city before we went back, but I need to go to SoHo. I've got an idea."

Jack was not impressed with my spoon. "You realize that's just asking for trouble, don't you?

Why don't we send Bo or Patrick? The police and vampires aren't looking for them."

"Mostly because I know what I'm looking for. If we left now, it'd be dark, and I doubt anyone at Chaz's gym knows what happened between us. Maybe I can bluff my way into his stuff and find some records that might help. Or see if anybody overheard where he went. The guys there know me, and they're more likely to talk to me than somebody they've never met."

He frowned at me, leaning his hip against the sink and scrubbing his chin absently despite the suds covering his fingers. The serious look in his eyes went so well with his soap beard, I couldn't suppress a giggle.

Jack's frown deepened, and he glanced at Nikki, who smirked as she reached over to flick his chin with a towel, getting rid of the worst of the suds. He then realized what he'd done and grabbed the towel from her to wipe his face. More's the pity. For a second I had mistaken him for a human being instead of a machine sent back in time to prevent anyone from having a good time or a sense of humor.

"It's risky," he muttered, returning his attention to the sink. "You can go, but not alone. Take Nikki or Bo with you."

Nikki scoffed. "Like hell I'm going anywhere at this hour. Not unless we've got a hunt."

I turned to Bo, knowing my expression must have been pitiful already, hamming it up even more by widening my eyes and letting my lower lip tremble. His laughter boomed through the room, loudly enough that Keith glanced with raised brows from over the top of his novel.

"With a face like that, how could I resist? Let me polish this off, then we can go."

Matching his grin with one of my own, I took a couple more bites of my own ice cream before rising. "I'm going to change into my gear. I'll meet you at the car."

Dashing upstairs, I forwent the body armor, but put on the belt and a *very* oversized sweater of Bo's that hung low enough to hide the stakes and had to be rolled up a half-dozen times at the sleeves to leave my hands free. It would make access to the weapons difficult, and made me look like I had the fashion sense of a four-year-old, but I doubted anyone at the gym would care. I wasn't planning on being there long, and the guys who knew me would probably assume I'd borrowed it from Chaz.

The belt took some time to examine my thoughts before it said anything, though it reveled in the exercise as I raced out of the room and down the stairs again. Keith dropped his book and flattened himself against the wall as I rushed past, and I barely remembered myself enough to throw a "Sorry!" over my shoulder before I was outside and breathing in the cold night air.

Bo was already warming up his car, a late model silver BMW. He took off as soon as I slid into the passenger seat, and I gave him directions to Chaz's gym, thinking hard about where I might search first. He didn't have an office, but he *did* have a cabinet with files on his clients near the front desk. Doubtless Kimberly's information was somewhere in those files. If I could get whoever was manning it to let me check it, I'd be golden. If not, one of the guys might have overheard something, and I could interview whoever was around. It was open twenty-four hours, so depending on who had taken the night shift this time around, there was a good chance one of the employees would know where I could find her.

If not, Chaz had said her office was "next door" to his gym. There couldn't be that many massage therapists with offices in that area. Process of elimination would serve just as well as digging up the info from Chaz's files.

It didn't take us long to get there. Traffic had died down for the most part by now, and we found a parking garage half a block from the building housing the Midtown Elite Fitness Center, not far from the Plaza District—or Royce's main office. The sign for the gym was clearly visible even from halfway down the block. There were some other businesses in the building, too, including some boutiques and a café on the first floor, but that was to be expected in this part of town. Chaz had a nice brownstone in Queens, not terribly far from here. It made me wonder how many times he'd brought his "work" home with him, which must have pissed me off more than I'd realized, because the oh-shit handle above my door cracked under my fingers.

"Hey, lighten up over there. Did you break something?"

I let go of the handle and concentrated on the

parking structure straight ahead, not meeting Bo's concerned gaze as he glanced at me. "It's fine. We're almost there."

Absently picking at the plastic now embedded in my palm, scowling more in anger than pain, I waited impatiently for Bo to find a spot and park the car. He'd barely come to a stop before I was out the door and moving.

"Shia, what the hell's gotten into you? Hold up!"

I waited impatiently for Bo to reach my side, hooking my thumbs over the belt under my sweater and drumming my fingers against the leather. Though he didn't often show signs of his earlier injury, his running days were long over, and when he tried anything faster than a brisk walk, he gained a limp. As he was sporting now while he hurried to catch up with me.

The belt chose that moment to make its first snide remark of the evening. *'Why do we need him again? He's just going to slow us down.'*

Don't you get started, I thought at it.

'There's nothing to start,' it complained. *'You're doing boring reconnaissance crap. What do you need me for? I'd rather you had me on while you sit and watch those chick flicks of yours than do this wannabe gumshoe crap.'*

Oh, for the love of—

"Are you okay?"

The concern in Bo's voice snapped me out of my murderous thoughts. Forcing a smile, I hooked my arm through his, tilting my head up to give him my best innocent look. "I'm fine. Just a little concerned to be out in the open, that's all. Let's get this over with."

'*The sooner the better.*'

He shook his head but didn't argue, and we made our way to street level. Gleaming towers of concrete and chrome loomed over us like giants in the dark, sharp edges and tinted glass lit by the advertisements and signs and headlights all around us. Even at this hour, the streets were packed with people, most headed to or coming from restaurants, bars, and nightclubs. This wasn't the best part of town for nightlife in the city, but it had its charms.

We made our way toward Chaz's building, but I was dragging my feet, looking around. Something felt . . . off.

Bo didn't notice. He seemed cheerful enough to have me on his arm, and to go at whatever pace I chose. He didn't argue when I paused in the middle of the sidewalk, though he did look down at me with mild surprise. The belt was practically thrumming with energy. Whatever was going on, it sensed it, too.

'*Were. Close. Keep scanning the street. It's here somewhere.*'

That sent a shiver of mixed fright and anticipation through me. I didn't have my armor or my guns. Though I was fast with the belt, I wasn't sure if I was ready to face a Were without any weapons but the stakes. Even if they were silver, I'd have to get far closer than was safe to use them—and, as far as I knew, Bo didn't have any weapons on him at all.

But then I saw what the belt and I were looking for, and forgot all sense of caution.

Blond hair in a ponytail and body encased in a pink, Juicy Couture velour tracksuit set, that boyfriend-stealing, two-faced, anorexic bimbo of a cheating whore, Kimberly, was just leaving the building Bo and I had been headed toward. If not for his sudden pained cry, bringing her attention our way, I might have had the element of surprise on my side.

Thanks to my sudden, unthinking rage, my grip had tightened so much that I'd nearly broken the radius of his left forearm. Even after I realized he was in pain because of me, it took me a second to remember I was supposed to let go.

The noise he made drew the attention of Kimberly, along with that of most of the other people on the street around us. Her brown eyes, wide with alarm, met mine for a split second—narrowed with recognition and anger—and then she was running. Away from me.

I didn't wait to see if Bo was okay. There was no time or room for second thoughts. With the help of the belt, I was after her, and wouldn't stop until my hands were wet with her blood.

Snarling, I dodged pedestrians and kept my gaze locked on her fleeing back, every step bringing me inches closer to bringing her down.

Distantly—very distantly—I recognized the path she was taking. It would bring us right to

Central Park. As a Sunstriker, she had to know that she was as good as dead if she didn't change direction, and soon.

If I didn't kill her, there was no doubt in my mind that the Moonwalkers would as soon as she set foot on their territory.

It only made me more determined to catch her first.

Chapter 11

The wind blew back my hair, and it probably outlined the weapons under the sweater, but I didn't care. I knew my expression was scaring people almost as much as my inhuman speed. They dodged out of our way, making a path for us, which was good. With the way I was feeling, I wouldn't have minded mowing a few of them down if it meant getting my hands on her that much sooner.

We cut across traffic, raced around and sometimes over cars, but the honking didn't dissuade me, either.

Kimberly was moving fast, but I was catching up.

She ducked around a decorative pillar in front of a bank and screamed over her shoulder, "Leave me alone!"

It gave me the opportunity to close the distance. I almost managed to wrap a hand around her upper arm, but the velour slipped through my fingers and she was off again, sprinting for the opening into the Grand Army Plaza in Central Park up ahead.

Apparently she didn't care whether she died at my hand or those of the Moonwalkers.

Though under normal circumstances I would happily have avoided any confrontation with Rohrik Donovan or his people, I wasn't in any kind of mood to pander to the werewolves or their territorial ways. If I had to drag Kimberly out by the hair, I would. If I had to fight the whole goddamn pack to have my chance at killing her before they could, I would.

Kimberly ran like she knew murder was on my mind. Maybe she did. There was a sense of desperation to it, a touch of panic. Not the smooth, even strides of a predator. Likely she realized there was something more to me since she hadn't left me behind, despite the fact that we'd run the course of several city blocks, and I wasn't even winded—though I felt a sudden and rather strange craving for something sweet. The gnawing hunger wasn't enough to distract me from my target. She moved like prey—and some sick, dark part of me liked it.

'*Move faster. Others are coming, I can feel it.*'

The belt didn't sound as excited as I felt. It didn't matter. There weren't as many people wandering around the park—we were now skirting the Pond, lights from distant buildings shimmering on the surface, with the zoo to our right—but there were a few dark bundles huddled on the benches overlooking the water. This wasn't the time to be visiting Central Park if you had good intentions. Even this close to Fifth Avenue, the park was dangerous, a hotbed of brutality and crime once the sun went down. Police and even the Moonwalker pack that claimed this park as their territory had been doing their best to clean it up, but thanks to decades of bad press, no one was surprised to hear about a rape, a mugging, or a murder on the verdant grounds.

Though from what I'd heard, the Moonwalkers contributed to that violent reputation whenever an uninvited werewolf from a rival pack stepped foot into the park.

Dry autumn leaves scraped along the cement, whipped into a whirling frenzy by our passage. Over-bright eyes watched us pass, but no one interfered. Perhaps the criminals who haunted the park at night knew better than to mess with the supernatural element of the city.

Kimberly twisted to one side, and I skidded, not expecting the move as she scrambled over some benches and deeper into the park, off the trail.

An ominous howl sounded from somewhere nearby. Kimberly froze for a second, then bolted back the way she had come, skirting the benches so she could avoid me and flee the park.

I'd only lost my footing for a brief moment, so her frightened reaction gave me the edge I needed to rush over the bench, using it to leap the distance and tackle her into the flower bed she was trampling in her haste to escape.

We rolled in the dirt and leaves, and I could barely see a thing around the tangle of knotted hair in my face. She used my momentum against me to force herself on top, and I cried out as she gathered enough of my curls in her fist to yank my head back. I retaliated by giving her a resounding slap that sent her sprawling to one side.

Something fell in the dirt, a bit of metal catching the light, but I didn't pay it any mind.

Crawling on top of her, I reached for her throat, but she flailed at me, forcing my hands off and making me defend my eyes as her nails slashed at my cheek. Christ, this was so high school. If I hadn't been so mad, I might have laughed.

'Why not? I'm finding this girl-on-girl action amusing.'

For a brief second, my murderous thoughts were aimed at the belt instead of Kimberly, and it distracted me enough that she got another good handful of hair to yank on again.

I screamed and tore at her wrist, my own nails biting into her skin. "Get your hands off me, you tramp!"

She gasped, shoving at me. "Trailer trash!"

"Town jizz jar!"

"Prude! Tease!"

"Cum-dumpster!"

"Skank-ass bitch!"

"Smegma-guzzling fire-crotch thunder cunt!"

That last was ridiculous enough that she paused to stare at me like I'd grown another head. Big mistake. It gave me the opening I needed to pop her a good one.

"Ow!" Blood spurted. She let go of me to clutch her nose and twisted away. "You broke by dose, you bitch!"

'*Nice work,*' the belt commented, though it didn't really sound like it meant it. '*Are you done with the hair-pulling and the girly fighting? Or should I put in a call to* Girls Gone Wild *to start filming?*'

"Oh my fucking God, shut *up!*" I cried. Then glared at Kimberly, who was crawling away, crying. I tried to get up—only to have to grab my stomach as some painful bruise or stretched muscle protested the movement. My words came out wheezed and breathless, but I was still determined to catch her and see this brawl to the end. "Stop running and fight, you fucking whore!"

Of course she didn't stop. Of course nothing could be easy. I reached for one of the stakes, fumbled with the edge of the sweater for far too long, then pulled one out. Maybe the threat of silver burn would get her to talk about Chaz's whereabouts.

Though I stumbled getting to my feet, I followed after her, giving her a kick in the side when she tried to get up to run. It sent her rolling down the slight incline until she fetched up against the bench.

She didn't fight when I crouched down and curled a fist in that stupid pink hoodie, stretching the stained material to the point where there was no hope of repairing the damage. Blood still gushed down her face, and she was sobbing, gulping for air. Particularly as I rested the very tip of the stake under her right eye, ensuring I had her attention. If I hadn't known what kind of person lay under that frightened mask, I might have felt sorry for her.

Might.

"Listen, you bitch," I said, my voice low and dangerous, mostly because I couldn't take a proper breath. "I want to know where Chaz is hiding. If you tell me, I'll let you go. I'll hurt you—but you'll walk. If you don't, I will happily kill you and leave you for the cops to find."

She inhaled sharply, then choked on some of her own blood. Brown eyes watering, she looked at me with greater fear than before. "You bade Vic disabbear, didb't you?"

I didn't say anything. I didn't have to. She sobbed and coughed again.

"Please, I dob't know abyding!"

My fist tightened. "You know where he is. Tell me."

"What the hell is going on here?"

I didn't recognize the voice, but cringed anyway, glancing over my shoulder to search the dark for the source.

Not a cop, thank God. He was bare-chested, wearing cargos and combat boots, with a T-shirt hanging out of his pocket. But the glowing eyes and the way the hair on the man's bare forearms bristled told me as much as the sick feeling in the pit of my stomach and the alarm radiating from the belt that I was facing another Were. He didn't look like much, but there wasn't a doubt in my mind that he was dangerous. One of the Moonwalkers out patrolling the territory, I was sure.

"She attabbed be!"

The guy was utterly flabbergasted by the blood, the no doubt strange sight of a *human* pinning a beaten up Were, and the silver in my hand. The flare of recognition in his eyes was even worse.

"Z! Isabelle!" Rustling in the bushes heralded the arrival of two more Moonwalkers, neither of them looking particularly friendly. The first one took a step closer, the glow in his eyes becoming more pronounced. He still kept a healthy distance between us—most likely because I had a silver weapon in my hand and was making no move to sheath it. "You're Shiarra, aren't you?" No point in denying it. At my nod, he gestured at Kimberly. "Not that we mind some help now and then keeping trespassers off our territory, but that seems a little extreme. You mind telling Rohrik what's up before you use that?"

Kimberly shifted uneasily under my hand. My gaze swiveled back to hers, pinning her in place with no more than the force of my stare.

"She took something of mine. I want it back."

"Easy, lady," said the other man—Z—who'd eased himself behind the first, watching me with the wary eye of one who is certain he's dealing with a crazy person. Aside from the glowing eyes and the claws tipping his fingers, he could have passed for your average, everyday lumberjack. "We won't let her go anywhere. Put the weapon down, back away from the girl, and tell us what's going on."

I considered my options. *What are the odds I can take these three down before Kimberly gets away?*

'*Slim to none. You're not armored and that one can partial shift. Usually only alphas can do that.*'

I know, I thought, searching Kimberly's face.

But what does that matter when I've got you? What does it mean?

'It means you've got at least one powerful dominant on your hands. If one of them manages to fully shift—and considering there's three of them, that's a high probability—you wouldn't make it out alive.'

Hell. Any other suggestions?

'Play nice. For now.'

Slowly, and with great deliberation, I loosened my grip on Kimberly's hoodie and stepped back. I kept the stake on her cheek as long as possible, leaving behind an ugly blister that she was quick to rub as soon as there was a little distance between us.

I wasn't stupid enough to put the weapon away, though the Moonwalkers were eyeing it like I was holding a poisonous snake that might lash out and bite them at any moment. Lowering the stake, I took my eyes off Kimberly to see where the Moonwalkers wanted us to go.

It gave Kimberly an opening to run. Damn it. She was on her feet in a flash, zipping over the benches and down the path like a shadow. One of the Moonwalkers—the girl, Isabelle—went after her. I felt an arm on my shoulder as soon as I turned to give chase.

"Don't—" he started.

My stake flashed up, scraping along his arm, leaving behind the sizzle of burned skin, but no blood, as he whipped away too quickly for me to do much damage. Fangs sprouted as he snarled at me, the formerly reasonable façade vanishing. I scrambled back, putting some distance between us, but Z was coming around to flank me.

"You are one ballsy bitch," the shirtless guy said, rubbing his arm. "What the fuck does Rohrik see in you?"

"She's a hunter, you dumb shit," said Z. Every time I moved to keep him from getting behind me, the other guy shifted, getting just a bit closer. Soon he'd be in arms' reach. They'd done this before. Classic hunting tactic. "Why else would she be here with those? He's probably thinking of recruiting her."

"I'm not here for any of you," I said, skittering to one side as Z made a move to reach for me. "I just want *her*."

"Yeah? What's the girl to you?"

"She's a Sunstriker. She can tell me where to find her pack leader."

Shirtless sidled closer, moving into a crouch. He was going to spring at me any moment. "What's the big deal? Why do you want to see Chaz?"

"Payback," I replied, wiggling the stake in my hand for emphasis.

That brought him up short—but Z took advantage of my divided attention and wrapped his fingers around my wrist, his thumb digging into my tendons until I had to let go of the weapon. It fell with a dull clang to the hard-packed dirt. I wasn't worried, since the runes branded into the belt would summon it back to its holster as soon as I moved a few yards away from where it landed.

The belt finally decided to chip in, though I could feel its reluctance. Why the hell it didn't want to participate in this fight was beyond me, but it wasn't about to let me be taken by the Moonwalkers. I kicked at Z's instep, but he shifted his foot. Clever. Not clever enough to avoid the sucker punch to his ribs, though.

His grip loosened just enough for me to pull away. Shirtless was closing in, but I didn't bother to engage. With a move that made my back and calves burn from strain, I slid under his outstretched arm—grabbing whatever it was that Kimberly had dropped, still shining merrily amidst the dirt and leaves—and pushed myself upright so I could launch my body over the benches and back onto the path.

I didn't look back until I reached Fifth and Fifty-Ninth. The Weres apparently didn't give chase, for which I was thankful. Didn't mean it was time to slow down. Though I'd lost my shot at interrogating Kimberly properly, and surely had made some new enemies out of the Moonwalkers, it helped to know that Chaz couldn't have gone too far, as he wouldn't have let his piece of ass wander beyond his reach. More than likely, he'd sent her out to play fetch on his behalf. It was a good sign, as I was positive that meant he was still somewhere in the Tri-State area.

Undoubtedly, that little fiasco back there would strain any future relations with Rohrik—but then, I strongly doubted I'd live long enough to have to explain myself to him. Though I grimaced at the prospect of having to apologize to Bo for leaving him in the lurch. No doubt he was back at the car waiting for me and wondering what the hell had happened.

Slowing to a jog, brushing absently at the leaves in my hair with my free hand, I looked down at the small piece of metal and plastic I'd scooped off the ground.

Kimberly had dropped a flash drive.

A dark, cat-that-ate-the-canary smile curved my lips. Maybe this night hadn't been a complete waste after all.

Chapter 12

I tucked the USB drive in my jeans pocket, slowing my pace once I'd put a little distance between the park and myself. Facing Bo wasn't going to be fun.

People were giving me odd looks, but I didn't pay them much attention, brushing absently at the borrowed sweater as I walked, trying to get rid of some of the clinging dirt and brush. The brick-red fabric, which clashed with my hair even without the additions of flecks of blood and mud, was pretty hopelessly stained. Hopefully Bo wouldn't be too pissed about that, on top of my leaving him behind.

"That look really does not become you, Ms. Waynest."

I froze, every hair on my body standing at attention as terror—and something else, something I didn't dare name—bolted down my spine. The bones in my neck creaked with tension as I slowly turned my head.

The vampire was leaning in the shadows of a recessed doorway only a few feet away, hands pocketed, one booted foot resting on the door.

He looked the same as always, dressed casually in a loose-fitting gray fisherman sweater and designer acid-washed jeans. No doubt that outfit cost more than my car. His black, shoulder-length hair swayed idly in the wind, obscuring what the darkness wasn't already hiding of his swarthy features. All I could make out clearly were the sharp line of his jaw and the sardonic curve of his lips, etched in stark relief by the shadows.

Someone plowed into me, knocking me aside as he bustled by. It broke my paralysis, but the guy did no more than flip me off when I cursed at him for his carelessness. Royce laughed softly, drawing my attention back, and I inched out of the way of the foot traffic to get closer despite every instinct I had screaming at me to get away.

'*Kill it,*' the belt demanded, a surge of something very much like desire radiating from it.

No, I admonished, clenching my hands into fists at my sides so I wouldn't succumb to the burning need to grab one of the stakes. *He'll kill me, Isaac. Stop. Now.*

The belt quieted, but my muscles still twitched with the urge to *move*. Hunt. Kill.

"What do you want?" While I managed to stand my ground and keep from running flat out to escape, I couldn't hide the quaver in my voice. Damn it.

The vampire lifted his head, his black eyes locking onto mine, drawing me into a quiet place until I heard nothing—not the cars zipping by, the rustle of wind, or the voices of passing pedestrians—nothing but his voice. My world dissolved around me until the two of us were all that existed.

"You. I want you. Come back to me."

That sent a jolt through me. I backed up a step. The movement was slow, jerky. Like moving through molasses. The sounds coming out of my mouth felt more like mush than words. "You—what you said . . . you said . . ."

"Yes, I know what I said. As much as I'd like to hear you make that apology, I'm not angry with you anymore." He sighed, a breath of air so light I barely heard it. "I sense when you're distressed, Shiarra. We're in each other's blood. You've been so afraid. Stop running, and let me take care of you. Let me put an end to this."

He held out his hand, and I couldn't resist the need to take it. His skin was cool against mine, like melting ice sliding along my skin, wrapping around my fingers. When he urged me closer, I went, drowning in the dark depths of his gaze.

"Tell me first—you did something with the Moonwalkers, didn't you? Just now? What were you doing with Rohrik?"

'*Don't! Don't say a word,*' the voice whispered, even as my numb lips moved on their own.

"It wasn't Rohrik." The need to pull away was growing. In the back of my mind, the belt was clawing its way to the surface, pushing its will into my limbs. Making my words slur. "Kimberly. Kimberly was there. Chased her."

Royce drew me closer, his hands sliding up to cup my cheeks. His eyes, framed by thick lashes, were so dark, glinting with cold red fire in their depths. Would it set me ablaze if I looked deeper?

"Did you kill her, sweet? Or did the Moonwalkers take her?"

'*Keep your mouth shut. Don't answer him.*'

I stared up at that beautiful face, into those ancient eyes that had seen the rise and fall of civilizations. He smelled of spice and mint, the scent of it drowning out the burn of the city smog in something cool and dark and wonderful. My mouth opened, but no sound came out, my vocal cords knotted tight.

Royce bent closer—his lips would brush against mine if he moved just a little more—and the red in his eyes became brighter, compelling, *demanding* an answer.

That was enough to make me instinctually balk against him. That heat burned my irises, and I closed my eyes, turning my face away.

"If you wanted information," I said, reaching up to grab one of his wrists, "all you had to do was ask."

Vampires as old as Royce do not startle easily, but I felt him flinch under my touch. Clearly he was not expecting me to resist his . . . charms.

'*Hurt it. Drive it off. Get it* away.'

He recovered quickly, once again assuming that cold mask of indifference I was so familiar with. By now I'd come to realize it meant he was hiding a great deal of emotion under the surface. A weakness he didn't want exploited.

"You," he said mildly, "are in a great deal of trouble."

"No, really?" My hand tightened around his wrist, and I bared my teeth in the semblance of a grin. A rush of energy blazed into me as the belt flooded my veins with adrenaline. "Has anyone ever told you it's rude to fuck with a girl's mind?"

My fist flew toward his face—the strength and anger behind the punch had sufficient force to crush a human's skull—but he caught my hand, closing his fingers around mine before the blow could land. Eyes narrowed, he examined my features and dropped his attempts to worm his way into my head. The sounds and sensations of the world abruptly starting around me again struck with all the force of a freight train. The severance was so complete, I sagged, muscles going slack from the shock.

"Perhaps, Ms. Waynest, I might have asked if you had given me any indication that I could trust you without the necessity of forcing you to divulge every ounce of information or cooperation I desire. You can hardly blame me for looking out for my own interests."

I tugged to free my hand from his, but he held fast, grabbing my other hand in a move so deft and quick I hadn't even noticed until I felt his fingers tightening around my wrist. He twisted my arms to trap both wrists at the small of my back with one hand and leaned in, taking a deep breath. Breathing in my scent? God, his fingers were so cold. . . .

"Shiarra." He said my name in a voice dark and

husky, sending an altogether different kind of shiver tracing its way over my skin as he nipped at my earlobe. "You don't know what you do to me. Feeling you day and night, tearing yourself apart. And for what? What are you seeking? Revenge? What good will it do? Come home with me."

Oh, my God, he could sense my emotions? Even after this long, though I hadn't had more than a few drops of his blood? Was that how he found me? His touch—oh, *God,* it made every joint in my body go liquid. If he hadn't been supporting me—trapping me—I would have sunk to my knees. He held me so tightly, I knew he'd never let me fall.

'*Don't.* Don't.' The belt beat at my consciousness, tearing away the layers of hunger and need Royce was making me feel to instead imbue me with a sense of purpose that felt too forced, too fake, to really impinge. '*You can't. You know you can't. He's using you. Again. Don't let him.*'

The mixed feelings clawing at my insides were becoming painful. It was getting hard to tell which thoughts were the belt's and which were mine.

"I can't," I mouthed. Not sure why. Not really meaning it.

"Tell me," he said, cool lips traveling down my jaw and sending tremors through what little of my muscles was left to respond. "Tell me why it would be so terrible. Tell me why you can't."

'*Don't forget your promise. Don't you dare.*'

That was enough of a reminder for strength to come back to me. Filled with a heavy sense of regret, I tilted my head just enough to meet

Royce's lips with mine, my tongue flickering out to taste the hints of smoke and brandy and mint lingering there. He stilled, frozen, as if either shocked or afraid of driving me away if he returned the gesture. My heart seized up in my chest as the belt protested, but it was far away, somewhere else.

Slowly, carefully, Royce released my hands to slide his own around my waist, cradling me to him. If I'd ever doubted his need for me, it was all washed away in that moment, in the feel of every contour and hard angle of his body meeting mine as he angled his head to deepen the kiss. Despite the chill in the air, and his cold touch, I was aflame, wanting more than anything in that moment to let him take me away from everything.

With a parting nip, I turned my head away, breaking the kiss and closing my eyes against the burning desire to weep into his sweater.

He didn't press me to continue, though I felt his hunger—a kind that had nothing to do with blood—as acutely as my own. "You don't have to do this alone. You don't have to push me away."

'*Yes, you do. The vampire can't help you now.*'

I pulled back, sliding out of his grip. Despite his words, he didn't try to stop me.

"I feel how torn you are inside over this—let me do something about it. Come with me."

I backed up another step. Another.

"Please, Shiarra."

I raised my eyes to his, meeting his gaze with difficulty. The words were forced, and they hurt, but they were mine. "No, Royce. No."

I took another step back. It wasn't getting any easier.

"At least tell me why. What you're looking for."

I bit my lower lip, tasting the remnants of him there, a ghost of him left behind on my skin. "Redemption. I won't find it with you."

He said nothing.

"If I live . . . I promise, if I survive this, I'll come back. I swear it."

'*You won't. You're only making that promise because you know you can't keep it.*'

What the belt said might have been true, but my words seemed to satisfy Royce anyway. He nodded, melting back into the shadows. "I'll wait for you, Ms. Waynest. But my patience isn't endless."

Whether that was a threat or a simple word of caution, I didn't feel up to analyzing it any more deeply. He'd said it before, and I had no doubt I'd give him reason to say it again before this was all over. Without another word, I spun on my heel and took off, running the rest of the way through a blurred haze of shame and regret.

Bo was waiting by the car, as I'd thought, and furious with me when I returned.

"Where the hell did you go? What were you thinking?"

I flushed as he glared at me, feeling more like an errant kid than a grown woman. The belt chattered mocking laughter and insults in the back of my mind, not helping matters. With a few hissing breaths taken between my teeth to collect myself, I affected a much lighter demeanor than I was feeling.

"Sorry, Bo," I said, flinching when he reached for me. His expression hardened. Jesus, I hoped he couldn't smell the vampire on me.

I forced myself to stillness as he pulled a twig complete with attached sugar maple leaf from my hair. The heat in my cheeks grew with the mounting disapproval in his eyes. Were my lips still red from the kiss?

"That was the girl who Chaz was boinking on the side," I chattered lamely, rubbing the back of my neck. Could he tell what else I'd been doing? "She's a Sunstriker. I didn't want to let her get away."

He frowned at me. "Did she hurt you? What happened?"

"No. We did fight a little. I'm fine, but she escaped." That nagging pang of hunger reared its head again, and I gave him a hopeful look. "Hey, you don't have any chocolate in the car, do you?"

Some of his anger and tension melted away. He put an arm around my shoulder, hugging me to him. The belt made a gagging sound that made me heartily wish it had some kind of physical form so I could forcibly shut it up.

"No, I don't have any sweets with me. Look, kiddo, I'm supposed to be your bodyguard when you're out on the town. I can't do much for you if you run off like that. Stay close next time, okay?"

As much as I hated being called "kiddo," I didn't want to antagonize Bo any more than I already had. "I will. Really, I'm sorry. It won't happen again." I held up the USB drive. "Hey, at least I've got something to show for it. Let's head back so Keith can find out what's on this thing."

He gave the flash drive a dismissive glance. Clearly he wasn't well versed in electronic devices or their uses. The tiny piece of plastic and metal might not look like much, but it could potentially have hundreds or even thousands of files on it that could help in my search for the Sunstrikers. Since Chaz hadn't shown up to retrieve it himself, presumably sending Kimberly in his stead, I didn't want to get my hopes up too high—but there was still a chance it contained something useful.

I only prayed that refusing the vampire for the sake of staying with the hunters was worth it. Staring out the window at the passing traffic through the blur of tears, it was only then that I realized I had never asked Royce what had happened to Sara.

Chapter 13

Panic was setting in. Days had passed, but I had yet to find Chaz. Hawk hadn't sent me any replies since his last message, even though I'd sent a few follow-ups. Jack and Nikki were pissed at me for trying to hunt by myself, and at Bo for losing me in the city. Bo was still pissed at me for ruining his sweater and running off. And Keith wasn't being very helpful about the USB.

Keith wasn't being that way on purpose. He'd been assigned to some other duty by Jack and couldn't devote much time to me. Though I couldn't imagine what was more pressing than the need to find Chaz before the full moon, it was taking up a great deal of Keith's attention. He'd opened up the USB, only to give the thoroughly disappointing news that it included copies of invoices, some tax documents, and a host of pictures of Chaz in . . . shall we say . . . "compromising" circumstances.

It appeared Kimberly wasn't the only one who had been on the receiving end of Chaz's attentions. Even though I hadn't been wearing the belt, it was a good thing Patrick had been around when Keith unlocked the encryption on the disk. Patrick had to put me in a headlock so I couldn't destroy a second computer in my rampage.

Now that I thought about it, that might have had something to do with why Keith wasn't in a mood to help me lately.

After I'd bugged him a number of times, he'd given me a laptop to use, warning me not to break this one and to stay out of my own e-mail accounts so authorities couldn't track my IP address. I already knew better than to do something that stupid, but I let him lecture me on Internet security for about half an hour (tuning out most of it, to be honest) and then snatched up the laptop and took it back to my room.

There were a number of things I wanted to do, but first I went through the USB drive a second time. A few times, I dug my fingernails into my palms hard enough to make them bleed, but I went through every file, including the pictures.

If I hadn't wanted to kill him before, the images of him with all those other girls now guaranteed I'd rip his nuts off and feed them to him when I found him. He might have been dating me, but it was now obvious that Kimberly wasn't the only girl he'd been plowing on the side. Each was sorted by date and a name. There were pictures of him and I together, but what killed me were the ones he'd taken of himself with four other women—not including Kimberly—tagged with dates during times that we had still been a couple. Some from before I'd even known he was Were. He must have been storing the flash drive at work so I would never find these photos. No wonder he was always so "busy."

The only bright side to any of it was pay dirt in the form of pictures that matched up with some things on his tax return from 2006. He'd somehow come up with the collateral and purchased a piece of property somewhere on Long Island, another plot of land in Buffalo, and another one just outside of some town in the Hudson Highlands. If I recalled correctly, that was right around the time he'd told me he'd become the pack leader of the Sunstrikers. Maybe that meant he'd inherited the lands from the previous pack leader or that his new position came with some financial perks; I doubted he had the kind of money or credit to buy those properties on his own. The addresses were worth checking out, if only because he could be hiding at one of those locations. It was the only good news I'd come across in days. Which was good, because I was running out of time to hunt.

Rohrik Donovan had warned me about the symptoms of the virus taking root. The words he'd spoken were practically seared into my brain.

"Without blood tests, you won't know for sure right away. Symptoms don't usually appear until seven to ten days before the next full moon. You'll crave rare or

uncooked meat. You'll find your temper snapping at things that at any other time would be insignificant. Some environmental triggers, mostly scents, may make you feel nauseous or uncomfortable. As it gets closer to the full moon, you'll develop a sensitivity to loud noises and may run a fever. Bright lights will hurt your eyes. The first change is painful and disorienting, so don't wait to contact me if you start showing symptoms. Too much stress, and you might change before it's time."

My temper had certainly morphed me into something resembling She-Hulk the last few days. Though it was usually only when I woke up, bright lights *had* been bothering me. My appetite had been a bit off, and I'd been craving odd things, but so far I hadn't had any desire to bite into a bloody piece of steak at the dinner table.

There was no way to know yet if it meant I was turning. Not unless I got some blood tests done by a doctor who wouldn't report me on that national registry the government had instituted, requiring anyone with a license to practice medicine or blood pathology to alert the Feds if someone had a potential or confirmed infection. When I'd asked Dr. Morrow if he could do it, he said he didn't have the equipment he needed here, and that he'd have to take a sample to a lab. Explaining away where he got the blood would be too risky.

Rohrik was unlikely to still be in a mood to help me after that stunt I pulled at the park. He owed me, but there was only so far I could push him or so much I could ask in return.

The not knowing was killing me. The combined worry of wondering what had happened to

Sara, where Chaz was hiding, and whether or not I was infected had driven me into a frenzy of research and constant irritation. The White Hats had mostly left me to my own devices once Keith gave me the computer, probably happy that I was out of their hair.

Patrick, Jason, and Adam had been coming and going the last couple of days, gearing up for something Jack, Nikki, Keith, and Bo hadn't bothered to tell me about. I gathered from the looks I was given when I happened to wander downstairs during the few times the three other White Hats stopped by that I wasn't welcome to join in on whatever super-secret plans they were formulating.

As much as I was itching to check out those pieces of property from Chaz's tax returns *right now,* I kept my head long enough to go through the entire disk for anything else of use before bringing my findings to Jack. He'd given the paperwork I'd put together a dismissive glance, more interested in visiting Chaz's home address again than in searching those other properties. He didn't think the Sunstrikers would be hiding somewhere so easily linked to Chaz, still holding out hope that one of his contacts might come up with something more concrete, and didn't want to waste time going on a wild goose chase. Not that I blamed him much. Buffalo at this time of year would be miserably cold and rainy, and it was a seven-hour drive, minimum, one way. Taking an entire day to most likely find a whole lot of nothing wasn't currently on my to-do list, though depending on how desperate I became over the next few days, I'd be willing to drive up by myself if only to be certain Chaz wasn't there.

Like Jack, I thought it would be a good idea to check Chaz's brownstone for clues before rushing off to visit these other properties. The hunter had also intimated that he'd come across other information of interest, but the bastard was playing everything close to his chest and wouldn't tell me what he'd learned. Jack's unwillingness to communicate useful information was driving me up the wall, and made it clear why Royce had made a deal to keep the guy alive with Royce's own blood. The mind games and manipulations Jack pulled would do the vampire proud. The two of them would make quite a pair considering how much they both liked to play the I-know-something-you-don't game.

If Royce turned him, Jack was going to be one hell of a scary vampire.

With ten days until the full moon, I wrapped myself up in a borrowed parka and gloves of Nikki's and followed Jack, Bo, and Patrick out to the car. We'd waited until dusk to make the drive, partially to avoid the chances of prying eyes or being recognized, and partially so I could be prepared with the belt.

I hadn't told anyone—not even Jack—about what the belt could do. I didn't want it taken away from me or destroyed. The White Hats were already assuming I was turning Were no matter what, so I let them think that my extra strength and speed came from my growing (hopefully nonexistent) furry side. When I told them I needed to work after sunset because I "felt stronger then," they exchanged knowing looks I couldn't fail to see, and agreed to limit any forays into the city in search of Chaz and the rest of the Sunstrikers that included me to after nightfall.

Jack took the wheel and Bo took shotgun, which disappointed me. I wasn't looking forward to sharing the backseat with numbnuts.

Patrick, for his part, didn't seem too thrilled to be seated next to me either. Though I wasn't interested in him as anything more than a distraction from the circular thoughts about what the hell was going on lately, I did find he wasn't too unpleasant to look at. He had the toned body and chiseled jaw complete with stubble that seemed requisite in any man who deemed himself badass enough to hunt supernaturals. His hair was a pale reddish color, and I spied some kind of tribal tattoo peeking out from under the collar of his sweater.

More interesting were the weapons making slight bulges under his track jacket and outlined against his pants. Apparently he was more interested in looking good, showing off his assets, than in wearing something loose enough to hide that he was carrying concealed. He'd probably watched one too many action flicks.

Then again, considering how I'd dressed during my showdowns with the Borowsky kid and Max Carlyle, I wasn't in a position to be pointing fingers about the latest in chic hunter fashion.

When he noticed I was checking him out, he fixed me with a steely glare. His eyes were a lovely hazel color. If he hadn't been such an ass, I might have found him attractive.

"What are you looking at?"

Bo glanced back at us, concerned despite being pissed at me. It didn't matter. Patrick might have pumped iron, but he wasn't a match for me when I was wearing the belt.

I smiled sweetly at him. "You."

He didn't seem to know how to take that. I'd deliberately kept any hint of sarcasm or mockery out of my voice. Coupled with the smile, my response no doubt made him think I was a few beers short of a six-pack.

"Well, knock it off," he muttered, shifting his weight and turning his glare to something on Bo's headrest. He'd also started fingering the hilt of a blade tucked up one of his sleeves. Funny to think I made the big man so nervous.

'*You know what he's thinking, don't you?*' the belt asked.

Oh, I can imagine, I responded mentally. *Something along the lines of "creepy, leech-loving bitch." Or maybe he's thinking about how the signs of turning are getting stronger.*

The belt laughed and sent a wave of warmth into my belly and cheeks, shifting its awareness to my insides. '*He must see something I don't. I haven't noticed any changes.*'

Yeah, but you aren't around me all the time. The days have been getting pretty hard to bear without you, Isaac.

'*How sweet. Don't tell me you're falling for this old ghost.*'

My smile widened, and I turned my attention to the world passing by the car outside. *You're the closest thing I've got to a friend here. You're the only one who hasn't been pretending to be something you aren't, or been planning to kill me when you're done using me for your own ends. It's got to count for something, right?*

The belt didn't respond right away. *'You're the only person who has worn me and not judged me for sacrificing myself to this life. Whether or not you turn, I've considered this time together an honor.'*

It was my turn to go quiet. It was hard to reply to that.

Of course the belt had to ruin the moment. *'And if I was corporeal again, you'd be the first person I'd come to so I could get laid.'*

Gee, thanks.

'I don't suppose you'd consider—'

Don't even think about it. It's creepy enough that you read my thoughts and memories. There's no freaking way you're going to be around my waist while I do that.

It made a harrumphing sound in the back of my skull. *'Fine,'* it sulked. *'Can't tell you how awful it is being stuck without a body and with no way to find release. That kiss you gave the vampire was the closest thing I've had to action in centuries.'*

Oh, my God, do not *talk to me about this!*

"We're here."

Blinking the haze of worry and guilt away, I focused on my surroundings. Chaz's brownstone, identical to all the others on the row, was dark and, as far as I could see from the outside, empty. There were no marked cars parked outside, so unless someone was pulling undercover surveillance, the cops weren't still looking for him here.

Patrick got out first, speaking over his shoulder in a gruff tone that made me wonder if he was just itching to get away from me or if he really wanted the duty. "I'm going to take a quick stroll to make sure there aren't any plainclothes watching the place. Wait here."

We did. The silence was neither awkward nor comfortable. Patrick walked slowly up the sidewalk, looking at the houses, then at the cars, then back to the houses. He crossed the street and did the same on the other side, doing a fairly convincing job of looking like he was lost and a bit slow in the head, unable to figure out where he was going.

Maybe that wasn't so far from the truth.

The belt laughed at the thought, then indicated it was time to pay more heed to my surroundings as Patrick waved to get our attention and signal that it was all clear. Jack, Bo, and I got out of the car and headed over.

There were some kids playing down the street, and there were sounds of TVs, chatter, and the clatter of pots and pans as the people in the surrounding homes prepared or cleaned up after their dinners. It was a peaceful place, lined with trees that made it smell more like autumn than the heart of Queens, beautiful despite the row houses crushed against each other. Chaz's row all sported a similar faded brick façade, the doors a lovely stained maple inset with frosted glass panels. There was a business card with a police badge prominent on it tucked into one of those panels on Chaz's door, so he couldn't fail to see it should he return.

We all crowded onto the tiny porch. Patrick tried the handle and found the door locked. He lifted his elbow like he was about to bust the glass, so I grabbed his arm. He snarled something at me, and I held up a hand for him to wait. The men watched as I reached over to the array of plants lining the porch (*And just who is watering those?* asked a cynical voice in the back of my head) and tilted up the heavy base of a potted tree. The extra key was still there, tucked into the irrigation hole at the bottom of the pot.

Bo and Jack pointedly didn't meet my eyes. Patrick sneered, and I returned his look in kind as I unlocked the door and stepped inside.

Chapter 14

We stepped directly into the living room. It was empty of furniture except for some weights, a single, small couch to one side, and a flat-screen TV bolted against the opposite wall. Spartan, thy name is Chaz.

The men spread out, searching the tiny house. I stayed by the entrance, taking in the details. Though the reek of Were habitation permeated the place, laced with old pizza and gym socks, it wasn't as overpowering as it would have been if he'd been spending time here recently. His indoor plants were still alive. We weren't tripping over stacks of mail on our way in. There was a glass on the windowsill—very out of place and unlike him. Someone else had been stopping by to take care of his things.

I checked the kitchen next. It was only slightly more homey than his living room, since he had a blender and a juicer along with some cooking utensils, a spice rack, and a huge jar of protein powder on the otherwise empty counters. There was a small stack of mail on top of the breakfast nook table. I flipped through the envelopes briefly. Bill. Bill. Spam. Bill. Credit card offer. *Penthouse* magazine. Yeah, not helpful.

Patrick started to reach for the mag. I took great pleasure in smacking the back of his hand. "Don't touch anything. You're not wearing gloves. You want to leave fingerprints for the cops to find so they can book you on a B&E charge?"

Rubbing the back of his hand, he gave me a sheepish glare, a touch of red showing high on his cheeks. "Yes, Mom." His reply was sarcastic, but hopefully he wouldn't be so painfully stupid again as to leave evidence behind.

Bo grinned and rolled his eyes at me. Good to know he couldn't stay pissed at me for long. Shaking my head, I stalked out of the kitchen and worked my way over to the stairwell leading to Chaz's bedroom. Jack was examining some picture frames on the wall. Having seen Chaz's credentials any number of times, I wasn't particularly interested, and doubted the hunter would find anything he could use among them, either.

Taking the stairs two at a time, I pushed the door to his bedroom open, half expecting to find somebody inside.

Nothing. His bed was made, nothing but a couple of magazines and a wilting fern on top of his dresser. All that told me was that Chaz wasn't the one who was coming here to see to his mail and his plants downstairs. Most likely he'd forbidden whoever it was to come up here to fiddle with his more personal effects in his absence.

The computer I'd urged him to get was off, a few DVDs stacked next to it. The last movie we had watched while in his bed had been on that cheap piece of crap. He'd gotten rid of the TV up here as soon as he figured out how to play movies on his computer. It had taken me a few months to cajole him into trying paperless bills, too. I knew some of his passwords—I'd been the one to set up the online accounts for some of those bills. He also apparently had learned how to take the pictures off the digital camera I'd bought him for Christmas last year to save them on that flash drive so I wouldn't find anything on the computer.

Fucking bastard.

It took me a few counts to ten before I was calm enough to sit down at his desk and turn the computer on. The log-in password, as I'd figured, remained unchanged. When I opened his e-mail program, it didn't prompt for a password, just downloaded a series of new items.

Most of it wasn't of interest. Billing notices. A couple of updates from a physical fitness magazine. A whole lot of offers for Cialis, Viagra, porn, winning notices from the Swiss lotto, requests to act as the recipient of some dead or dying official's millions, and enough viruses to set his scanning program to light up with alarms. If I had to hazard a guess, I'd say Chaz had posted his e-mail address somewhere public online. Also, he hadn't checked this account in almost two months, so there were a formidable number of messages to wade through.

Once the virus scanner settled down, I skimmed through the downloads until I spotted the latest e-mail from his bank. Crud. They'd switched to viewing the statement on the Web only. When I clicked the link, of course half a dozen pop-ups opened with his browser. Grumbling under my breath, I ignored them and tapped in his social security number and the same password he'd asked me to set up for his computer log-on.

Invalid.

Hmm. He'd always complained about how hard it was to remember his passwords if they were all different. It had taken me a while to convince him that he needed to think about digital security by using different passwords for different Websites and programs. He'd protested, didn't know how he was expected to remember them all, and wanted me to sort it out for him.

Narrowing my eyes, I opened up the desk drawer, and nudged around the pens and paperclips. There was a small notepad inside. Much as I'd guessed, he'd kept the page where I'd written all of his user IDs and passwords, and then added a few of his own, instead of destroying it after memorizing them like I'd instructed.

The porn Website log-ons explained all the pop-ups. Ugh.

I tapped in the password, breathing a sigh of relief that it worked, and immediately went to his checking account to see if there'd been any recent activity.

Jackpot! He'd been using his debit card almost every day for the last two weeks to buy something from a store in Peekskill. That could mean he was staying at the property in the Hudson Highlands. Thank goodness I wouldn't have to chase his ass all the way to Buffalo. Forty miles was a lot more feasible than four hundred.

I printed out the statement—then cursed when I noticed the last two purchases.

One at a gas station in White Plains, and another at a mini mart down the street from my apartment.

He was back in town. Or he had been, as of two days ago. It was entirely possible he had come back to retrieve the USB before either the police or I could get our hands on it. No doubt he knew he was being hunted. If he hadn't known I was after his ass before, he had to know now that I'd beaten Kimberly ten shades of black and blue.

Though I was still mightily pissed, I kept my temper in check long enough to check his hard drive for any other clues. Nothing important. The page of passwords would serve me in better stead. All I found were more pictures—oh, holy hell, one of them was of *me*—and a rather impressive collection of porn. The picture of me had been taken while I was asleep on the bed right behind where I was currently sitting. He'd captured me without clothes, the scars on my stomach and ribs plainly visible.

Seething, I proceeded to reformat his hard drive.

Once the process was well under way, I spun away from the computer and looked up into Jack's eyes. No telling how long he'd been there, watching over my shoulder. I couldn't help but wonder if he'd seen the picture of me.

He didn't take his gaze off mine. "You finished here?"

Flushing, I looked away first. That was good, because it reminded me to grab the pad and the printout of the statement. "Yes. I found some useful stuff."

"Good," he said. "So did I."

Neither of us elaborated. Neither of us spoke.

Bo broke the thoroughly awkward silence by poking his head in the door. "Hey, you ready to go? Patrick says he thinks someone might have noticed we're here."

Most of the neighbors were likely to assume it was fine we were here since a number of them knew me. Not too many people had a head of long, curly hair quite my shade of fire engine red, so no doubt if anybody had been watching, they'd recognized me. Then again, if some beat cop had been knocking on doors, one of them might have called to alert the police I was here. Peachy. Wish I'd thought of that sooner.

We didn't run, but we moved rapidly out of the place, turning off the lights and locking up behind us. I returned the key to its place under the pot, then hopped in the backseat, pleased to see Bo had decided to let Patrick sit up front this time.

"We have one more stop," Jack said.

Patrick shoved his seat back, narrowly missing my knees. "What's the plan, chief?"

"One of my contacts said he'd found a lead on the Sunstrikers and that other group we've been looking for." Patrick and Bo nodded, the three of them leaving me adrift. What other group were they searching for? "I'm supposed to meet him at the Carl Schurz Park. It's on the way back if you take the Midtown Expressway."

It added a bit of time to our route, but none of us had any objections. Though I was curious, I didn't pry into this other group they were after. It probably had something to do with whatever that project was Jack hadn't wanted to tell me about.

I did want to let them know what I'd found, though. "Hey, Jack? I know where Chaz has been hiding the last few weeks. He was only a few miles outside of town, over in Westchester County. He's somewhere in town now, though."

Patrick glanced back at me, his brows nearly raised to his hairline. "No shit? You found that crafty fucker?"

"Watch your language around the lady," Bo admonished.

I grinned. "Almost. I'm getting closer. I've got access to his bank activities now. I can see when he makes a purchase. The last one was two days ago—right by my place. So he's probably back in the city, staying with one of the other Sunstrikers."

'*Probably shacking up with Kimberly,*' the belt said.

Nobody asked you. Out loud, I said, "It's only a matter of time before he uses his card again."

"Good," Jack said, semi-distracted by traffic. "When we get back I'll put Keith on it. He can cross-reference what we know of the pack members. Maybe we can narrow down the neighborhood to a street or two, see if we can pinpoint where he's staying."

It didn't take long to reach our destination. We piled out of the car and huddled in our jackets, working our way to the Peter Pan statue in the park plaza. Some of the flowering plants in the landscaping were wilting with the onset of winter, and this close to the water was bitterly cold at night, but it was lovely and quiet. We didn't see many people on our way to the rendezvous point, only passing a jogger and a couple of late-night dog walkers. This place was nothing like the tourist trap that Central Park had become.

At Jack's command, Patrick broke off from us to scout the area and ensure we were alone. He melted into the shadows and was gone.

It might have been the cold or the city smog, but something was making Jack cough more than usual. I gave him a careful pat on the back when he doubled over, a fist held to his mouth while he struggled to catch his breath.

The wet sound of his breathing wasn't good. He was running out of time, as surely as I was.

When he'd stopped gasping so much, I pulled away, giving him some time to collect himself. After a minute or so, he straightened, running a hand over his face. Some distant part of me noted the scent of blood on the air. On his hand. His lips.

Maybe he had less time than I did.

None of us acknowledged the weakness. Once he caught his breath, he resumed stalking down the path that led to the plaza like he owned the place, acting like nothing had happened. If that was how he wanted to play it, more power to him. Bo and I trailed behind.

The few lights didn't seem to banish the darkness here. Though I had no trouble seeing in the dark, thanks to the night vision the belt granted me, I wasn't sure how well Bo, Patrick, and Jack were doing. Jack seemed to know where he was going; he found the steps leading down to the circular plaza containing the bronze statue of Peter Pan and his four-legged friends, a deer, and a rabbit. Someone was seated on one of the benches across from the graceful arch of a bridge overlooking the landscaped depression. It was an excellent place for a clandestine late-night meeting: quiet, peaceful, and right in the heart of New York City.

The person Jack was here to meet was bundled up in a long trench coat, a fedora, and was smoking a cigarette to boot. Clearly we had a Humphrey Bogart fan on our hands.

Whoever it was tipped their hat down, hiding their face as Jack approached. He made a slight gesture that Bo and I took to mean to wait by the stairs. I assumed as badass a pose as I could while being bored and cold in an ill-fitting, fake fur-lined parka. Bo did a far better job of looking menacing as he folded his arms and adopted a bodyguard stance.

Jack muttered something so quietly, even with the help of the belt attuning my senses, I couldn't hear what he said. Whoever was sitting on the bench responded in kind.

A few things happened at once. Patrick's body landed with a sickening crunch on the flagstones between Jack and me, apparently thrown from on top of the bridge. At the same time, a group of shifted Weres hopped off the top of the arch to follow Patrick down, while others loped down the steps from the other side of the park. As far as ambushes went, this one was certainly planned out well. Fuck.

Worst of all, whoever that was who'd been sitting on the bench moved with liquid speed and grace to their feet and sucker-punched Jack. When the hunter staggered back, turning around, his shirt had a growing red stain between his ribs—and just before he went to his knees, above the cherry glow of the cigarette, I caught the sight of flashing yellow eyes staring at me from the darkness under the fedora's brim.

Chapter 15

Bo and I immediately went back to back so we couldn't be flanked, preparing to meet the rush. I hadn't expected a fight, so all I had were the stakes. As far as I knew, Bo only had a Glock tucked into the small of his back and a silver-coated hunting knife. Three—no, four—Weres had hopped down from the bridge, and two more had come down the opposite steps, plus the fucker in the trench coat.

Patrick's sightless eyes and the blood staining the stones under him were hint enough that this ambush hadn't been planned so whoever was after Jack could take prisoners.

'*Not good odds.*'

No shit. Any ideas?

'*Let me take over. I'll handle it.*'

There wasn't time for me to argue or reflect. The moment I started contemplating agreeing, I found myself trapped in my own head, a bystander to the belt's special brand of madness.

Though I could feel the stretch of my muscles, the pain of impact when one of the Weres managed to punch or scratch me, and the cold wind blowing my hair around my face, I had no more say in what I was doing. The belt forced me to move away from Bo to meet my attackers head-on. Though I felt a pang of conscience for leaving Bo to fend for himself, I spun, twisted, ducked, kicked, punched, and basically put some of Neo's moves in *The Matrix* to shame. Everything moved in a blur—and I found I wasn't as worried about those scratches as I probably should have been.

One of the Weres swiped claws at my face. I caught its wrist and hurled it into another one of the beasts. Another snapped its jaws at my ankle, aiming to incapacitate me. I kicked it so hard, fangs scattered like marbles, clacking over the stone pathway. It fell back, only to be replaced by another, which I cracked in the sternum with my elbow, driving the breath out of it.

I hadn't even pulled one of my stakes yet.

Bo was just as busy as I was. He was using the gun to keep the Weres from descending on Jack, and the hunting knife as long as my forearm to slice and dice any of them that got too close to him. I'd never seen him in action before. His leg had already been in traction when I first met him, when I was taken to the White Hat's hideout back when the hunters saved me from Max Carlyle.

He showed no signs of his earlier injury. The moves were calculated, fluid, and deadly. One Were was already breathing its last by his feet. Others sported wounds on their furry muzzles, throats, and chests. He was going for the kill, not to wound. Excellent.

Considering the Weres put the majority of their attention on me once they realized I was a greater threat than Bo—that I was more than human—I was holding my own. My back was burning with pain from some shallow claw wounds. My ankle ached from kicking the Were, my arms were bruised, and my knuckles were raw and bleeding. Other than that, I wasn't doing too badly.

Time to break out the big guns.

A pained yelp was startled out of the Were in front of me when I embedded one of the stakes in its chest. I shoved it aside as it fell to its unnaturally jointed knees, and worked my way closer to Jack and the thing in the trench coat standing over him. Bo was out of bullets, unable to drive it off.

The stakes were not only silver, but imbued with magic. As soon as I went more than a few feet from the body they were stuck inside, they popped out of existence and teleported back into place in their holsters on the belt. The glory of magework. The belt used its knowledge and skill to kill and incapacitate the remaining Weres until only the leader remained, one hand formed into monstrous claws hovering over Jack's throat.

"Step no closer."

The voice was low, guttural. A male on the verge of shifting.

I—or the belt—didn't give it a chance to hurt Jack. With a rather impressive roundhouse kick (if I did say so myself), I sent the creature flying a good thirty feet until it slammed into the base of the bridge, leaving a deep dent in the concrete and stone. Dust and pebbles rained down onto the stones of the path below.

That might have slowed the creature, but it wasn't down for the count. It was already staggering to its feet. As much as I wanted to prolong the fight and finish the thing off, sirens were blaring in the distance, growing closer. The gunshots must have been reported by someone.

Scooping Jack into my arms, I fled back the way we had come, shouting at Bo, who was staring at me instead of hightailing it as he should have been. "Come on! Move your ass!"

With a start, he bounded after me, hot on my heels. I had to slow down so he could keep up. Jack was groaning and clutching his wound. He hadn't quite seemed to notice yet who had picked him up. That wasn't a bad thing in my estimation. He already thought poorly enough of me. No telling how he'd take it or respond once he realized he'd been rescued by an Other-tainted girl.

Of course that asshat in the trench coat couldn't stay down. Bo made a strangled sound before he was pulled back, cracking his cheek on the steps when he failed to catch himself as it yanked one of his legs back.

Though I wasn't as gentle with Jack as I wanted to be, I put him down as carefully and quickly as I could before leaping over Bo to tackle the creature. Claws dug into my ribs and hip as we rolled down the steps in a mockery of a lover's embrace. We were both snarling and clawing at each other.

Its much heavier weight allowed it to come to rest on top when we finally stopped that painful roll.

I shoved and clawed at it, writhing under its bulk, but it didn't let up in the slightest.

Its hands immediately went for my throat, putting pressure on my windpipe while those talons dug into my skin. My vision was going gray around the edges, but the belt still radiated confidence.

Abruptly, the creature let loose an agonized howl, falling back as the stake shoved into its gut dug deep enough to scrape along bone. Blood and some other fluid gushed out of the thing, coating me in foul-smelling, hot ichor.

It twisted off of me and leapt to its feet, fleeing into the darkness, one hand holding its guts inside. Coughing and rubbing at my throat, I cautiously sat up, feeling around my chest to make sure I hadn't rebroken any ribs in the tussle. There was pain and tenderness, but it didn't feel like anything was out of place.

Lurching to my feet, I shuffled up the stairs as rapidly as I could, considering my head was spinning like I'd just taken a few shots of green death Nyquil. Bo had gotten back to his feet and had Jack in a fireman's carry. That couldn't have been comfortable for either of them. Bo's cheek was still bleeding, too. He shook his head when I caught up and tried to help, jerking his head in the direction of the car.

"Take the keys and get it started. I'll be right behind you."

I pulled the keys from Jack's back pocket and took off at an unsteady trot for the car. The sirens were getting pretty deafening, and red and blue lights were now flashing through the trees over my head. I veered off the path and cut into the bushes, sticking to the dark and moving from tree to tree, trying to stay concealed. I hoped Bo had thought to do the same.

A few uniforms raced past me, some unnervingly close, but none seemed to notice me in the shadows. They all had their hands on their guns and were booking it for the plaza. The bodies would cause quite a stir. Six dead or dying Weres beaten to a pulp and one dead White Hat were no doubt an unusual sight, even for New York's finest. They'd have to call in supernatural consultants to check the scene, but Patrick's body meant civilian involvement. It would be a public relations nightmare for the Others in the city once word got out.

I was sure Bo had had alterations done to his gun and ammunition so the bullets and casings wouldn't be traceable. None of the hunting activities of the White Hats could be considered legal, and they'd had years to learn the pitfalls of dealing with police interference and investigations. The kind of damage we'd done and lack of human bodies on the scene would most likely make it appear to be an Other-related fracas Patrick had unwittingly stumbled upon, so hopefully that meant little suspicion would fall on the hunters. Or on me.

Once the cops were well past me, I counted to fifty under my breath, then huddled into my jacket and headed at a good clip toward the car. The image of a civilian trying to get away from a scene of violence and bundled up against the cold should work as long as no one looked too closely, noticed the blood or the way the parka lay in tatters on my back.

Luckily enough, no one called out for me to halt or to say that they just wanted to ask a few questions. Most of the cops must have gone straight to the scene. They'd left their vehicles parked haphazardly on the street, only one policeman left behind to keep an eye on things. He didn't appear to notice me—his attention was on whatever was coming out of the radio.

I held my breath as he looked my way, noting movement or maybe hearing something in the park. He scanned the area for a heart-stopping twenty or thirty seconds, then looked elsewhere, once again distracted by some report coming in over the horn.

Bo must have been making some noise. As soon as the cop wasn't looking his way, he rushed out from behind a bush to crouch behind the concealment of the car, easing the door open and shut.

"Don't go back to the house," Jack said, his voice weak with pain. I jerked around in the seat to look him over, examining his injury as best I could. His hand was over the wound, putting pressure on it, but it appeared to have stopped bleeding. Couldn't be that serious then. "That ambush . . . somehow they knew. Ricky betrayed us. Who knows what else he's told them."

With a grimace, Jack tried to sit up but settled back when Bo pushed him down.

The belt released its hold on me, now that its skills and stealth weren't needed, but it was still projecting excitement and satisfaction. Creepy thing.

I started the car and eased out into the street, careful to avoid the cop cars. Wouldn't do us much good to have gotten this far without attracting notice just to end up having the cop read the license plate and put out an APB for suspects in a multiple homicide. Self-defense would come across like a pretty lame excuse when faced with the mess we left back there. Our combined documented histories with Others also wouldn't help our case. Oh, and let's not forget that I was already considered a suspect or at the least a person of interest in the murder of Jim Pradiz. This was looking better and better by the moment.

Fingers tight on the steering wheel, I didn't focus much on where I was going other than to ensure I didn't plow into somebody else or run any lights. My attention kept flicking to Jack through the rearview. "Where the hell do we go? What do we do, Jack? We need to get you to Doc Morrow."

He coughed, then wiped his mouth with his sleeve. He examined whatever rubbed off with dull eyes, then closed them, his features twisting in pain. "Take the next left. Head toward Times Square. There's a safe house downtown. We'll call the others over when we get there."

I did as he bid, getting the address when he started fading so I could find it if he passed out. His normal pallor had become sallow and worried me. It was possible he needed more than Dr. Morrow's attentions. What if he needed another infusion from Royce?

Jack was clearly fading. I doubted he went to the vampire except when he had to. Nikki would never forgive me if I let him die—but Jack might never forgive me if I told Royce where the hunters' hideout was, or let the other hunters find out that Jack was playing both sides.

Plus, facing Royce right now did not seem like the best idea. He'd wormed his way into my head, right there on the street, and I knew he was losing patience with me. No matter what he said, he wasn't interested in letting me run around on my own much longer. I had to finish this business with Chaz before I went back to Royce's place, or he might never let me go.

'*Might? You* know *he wouldn't. If not for the vampire, you never would have gotten in this mess.*'

It's not Royce's fault Chaz cheated on me, I replied, keeping a tight lid on the explosive rage behind that thought. *I can't do this right now. Let me concentrate on driving.*

'*All I'm saying,*' the belt whispered, barely there in the back of my head, '*is that you need to start considering what you're going to do about the vampire once this business with the wolf is over. You know it won't let you go. It'll enslave you, just like it did before. Is that what you want?*'

I didn't bother responding.

'*You know it's true. Look at what it tried to do right in the street. What do you think it will do to you once you're alone with it? It doesn't care about you. All it sees is an asset. An expendable one.*'

My grip tightened on the steering wheel. *Stop. Talking.*

'Just think it over. Consider your options. The longer you wait, the less choice you'll have.'

Story of my life.

Chapter 16

(Days left to full moon: 6)

Less than a week left. I hadn't been sleeping or eating for the last two days. Ever since we had come to the loft apartment Jack had directed us to, he'd forbidden most of us to leave until he was back on his feet.

The doc didn't want Jack moving around or doing anything strenuous. The damage the Were had done was minimal, but the blood loss combined with the lung cancer had set Jack's recovery back a long way. There was little Dr. Morrow could do, as all of his treatment had to be off the books, and there was only so much equipment and medicine he had to work with there. Jack kept insisting it wouldn't be much longer before he was ready to fight, but from the look of him and the sound of his breathing, I wasn't sure he'd ever get back on his feet again.

Nikki was falling apart. She wouldn't leave Jack's

side and ran the other hunters like she owned them. When she tried to boss me around, too, I walked out. It pissed her off, but I wasn't going to pretend even for a minute that I considered her fit to lead this outfit once Jack was gone. If he died before this was over, I had no doubt Nikki's first order of business would be to kill me, even if I hadn't shifted yet.

Jack was situated in the master bedroom. Bo and Keith had set themselves up on cots downstairs, while I'd set up camp on a couch and Nikki had taken the other bed upstairs. Keith had taken as much equipment as he could carry from the hideout on City Island and met up with us within a couple hours. There were extra sets of clothing, weapons, ammunition, and food stocks in the loft. It was a little cramped considering we were all supposed to stay put, and no one other than Keith was happy to be here. The only reason the computer geek liked it was the discount electronics shop right across the street.

I might have liked the place better if I could have parked my ass at the Starbucks or the Dunkin' Donuts down the block instead of having to wait out Jack's recovery day in and day out inside the apartment. Bo, Nikki, and Keith could come and go as they pleased, but I wasn't allowed to step foot beyond the building's front door. No one wanted to risk my being seen by cops or anyone else who might recognize me. It didn't help my temper that Jason and Adam were also forbidden to wander around. We were the biggest security risks, according to Jack.

Plus we were technically in Moonwalker territory, and who knew what connection, if any, the werewolf pack had to the Weres who had attacked us in the park or what they'd do if they knew I was here. I was reasonably certain I was now on Rohrik Donovan's shit list, and the local and national news was abuzz about the bodies found in Carl Schurz Park that night. While Patrick's death was regrettable, it didn't appear too many people were up in arms over one more dead extremist hunter. Rather, the buzz was focused on speculating about an Other war brewing on the horizon, and that this was just the first skirmish of many to come.

If only they knew.

As often as I put up the argument that I could have been doing more good on the streets, following up on the leads I'd gleaned from Chaz's computer, Jack wouldn't hear of it. He sent Bo, Adam, and Jason to check them out instead. Keith let me use one of his laptops so I could keep tabs on any purchases made by Chaz, but other than that I was feeling useless.

Bo had followed my instructions and found what we thought was Kimberly's office, pretended to be a potential client, and got some song and dance from the answering service that she was currently out of town. It didn't matter. I used my own resources to find her home address once Bo confirmed her last name for me.

Like with Chaz's home, it appeared someone was stopping by to handle minor matters, but that nobody had been occupying the place for at least a week or two. It was incredibly frustrating not to be able to go myself and having to rely on the information the men gathered. They were good, but they weren't private investigators or cops, and didn't know the little telltales to look for or have the patience for traditional surveillance work. That was a staple of my business.

I didn't want to cause the bank to flag Chaz's account for suspicious activity by checking it too often. I limited myself to twice a day, tempted as I was to check it every fifteen minutes to see where that bastard was hiding.

He made a few minor purchases. Fast food, mostly. It wasn't always in the same part of town, but he was still on Long Island, mostly in Queens and in Nassau County. He stayed roughly in the region of my house and Sara's. Hard as I tried, I couldn't think of any mutual friend or other Sunstriker who might be offering Chaz, Dillon, or Kimberly shelter. If he was staying at a hotel, he was using cash on hand, not his card.

If this had been a case for a client, I would have used my computer at the office to hunt down family to call and question. Without access to my accounts and programs, I couldn't do my job effectively. I couldn't risk logging in to any of my personal accounts on the Internet for fear of having my IP traced back. Chaz's car hadn't been parked by his home to allow us to install a GPS tracker, and I didn't know what Kimberly or Dillon's cars looked like, so I couldn't have the White Hats do an install on theirs.

While the belt had kept me company at night,

it wasn't much help. It kept insisting Royce was responsible for my troubles.

Problem was, I was starting to believe it.

If I hadn't taken the job for The Circle—my God, was it really less than a year ago?—I never would have found myself tied up with Royce. If the vampire hadn't become so interested in me, I never would have been beaten, hospitalized, kidnapped, bitten, and bound by blood as a mindless servant. Chaz wouldn't have been interested in rebuilding our relationship only to let it fail so spectacularly. The police wouldn't want me in connection with a murder I didn't commit. My father wouldn't have disowned me.

I wouldn't have killed anyone.

The more the belt whispered about all the things that had gone wrong since Royce came into my life, the more I wanted to blame him for my troubles. Which wasn't right. I knew it wasn't. But the belt's words still made me doubt, and that made me want to confront the vampire and find out if this mess he'd made of my life had been his plan for me all along. Had he meant for all these terrible things to happen so I'd be forced to turn to him for help again and again until I wouldn't—or couldn't—leave his side?

There was no doubt in my mind Royce wanted me to return. Hell, he was holding back the information on whatever had happened to Sara, most likely specifically to make me come back to him.

Of course, as soon as I showed up at Royce's door, he'd never let me leave again. The question remained: Why? What did I mean to him? Why was

I so special? No matter how I wracked my brains for answers, I couldn't figure it out.

So I took the time in confinement to learn about him. Study him. See if I could get into his head. I studied every interview and article about him I could find. He was artful and cagey in all of his responses. Very public relations-oriented. Nothing new there. Most of what I found was not at all useful, just statistics and speculations about his businesses, his charitable contributions, and his public appearances.

The OtherNet, though. That had a few more answers, and none of them were good.

Unsurprisingly, the vampire had an entire thread devoted to him, many pages long. He had even posted on it a couple of times. It was full of sightings, notes of his involvement in certain disappearances, and an estimate of the traffic his business was seeing, both in terms of finance and expansion of his ranks. His popularity was undeniable, as was the scary fact of his power, made clear by the documented instances of him or his minions laying the smack down on competitors. Someone had even posted a few pictures of the aftermath of a battle that Mouse and Royce's chief of security, Angus MacLeod, had participated in behind some club sometime back in the eighties. Some of the remains were barely recognizable as having been a person.

Royce's response on the message board was simple, elegant, and chilling, all at once.

We all do what we must to protect our own.

Yeah. Real charming.

It was frustrating that Keith still wouldn't let me post on the board. I was itching to ask questions. As many as the board answered for me—and make no mistake, it was *full* of information about Others and their politics that I probably could have happily done without knowing my entire life—it seemed that for every answer I found, two more questions formed in my head.

Out of curiosity, I checked the sub-forums for other cities, just to see what they might hold. There were threads on all of the big names in their local supernatural communities, too. Some were longer and obviously hotter topics than the others, like the ones on Rohrik Donovan and Royce.

Vampire-ville was what drew my eye.

Max Carlyle. Clyde Seabreeze. Ian Taft. Vampires I'd never heard of before—Chuck Masterson in Dallas. Fabian d'Argento in San Francisco. Theodore Welsh in D.C. Alejandro Vasquez in Las Vegas. On and on. A few of them were members of the message board, too. Clyde, the master vampire of Los Angeles, was more active than Royce. His thread was full of pictures of him modeling and posing for magazines and YouTube clips of him speaking on TV shows. Some of the links and pictures had even been posted by him. Overall, it wasn't very interesting, though he was pretty to look at in a blond, blue-eyed, chiseled, James Dean knock-off way.

Actually, I take that back. After taking a closer look at his latest picture, make that brown with frosted tips. Yeesh. In that pose, lounging shirtless on a plush couch in some leather pants, and with that gleam in his eye that said he wanted to do bad things all night long, he could have given Royce a run for his money in the smoldering looks department. The vampire was prettier than he had any right to be. Hell, most of them were.

Reading the threads took my mind off my impending change. Any doubt that I was infected had been wiped away once my body decided that it was switching to a nocturnal schedule. Daylight dug into the back of my skull like daggers. As Rohrik had warned, loud noises now bothered me, and I found myself getting nauseous at the scent of things the others didn't pick up on, even when I wasn't wearing the belt. The only symptom I hadn't shown yet, thank goodness, was a craving for rare or raw meat.

None of the hunters wanted to be around me while I was like this. Some of the threads on the OtherNet had confirmed my fears. I was showing almost every sign and symptom of having succumbed to the lycanthropy virus. My only consolation was knowing that, at least until I turned, I still had the use of the belt and I still had some time to find Chaz. Not much of it, and maybe no real leads to speak of, but I hadn't given up yet.

Though I thought about getting in touch with Arnold now and again about that cure he'd promised to hunt for, and maybe to see if he'd had any word from Sara, the belt strongly advised against it. Since the belt had been a mage in life, I believed it when it said he wouldn't have found anything that could help me. Plus the risks of being tracked by getting in touch with friends and family while so many were looking for me made it far too dangerous to chance. If Sara hadn't been keeping in touch with Detective Smith, she might not have been contacting Arnold, either. The only real way to be sure what had happened to her would be to go back to Royce's apartment building to see for myself—a prospect I knew I would eventually have to face, but was coming to dread.

Everyone else had long since gone to bed, and the moon had already set for the evening. The latest eye candy in Clyde's thread soothed the burning in my eyes—but not as much as the pop-up alert that Hawk had finally replied. I nearly dropped the computer in my haste to see what his message said.

Sorry for the delay. Family and pack emergencies kept me AFK, and looks like your boy does a decent job of pulling a Houdini when he needs to.

Anyway, looks like newbsauce is staying with a beta, along with most of the dominant wolves in his pack. I've got an address for you. Don't envy whoever they strong-armed into letting them camp. You need the Nightstrikers to help you raid? I wouldn't take him in PvP unless you're packing some heavy firearms. We can drive down to the city if you need us to get your back. Don't pull a Leeroy on this one.

I told myself the tears pricking my eyes were from the brightness of the screen combined with the lack of sleep, not the overwhelming gratitude that washed over me. As much as I could have used their help facing Chaz (and wondered what the hell a Leeroy was), I didn't want to pull the geeky Weres into my mess.

I typed back a quick "thank you," an insincere promise not to do anything rash, and asked for the address. He got back to me in less than a minute with the info and a warning.

I'm not j/k'ing. There's something bad brewing in town, and he has something to do with it. Watch your ass.

No kidding. Here's hoping I could pull this one off.

Chapter 17

My head was swimming with ideas, but I had to wait for Jack and the others to wake up before I could do anything effective. I spent the rest of the night on a stool in the kitchen, hunched over the laptop and impatiently checking the clock between scanning more threads on the message board for useful information.

There were some things I'd been avoiding. Digging too deep into the activity of one of my enemies, for one thing. Burying my head in the sand was no longer an option.

Now that I was looking, I almost wished that I could have remained ignorant about the issues involving the Others so that I wouldn't have had another worry added on top of what was already on my plate. For instance, it might have been nice to know sooner that Max had been spotted making the rounds in other territories—except there was no hint in any of the posts as to *why* he was doing it.

Aside from the gripes from someone who had been in Royce's building during Max's attack, Others from a few different cities made mention that they'd seen him in Atlanta, New Orleans, Los Angeles, and Las Vegas. Nobody seemed to know why he was there, or who he'd been there to meet with—only that he'd been in town. No attacks, no confirmed meetings with the power players in the area. It was worrisome in a distant, this-might-become-my-problem-later fashion.

What was he up to?

It was just my luck that Jack woke up in a bear of a mood. He was determined to get back on his feet and stumbled out of bed to join me in the kitchen, dressed in a loose pair of sweats and a navy wifebeater that didn't complement the pallor of his skin. Judging by the expression on his face, now wasn't a good time to ask him for any favors.

I waited until he'd made himself a cup of coffee and the spines had retracted a bit before I attempted conversation.

"Thought you might like to know I found the address where Chaz is hiding."

Jack grunted.

"I can take the guys and check it out today. We can make sure he's still there."

Another grunt.

"If he is, we can form a plan of attack, rally the troops, and get this over with tonight."

Jack sipped his coffee, then carefully set the mug down on the sleek granite countertop. "Where'd you get the intel?"

"A friend. An Other who has it out for Chaz."

He sniffed. Rubbed his face. "You never cease to astound me. Trapped in here with the rest of us, and you're still more effective than the men I've had combing this goddamn city all month."

As grudging as the praise was, hearing it from Jack made me glow with pride. Until he opened his mouth again, that is.

"Too fucking bad you're going to be one of them. You really would have made a good leader for this outfit when I'm gone."

To keep myself from saying something caustic, I got busy pouring myself a cup of the brew he'd made, gulping a few swallows. It didn't help in the slightest. I didn't open my mouth until I was sure I had a handle on my temper and wouldn't say something regrettable.

"You and I both know it's never going to happen," I said, staring into the depths of my mug like it might hold some answers. "You know, I haven't really thought beyond what's going to happen after the fight with Chaz. The full moon is only a few days away. Do you . . . I don't suppose . . ."

Jack pulled out a stool next to me and settled against the counter in a casual lean. The relaxed look was ruined by the sudden bout of coughing that had him doubling over. I thumped his back until the fit eased. He stayed bent over, and I left my hand splayed against his ribs once he got his breath back.

He didn't say anything about my touch or withdraw from me. The heat radiating from his body was unhealthy, but somehow I didn't think he cared much about that. His mind had always been centered on how to care for his people, and what I could do for him both in the short and long term. Nothing more, nothing less.

He took a deep breath, then another. It almost sounded like he was sucking in air through a wet cloth. His voice was soft, gravelly, and above all, tired. "We have a place. A cage. Sometimes we take the Weres there when we capture them alive. It's lined with silver, so you won't be able to get out. We can discuss what to do with you . . . after."

I nodded, too afraid to open my mouth, though his head was bent, so he couldn't see. He arched his back in a stretch as he sat up, and I withdrew to cradle my coffee in both hands and watch him over the rim.

Tilting his head back, then side to side to crack his neck, he closed his eyes. "I'll talk to the others. You're—even if you're one of them, you're too valuable to us."

Well, go figure. Either Jack was going soft, or he was starting to ease up on his hatred of all things Other. Hard to say which it was at this point.

"I see why Royce wants you."

I'm not sure if my coffee or my jaw hit the floor first.

He started as the cup shattered on the linoleum, coffee spilling everywhere. My face felt hot enough that I'm sure it must have been as red as my hair. Sending the stool scraping back to clatter on the floor, I jumped into action, grabbing a towel and kneeling down to clean up the mess. He eased off his stool and knelt down next to me, grabbing my wrist before I had a chance to sop up much of it.

I kept my head down, my fingers tightly clenched around the wet fabric.

"Shiarra, you may not think so, but you've got a great deal of potential that hasn't been realized. You're afraid of this life. Understandable. It's dangerous, often thankless—but there's no feeling like the hunt. You have a taste for it now. You're strong enough to handle it. That's a good thing to have in a soldier. It's no wonder the vampire wants you. That's uncommon enough in this age. That you're willing to deal with the Others—now that's rare."

Christ. Of course that's what he meant. Sure.

"Look," I said, voice shaking as badly as my hands, "I'm sorry, Jack. I never asked for this. I don't want this life for myself. I have no idea what I'm going to do after this business with the Sunstrikers is taken care of. I'm more afraid of thinking beyond that point than I am of facing a pack of angry werewolves. You can't imagine what this is like—"

His grip abruptly tightened on my wrist to a painful squeeze. I looked up, meeting his eyes. The dark circles under them were more pronounced this close up. His brows were lowered, his thin lips set in a hard line. "Don't think you know what my life has been like. You have no idea."

I wasn't sure how to respond to that.

"You're going to have to start thinking about it, whether you like it or not. Time is running out for you, Shiarra. You've got decisions to make. We'll discuss this again after tonight. I expect you to do your best to stay alive. You've got the instincts of a survivor, and you're not getting out of the hard decisions by taking the easy way out."

I flushed at the insinuation that I might consciously make a decision to put myself in harm's way so I wouldn't survive tonight's fight. Even if I'd been thinking that was what would happen all along.

"You," he said, looking down at his fingers on my arm, clutched so tightly that the skin around where they dug in had gone white and bloodless, "are not going to die tonight. If that means running from the fight, you do it. Do I make myself clear?"

I twisted my wrist around, breaking his grip and reversing it, so that I now held his hand in an iron hold. "Tell you what, Jack. I'll make that promise if you'll do the same. You stay out of the fight tonight."

He glared at me, a look I would have flinched from only a few days ago. That steely look was *scary*—but I'd now seen a side of him that was vulnerable and human, and there was no way he was going to be able to bully me while he was this weak. He kept it up for a good long while, but he also looked away first.

Holy shit. I'd just out-stared Jack!

"I can't make that promise," he said. He sounded as petulant as a kid who'd just been told Christmas was canceled. "You know I can't."

"Good," I said. "Then you realize I can't make the kind of promise you want, either."

He yanked his hand out of my grip, rising to his feet. He stalked on unsteady feet to the other side of the kitchen, slamming his fist down on the counter so hard his cup rattled. "Don't you blackmail me," he spat. "You don't have any idea what I'm capable of. I might be sick, but I'm not an invalid. As long as I'm on my feet, I'll fight. You can't take that away from me. Nikki can't. No one can."

"I'm not trying to, Jack. I just want to make sure you're ready for the fight before you go out there and get yourself killed. The White Hats need you a lot more than they need me."

That sobered him somewhat. The anger in him was brutal, but his body was too weak to hold it for long. As much as he visibly wanted to stay strong and keep arguing with me, he had no way of countering my logic or showing me just how much he was capable of doing while so sick.

His fists remained clenched, but some of the tension in his shoulders eased as he slumped over the counter. His words were bitter and grudging, but at least he was starting to see some reason.

"Fair enough."

I started wiping at the coffee again, careful not to cut myself on any shards.

"You go with Bo and Jason this afternoon to

make sure the tip pans out. How much do you trust your informant?"

"A lot more than I trust yours."

That prompted a small smirk out of him. I think that was the first time he'd ever shown any amusement at one of my lame jokes. "Good. That's good."

I snorted and finished mopping up the spill, tossing the shards onto the towel before taking it to the trash. Jack watched me, not saying anything else, making no move to help or to continue badgering me about my choices or his. This was just getting too weird for words. I grabbed the laptop and started to leave, intending to attempt some sleep before the afternoon's festivities.

He crowded me when I moved to exit the kitchen, stepping in my way until I stopped in front of him. I opened my mouth to tell him to fuck off, but something in his expression warned me against it. Though it was weird, to all appearances he wanted to say something more, but couldn't seem to find the words. His hand came up, hovering by my cheek, but he didn't quite touch me. Was it his illness, the awkwardness of the moment, or nervousness that made his hand tremble?

He stayed that way, indecisive, for a long moment. His eyes kept searching my face, looking for something, but never settling. Seeing Jack like this, like he wanted something more from me than cooperation in his plans, was a painfully surreal experience. He gave no voice to whatever thoughts were running through his head, couldn't say what he wanted from me aloud. There was more under that pale skin and more going on behind those icy blue eyes than he'd ever let on before.

Whatever it was he was selling, I wasn't buying.

Without a word, I brushed past him and stalked back to my couch, not wanting to face him or any of the other hunters until I'd had some time to think things over.

Chapter 18

(Days left to full moon: 5)

I was close to punching Adam. He'd been tapping his foot impatiently for at least half an hour. We were in Jack's white van, across the street from the house where we'd confirmed earlier in the day Chaz and some of the other Sunstrikers were currently using as their hideout. It was well past one in the morning. The combination of shitty sleep, lack of food, and stress from having to sit on my ass and wait while my target was so close I could practically smell his godforsaken aftershave, was hell on my nerves.

We were supposed to wait until everyone was asleep, then use a combination of gasoline, Molotov cocktails, and a few flash grenades to light the place up. In theory, it would incapacitate or kill the bulk of the Weres, and the few who managed to crawl out from the flames would come right to us, weak from smoke inhalation and disoriented from the grenades. Adam, Bo, Jason, and I would take our positions at each side of the house to mow down any survivors who tried to escape. Nikki would be mobile, rushing to help whoever needed it most. Keith was our getaway driver and would make himself available as a last resort to pop in and act as additional backup.

The problem with our plan was that the were-wolves were all still awake and moving around. We could see them in the windows. Lookouts, maybe, or possibly it was too close to the full moon for them, like me, to sleep at night. We'd been here since 11 PM, and there was still plenty of activity in the house. With their superior senses, there was no doubt they'd hear us coming long before we had a chance to set the place on fire.

"How long do we want to wait for these things to bunk down? I'm supposed to be at work in six hours. Can we try this again during the day, when they're all asleep?"

I turned a baleful look on Adam. He really was getting on my last nerve. "If you knew you were going to have to go to work, why did you agree to come on this run?"

He scoffed. "Lady, have you ever tried saying no when Jack asked you to do something?"

That wasn't a question I was about to answer. Not here, not now. Not after the conversation I'd just had this morning.

Keith was tapping an absent beat on the steering wheel with his fingertips. "You guys tell me. I'm just the driver. You want to call it a night and work out an alternate plan?"

The van wasn't made for pacing, but I wished I could get up and work off some energy. The need to move was driving me bonkers. The belt wasn't helping. It had kept quiet, not intruding on my thoughts, but it was radiating an emotional gamut that I was in no mood to deal with. Excitement, desire, hatred, bloodlust—all the emotions that I should have welcomed but couldn't stand to deal with—were rattling around in my head. Right now, I needed to be cold and calculating, or I wasn't going to come out of this fight alive.

"We can't walk away. We don't know how long they'll stay here. By tomorrow, they could be gone. This has to be done tonight."

Bo nudged me with his boot. "That's great, but we need to know what to do. Jack has always been the mastermind behind everything. He didn't mention any contingencies on this one. Somebody else feel like stepping up to bat?"

"I think we should go," Nikki said, her eyes closed and her head tilted back to rest on the wall of the van. "We didn't have enough time to call in backup from the units in Jersey or Connecticut, and we don't have the manpower to deal with this many Weres. They'll know something is wrong the instant we try to torch the building—they can smell it or sense it or something. I'm not interested in waltzing into a deathtrap. We have to call it quits and come back later."

Some big, brave hunter she turned out to be. I got to my feet, stalking to the end of the van and shoving the back door open. Jason grabbed my arm, his thick, tree-trunk muscles straining to hold me back despite the fact that I was less than half his body weight.

"Didn't you hear her? We're going back. Sit down."

I turned a contemptuous look on him, my lip curling as I shoved his shoulder, breaking his grip. He stared up at me in shock, mouth dropping open. No one my size should have been able to push off that mountain of muscle like he weighed no more than a child, but the belt made it all possible.

"I'm not going back. If I have to do this by myself, I will."

Bo clambered to my side, shooting a look at Jason, who was now watching me with the expression of someone who has just discovered that a poisonous scorpion has taken up residence between his legs in his bedroll. They might have heard some talk about my infection, but I suppose it was a different thing when you were faced with the reality of it staring you in the eye.

The others reluctantly followed me out, taking Bo's cue. Nikki, Adam, then Jason, dragging his feet and watching me warily. They kept their distance, occasionally turning a nervous glance to the house. The longer we were out in the open, the more likely it was one of the Weres or the neighbors would notice us.

While it was a flash of heated anger that sent me stalking out of the van, now I felt cold certainty. There was no way I was going to survive this fight. The odds were too steep. We'd counted no less than six dominant wolves, plus the alpha, and a couple betas. Maybe, if we'd been able to stick to the original plan, maybe I could have walked away from that.

Not this. Not with what I had in mind. We'd stick to the plan, for the most part. The only change would be my role in it.

Strangely, I wasn't afraid. My hands were rock steady when I held them up to get the White Hats to quiet down their urgent whispering amongst themselves. They shut their mouths and looked to me for direction.

Nikki's mouth was set in a sardonic smirk, as though she was certain I was going to say something stupid. Jason and Adam had matching distrustful expressions. Bo was the only one who regarded me in the same way as ever—with what was probably a severely misplaced trust and attention.

"Okay, listen up," I said, keeping my voice low so it wouldn't carry to the sensitive ears of the Weres. "Here's what we're going to do. Bo, Jason, Adam—carry out your parts in the original plan, no change. Nikki, you're going to take over for me."

They all exchanged confused looks, though Nikki was quick to recover her sarcasm. "And I guess you're just going to sit your ass out on this one, right? I knew we shouldn't have listened—"

"Be quiet," I said, the venom in those two words sufficient to make her take a nervous step back. "I'm going in the front. As soon as I'm in, hit the place with everything you've got. There won't be time to pour the gas, so stick with the cocktails and the grenades, then switch to your firearms. Concentrate the grenades in the back and on the upper floors so you don't incapacitate me along with our targets."

Bo was quick to come to my side and grab my arm, shaking me. "Shiarra, no!"

"Are you insane? They'll kill you! Tear you to shreds!" Keith stage-whispered from the front of the van. I hadn't realized he could hear us from there.

"Forget the Weres," Adam said, appalled. "What if you get hit by friendly fire? You can't walk into the thick of that mess and get out again in one piece!"

I looked up into Bo's face, something in my gut twisting at putting that worry and panic into his eyes. His dark skin was flushed; even in the shadows where we were parked, I could see it, clear as day. Smell the blood rushing to his skin. The thought of the fight to come hadn't worked him up, but the idea of letting me walk into that house alone terrified him. I put my hand over his on my arm, giving his fingers a reassuring squeeze.

"I have to do this. There's no other way to make sure the dangerous ones, Chaz and Dillon, don't escape. I won't let them walk away from this."

I didn't have to say they wouldn't let me out alive, either. No doubt the hunters knew it as well as I did.

Bo shook me again, not hard, but enough to

make it clear he wanted me to see sense and stop the crazy talk. "Look, I've seen you in action, but even you can't take that many."

Jason looked me up and down, fingering the bowie knife at his belt. "I don't know. She's capable of more than we thought. You have something up your sleeve, girl? Some secret weapon you plan on using while you're in there?"

I gave him a look, and he held up his hands. "Hey, no harm in asking, right?" I didn't dignify the comment with an answer.

"You're crazy," Nikki said, surprise and a grudging kind of admiration in her voice. "You really think you can survive this?"

I shook my head.

Adam gave a low whistle. "Man, didn't think you had this kind of dedication to the cause. We won't let you down."

Bo's fingers tightened painfully, even through the protection of my armor, pinching my skin. He didn't seem to realize he was hurting me. "Shia, you can't—you'll never get out alive—"

I looked up into his dark brown eyes, locking gazes with him. That same, weird calm flooded through me, a certainty of the inevitability of what was to come. Somehow, my voice stayed steady and composed, even though I was sorrier than I could say to hurt Bo like this. "I know. Tell Jack I'm sorry. And don't let any of them walk away from this. Burn it to the ground."

Without another word, I pulled away and jogged across the street, not giving them another opportunity to pull me into an argument or to come up with reasons to put this off until later. I wasn't sure how long this Zen-like state of mind was going to last. I needed to take advantage of it while I could.

I was dimly aware of the other hunters getting themselves into place. Bo tried to come to my side, but Nikki pulled him past me and shoved him toward his designated position outside the house. Front yard, hidden behind a bush lining the walkway leading up to the house. I'd have to pass him on the way. He might try to stop me, so I'd have to be careful not to give him an opportunity to give us away.

Taking a deep breath, I took stock of my weapons while I waited for the other hunters to get under cover. My guns were in their holsters, ready for easy access. The belt was cinched tight around my waist, thrumming with something bordering on lust for the coming fight. Extra ammo clipped to the belt. Borrowed knives strapped to my outer thighs, ankles, and another at the small of my back. With a few careful tugs, the turtleneck was pulled just a bit higher on my throat, protecting me from any new claw or bite wounds. Not that it mattered much at this point.

A dim light shone from the side of the house, over by the trash cans. Everyone was in place. It was do or die time.

Another deep breath centered me, helped me focus on nothing but the front door as I strode forward. If I looked into Bo's eyes one more time,

I might lose my nerve and call this suicide mission off. There was no way I could allow that.

The bushes rustled as if he reached for me, tried to hold me back, but I used a bit of the belt's gifts to speed past long before he could lay a hand on me or whisper at me to stop.

I took the few steps leading up to the porch one at a time, everything in that moment condensing into a need to face what lay behind that door. I could feel them in there. Their energy. Their smell; a tainted musk, unclean. Afraid of something. Maybe knowing I was coming for them.

Well. Wouldn't do to disappoint them. I lifted my hand, glad of the studded leather gloves that Jack had found buried in a drawer and handed to me before we left for the mission earlier this evening. The sharp crack of the metal studs against the heavy wood, just under a Halloween ghost taped to the door, echoed down the quiet street, loud as a gunshot.

All sense of movement and sound from behind the door ceased. The tang of fear grew stronger, more bitter, sharper. I could taste it on my tongue, burning my taste buds like sucking on a copper penny.

Someone was approaching the door. I could feel the heat of them. Closing the distance. I closed my eyes and took one more breath, holding it, hoping it wouldn't be my last. Drew my guns, running my leather-clad thumbs over the grips, before leveling them both at the entryway.

Slowly, the door swung open, the figure on the

other side a silhouette against the lights burning deeper in the house. He or she gasped, a sharp intake of breath, only managing a single step back before I pulled the triggers.

"Knock, knock, bitches."

Chapter 19

The gunshots would no doubt alert the neighbors that something was up, but I didn't plan on this taking very long. I stepped over the corpse in the entryway, still twitching, the acrid stink of silver burn heavy on the air. A niggling thought rattled around in the back of my head that I should be sorry or horrified, but I ignored it.

Another Were was scuttling around somewhere beyond my line of sight, running away from me by the sound of it. There were also the stomach-churning wet cracking and groans, and the telltale rip of tearing fabric, coming from multiple sources somewhere in the house around me. The dominant wolves were pulling quick shifts, preparing for battle.

I paid no mind to the bottles of alcohol stuffed with burning rags that shattered the windows and set the furniture on fire, using the belt's preternatural reflexes to dodge out of the way whenever one came too close. The picturesque, suburban perfection of the place was quickly being ruined by fire and ash. The added Styrofoam and dish soap we'd used would guarantee the house would be choked up with smoke in no time. The haze would provide cover, but could be more deadly than the Weres if I stayed inside too long.

Without hesitation, I pressed deeper inside, searching. There hadn't been any gunshots or sounds of brawling from outside yet, so the monsters were all still trapped in here—with me.

Claws skittered across linoleum. I kept one gun in front of me, aimed low, the other held at my shoulder with the business end pointed at the ceiling. The clicking and scraping sounds grew louder as I approached. Turning the corner, I barely registered what I was seeing before the gun popped again, impossibly loud in the enclosed space.

A wolf—silvery gray fur, not big enough to be Chaz—let loose with a howl, charging at me, its paws slipping on the slick tile as it shot around the table that still burned with the remains of a shattered Molotov. There was blood on its shoulder, but clearly the silver bullet wasn't enough to stop an enraged dominant Were. Jesus, the thing was *huge*—teeth as long as my fingers and a body that would put a St. Bernard to shame—and it looked like it was intent on latching onto my throat.

I barely had enough time to tuck the guns away before it bounded forward, knocking me back against the wall. It felt like the whole house shuddered under our weight. I got one arm under its mouth and the other hand buried in the fur on top of its skull, forcing its jaws shut. Claws raked down my chest, bruisingly hard, but the armor prevented it from flaying me open. Plaster dust drifted down around us like snow while we grappled.

The growls issuing from its throat were thunderous, so deep that my bones shivered in response. I voiced a low growl of my own, glaring into its yellow eyes with every ounce of hatred I could muster.

Tightening my grip, I gave its head a sudden twist, breaking its neck with a dull, meaty crack.

Satisfaction warred with relief and a dim sensation of horror at what I had just done.

The limp body slid to the floor with a thump. When I looked up, glowing green eyes were watching me from the shadows of a doorway across the room. The creature had fur so dark, it seemed to suck in the light, the shadowy outline of its hulking frame emphasized by the occasional spark from floating embers drifting through the open space between us.

It ducked its head under the frame and stepped into the room, having to stoop so as not to bang its head on the ceiling. Ropy muscle bulged across a thick chest and long, talon-tipped arms. Sleek black fur covered the vaguely humanoid frame of the monster before me. It moved with a smooth, deliberate grace as it approached me. A beautiful and terrible hybrid of human and wolf, like a magnificent living sculpture of pure, condensed predator, coming for my blood.

A predator I recognized.

Dillon.

The rat bastard. The asshole who had infected me.

His lip lifted, revealing yellowed dagger fangs, even bigger than those of the wolf I'd just defeated. Claw-tipped fingers spread, and he arched his back, dog-like head lowering until he was nearly my height and presenting a slightly smaller target. Say, the size of a VW Bug instead of an Escalade.

My own lips pulled back in a rictus grin, the skin stretched so tight over my teeth that my cheeks ached. As Dillon growled, so did I, one hand closing on a stake. He stepped forward with a heavy thump, spreading his arms and flexing his fingers so the light could catch on those obsidian claws. A challenge, daring me to come at him first.

There was no way in hell I was going down without taking Dillon with me. Now that he was within sight, all the bitter, hateful things that had brought me to this point rattled around in my skull, shattering that icy calm to release the rage frozen deep inside.

Jim Pradiz might have been a sleazeball, and his methods of reporting might have been deplorable, but he'd been a good man at heart. He'd tried to protect me in his own, twisted way. And he was dead because of the Sunstrikers. The belt whispered that Dillon might have even been the one to kill him.

My arm sported scars from those sickle-like claws. More than likely, I'd be some monstrous beast like the one standing right in front of me once the moon waxed full. Because of Dillon.

The mess I had gotten into with the Sunstrikers, including my probable infection, had made it into the papers, and had led up to my father's disowning me and telling me I wasn't his little girl anymore.

All because of Dillon.

An inhuman howl split the air, shrieking, earsplitting, shaking the house to its foundations. The very air vibrated with the sound, and Dillon cringed back from it, covering his tufted ears. It drowned out the sound of the crackling flames, the shouts of the White Hats outside, the answering cries of the other werewolves in the house.

It came from me.

I've heard people talk about a red haze taking over their vision in moments of extreme rage. That had always sounded stupid to me. An exaggeration, used as a way to say you were too stoked by anger to really notice what was going on around you during a battle, that's all.

Until that moment—that moment when I lived and breathed that furious beast, screamed to the heavens with all of the pain and anguish and hatred that had been stored in my mind, battling for release since the clusterfuck that my life had become began spiraling out of control less than a month ago—I'd thought the red haze of rage was nothing more than a joke.

It wasn't. The sound that came from me should never have come from a human's vocal cords. My eyes felt like they must be glowing like the fire licking at the curtains over the sink and eating away at the oak table a few feet away. There was no room in this body for all of the heat and rage it contained. This weak flesh was not enough to hold it in. It needed release.

It needed to punish.

Dillon retreated, lowering his head and skittering back from me like a giant, frightened dog.

I followed him, stalking forward with a slow, deliberate pace, knowing that this moment was inevitable. That it had been coming from the moment he scratched me. The moment he first tried to hunt me, back in that filthy, dark alley outside of Royce's restaurant, back before we battled the crazy sorcerer. He could run. He could hide. But I would find him, and I would end him, just like I'd find and end Chaz.

He fell to all fours and loped out of the kitchen into the room he'd been watching from, where it was dark and presumably safe. His claws left furrows in the tile. I followed, moving with a kind of single-mindedness I'd only experienced once before, while chasing after Kimberly.

Hopefully she was here, too, so I could finish what I started with her back in the park.

Dillon was hauling ass, but I never once thought he'd escape me. When I reached the doorway, I tucked the stake away and drew my gun. In the back of my head, I knew we were moving at hyperspeed, but it *felt* like everything was moving in slow motion. He sailed over a couch, forepaws landing with a heavy thud that I felt through the soles of my boots. In that short span of time, I'd already locked on my target and popped off a round aimed at the back of his left leg.

He made a sound I barely heard, his hind leg collapsing under him as he landed. It wouldn't hold his weight with the silver frying all of the nerve endings in his upper thigh.

As he twisted around, I calmly put a bullet in his other leg, shattering his right kneecap. He curled up on himself with a shriek, so I walked around the couch and pressed my boot into his thick neck. He made a gasping, choking sound, wildly rolling eyes widening as I lowered the gun until it was aimed at his temple. From this close, I couldn't possibly miss.

"Why did you have to make it this easy?" I asked, distantly noting how cold and lifeless my voice sounded to my own ears. "Why couldn't you have at least put up a good fight?"

The Were swung one arm, as thick around as both my thighs, his closed fist slamming into my stomach and sending me into the couch. It fell over backwards, sending me with it. The gun fell out of my hand and disappeared somewhere in the dark.

The belt loved it. My back, not so much.

Deep inside, the power of the belt uncoiled like a serpent, flooding me with power and adrenaline. Another giant wolf shot out of the darkness toward me, and while I was still on my back, I lifted the other gun and got it right between the eyes. The body, still twitching, tumbled forward and slid into me.

With a groan, I pushed it aside, coughing on the smoke drifting into the room from the kitchen. The fur was thick, warm, and my gloved hand came away sticky with blood.

I staggered to my feet and pressed my palm to my forehead. All the energy rushing through my bloodstream combined with the chemical smoke and the tumble was making for a horrible head rush.

When I focused on where Dillon had fallen, he was gone. A trail of blood and claw marks led me into the next room. Though I was swaying slightly, the vertigo faded as the object of my current obsession came back into view. He was dragging himself to stairs leading up to the next floor.

He pulled himself one slow, painful step at a time, his talons digging into the stairs one by one. I came up behind him on silent feet, so quiet and swift that he didn't notice me until my hands were in his scruff and hauling him back to the first floor. His claws hooked into the wood, trying to stay put, but with the help of the combined rage and strength I was channeling from the belt, he took most of the step with him when I threw him against the wall. It buckled and cracked under the impact, and he lay where he fell, luminous green eyes blinking stupidly up at me as I descended upon him like an avenging angel.

His eyes drifted shut once I was close enough to stand over him, the tips of my boots stopping at the growing pool of blood. The thick crimson liquid kissed the edge of my steel toes, seeped between the treads.

I knelt down, waiting until Dillon opened his eyes again to look at me. Waited for the dilated irises to focus.

"Dillon," I said, soft, gentle, just loud enough to be heard over his labored panting, "I want you to know that I did this for me. For my family. For Jim Pradiz. For everyone else whose lives you ruined or took, whether I knew them or not. You're never going to hurt anyone again."

He blinked and made a faint whining sound in his throat. The sound of a lost puppy.

It was the last sound he made before I shoved the silver stake into his heart.

"Shia, no!"

That anguished, broken voice came moments too late. Not that I would have stopped. Thick, almost black heart's blood dripped off the tip as I pulled it free, dulling the metallic sheen of the silver. My fingers tightened on the leather grip until it squeaked as I slowly got to my feet and turned around, lifting my eyes to focus on the figure at the head of the stairs.

He was dressed only in jeans, his bare toes curled over the edge of the top step and his crystalline blue eyes wide with shock. That tousled blond hair was sticking up in all directions, in desperate need of a trim, his tanned chest and arms thick with hair, and his jaw covered with stubble. Maybe he'd just shifted back to human. Or maybe he'd been on the run for so long that he hadn't been able to see to those simple, mundane necessities of personal grooming. It didn't matter. Even now, after all he had done, he was beautiful, a golden god among mortal men.

He stood there, watching me, unmoving as I approached. My world narrowed down to a tunnel. Nothing else mattered. Nothing else existed for me. The patter of the liquid dripping off the stake in my hand. The stink of Were and smell of burning things, stinging my eyes. The embers floating like fireflies, winking in the space between us. None of it.

I'd found Chaz.

Chapter 20

He stayed frozen in place as I stalked up the stairs. I had eyes only for him. I didn't even realize I'd tried to stab him with the stake until I felt a sudden shooting pain in my wrist, noticed his hand had closed around my arm and his fingers had dug into my tendons until the silver thudded against the floor and rolled down the steps.

A sound bordering on a sob died in my throat as I rounded my other fist and threw a punch at his jaw. It connected, the silver studs on my knuckles cutting into his cheek, throwing his head to one side.

With a snarl, he yanked me up into his arms, trapping me against his chest as he pulled me onto the landing. "Jesus *Christ*, what the fuck's gotten into you? Are you on vampire blood again?"

I squirmed and fought, landing a pretty decent blow to his nuts before he slammed me against the wall hard enough for a couple framed pictures to fall and shatter at our feet. The belt was a huge help, but when he pinned my hands at the wrists and used his lower body to pin my legs, pressing against me like he had the right to be as intimate as a lover, his superior weight won out. Still, I struggled, my hands curled into claws as I strained to escape, hoarse sounds that might have been screams of fury passing between my clenched teeth.

"Stop it," he hissed, staring down at me with eyes that glowed with an inner light. "For God's sake, stop! Listen to me! We've got to get out of this house or we're going to die!"

With an anguished moan, I shoved at him, succeeding in making him take a step back to readjust his position. I had to get him off of me. *Had to.* If I didn't, I'd die, and he would live, and all of this would have been for nothing.

His shock was fading. Calculation was setting in. He looked down at me as though he'd never seen me before, while all I saw was a lying, cheating, murderous scumbag—a walking plague upon this earth.

"Shia," he whispered, "what's happened to you?"

I headbutted him. He reeled back with a curse, letting me go so he could press a palm to his forehead. With a sweep of my leg, he fell on his ass with a startled yelp.

At that point, I was too far gone to think to use any weapon but my hands. I fell on him in a straddle, one hand under his jaw to hold him in place, the other settling into a steady rhythm of pounding his stupid, perfect face into the back of his skull.

He flailed under me, struck me, but I barely felt it, even though I heard a distinct crack that came from somewhere inside my own body. It wasn't until he loosed a roar and rolled that I stopped, and then only to catch my balance as I arched my body to avoid his grasping hands.

I fell onto my back and shot a kick at his jaw as he surged to his knees. His head snapped to the side, blood spraying the wall and a tooth rolling across the floor. His lip lifted in a gap-toothed snarl, and his eyes literally glowed with rage. He hefted himself up on his arms, and then to his feet, the floor shuddering under his weight with each heavy step.

He was after me now.

Once again, that deadly calm stole over me. I knew what needed to be done. I knew neither of us was going to live through this.

His nails were growing—not quite talons, not yet—as he reached down to grab hold of me. With a sinuous twist, I avoided his grasp, moving out of the way and landing a sucker punch just below his ribs. He gasped and rounded on me with a wild swing that managed to clip my shoulder and numb my arm.

Quietly, in the back of my head, the belt was whispering a litany ('*kill-swing-kill-kill-kill-it-duck-kill-kill*') that was like a mantra, keeping me focused through the pain and the shortness of breath. The fluid movements were mostly the handiwork of the belt. I was long beyond the point of sanity, my only desire in that moment to take Chaz down with me before I died.

We exchanged blows. He didn't fight dirty. I did. At one point, I had a good grip on his inner wrist with my teeth, and he made a sound that nearly busted my eardrums.

When he clipped the side of my face with an uppercut, making my eyes water and everything wobble in my vision for a second, he seemed to come to some kind of realization about what he'd done. He grabbed my shoulders to steady me. I used the grip and his uneven footing to topple us both to the ground again, but miscalculated the distance to the stairs.

We tumbled down in each other's arms, the wooden steps snapping under our weight.

Though my ears were ringing and everything *hurt* from that fall and my skin was stinging from the heat of the nearby fire—which had spread and was now creeping up the walls near the doorway to the kitchen—I was amazed I was alive. Chaz had put his hand behind my head on the way down so my skull wouldn't be crushed.

It was a terrible tactical error on his part. I might have been shaky, but I was still functioning, and the fight wasn't over yet.

He blinked down at me through watery eyes, his hand going to my cheek where he'd landed a good one. I stabbed him in the side with a stake while he was distracted.

A pained howl was torn out of his throat, and he flung himself to the side, grabbing the weapon and tossing it away in the process. His palm was singed from the brief contact, even through the leather grip. I reached for another stake.

"Chaz! Chaz, the passage is open, we can leave—"

Kimberly's voice abruptly cut off as she noted exactly what he was up to. Seeing her readjusted my priorities a tad, considering he was down for the count. She must have escaped from Isabelle when the Moonwalker chased her in Central Park.

The shock on her features, combined with the new angle of her formerly pert and perfect nose and the scarring on her cheek from the silver I'd pressed against her in the park, made my day. I gave her a bloody smile, spitting some of the copper taint out of my mouth before advancing on her. She squealed and retreated back into the basement she'd been hiding in, slamming the door behind her.

Just before I could reach the knob, Chaz grabbed me around the waist and flung me back, sending me skidding over the floor until my head and spine connected painfully with the wall. It was hot enough to the touch that the heat of it was burning my back through the armor. Everything went dim for a few seconds, and my body ached abominably, but I was conscious enough to keep going.

There were stars in my eyes as he limped closer, but I still got to my feet, ready to meet him. He eyed me warily, his fists up in a defensive position, but made no move to strike me again.

"Listen," he said, voice thick and raspy from blood and smoke, "just stop for a minute. Stop

it! I don't know what the fuck bug has crawled up
your ass, but you're going to knock it off and
come with us. You hear me? You're not dying in
this house. I want to know how you found me,
why you're doing this, and what the hell you have
to do with the hunters outside when you're so
obviously tainted with Other blood."

Tainted. There was a word for it. I was tainted
all right.

*'Tainted with the blood of thy enemies, perhaps, but
you have the upper hand here. He wouldn't be calling for
a truce if he thought he could win by force. Take him
now. Don't let him get away.'*

My chest heaved, every breath burning both
inside and out. I used my arm to wipe some sweat
and blood off my brow, flinging sweaty curls out
of my eyes. Chaz took another step closer, edging
nearer bit by bit, while blood turned black from
silver taint slowly leaked down his side, staining
his jeans.

"I don't care if it's the vampire, Shia. I really don't.
I don't want you to die in here. Come with me."

I blinked slowly, not quite processing that last.
My jaw hurt, the words coming out haltingly and
with a wince or two in between. "What do you
mean, 'if it's the vampire'? What the hell are you
talking about?"

He waved some of the smoke out of his face,
then held out his hand. "Whoever made you
Other. You smell more like him than like a Were.
Come on, let's go!"

I ignored the offered hand. Stepped closer, fingers twitching above the handles of the stakes.

Had to wait to use them until I was close enough that he couldn't stop me.

"Dillon changed me. Dillon infected me," I spat.

That seemed to throw him through quite a loop. Hell, I almost believed his nonplussed expression, though it was a little hard to see under the mass of cuts and bruises on his face. "What?"

"You heard me. Don't tell me you didn't see it in the papers. The picture Pradiz snapped of my being scratched back at the cabins. Dillon did it, Chaz. If not for your fucked-up pack, and their fucked-up politics, and your fucked-up sense of responsibility, my life wouldn't be a complete fucking mess right now. J.P. would be alive. You and your whole goddamned pack have a lot to answer for."

He stared at me, thunderstruck.

It gave me the opportunity to step in close enough to draw a stake and go for his chest, hopefully to land a clean kill as I had with Dillon.

Chaz twisted his torso back, avoiding the killing blow, though the sharp tip still sliced him open across the chest. He slapped my hand aside, then rushed at me, nearly cracking my ribs as he slammed me into the wall again.

Embers and flaming bits of plaster rained down on us, stinging my eyes, burning my cheeks. He ignored the pain he must have been feeling from the fire licking at his skin, one large palm holding my head steady so I had no choice but to look into his eyes. He had to blink away blood from the cuts I'd inflicted when I'd whaled on his face. His voice was a low, husky growl, and I could see the tips of upper and lower fangs peeking through his lips as he spoke.

"Listen to me, Shiarra, and listen good. My pack isn't perfect. Never claimed it was. But we're not murderers. I know who killed Jim Pradiz, and I've been trying to find him for the last three weeks so I can clear myself. This isn't the time or the place for me to explain all this to you. Stop fighting, *now,* and come with me!"

All the while, the belt was speaking, too.

'See how he lies. What story do you think he's cooked up to save his ass this time? Do you think it's as convincing as what he tried to tell you about why he was sleeping around behind your back? I wonder . . .'

Blinded by tears of rage, I lashed out, renewing my earlier attack of punching, kicking, and biting, even though I wasn't in a good position for it. He'd never stop lying. He'd never stop trying to find a way to make me fit into the mold of stupid, human girlfriend. From the very beginning, all he'd ever done was lie and cheat and manipulate me. And I hated that I was so dizzy I could barely stand up, choking from the smoke in the air, my vision blurred with tears and ashes.

'Just a little more. Find that well of strength. The one deep down. Right near your heart. Draw on it.'

Sobbing, I struck at Chaz with all the force I could muster, though everything was going hazy and black at the edges. All he did was hold my upper arms so I couldn't hit him too hard or grab one of the stakes or guns again. I was on the verge of passing out, and even with the belt's help, I wasn't coming back from that precipice.

Still, I kicked at him, each strike a little slower and less powerful than the last. Mostly I went for his shins and knees, hoping that would force him to step back and give some ground.

'*You're wearing yourself out. Concentrate.* Think. *Aim for his weakest spot.*'

I went for another cheap shot between his legs, lifting my knee, but he swiveled his hips to avoid it, then shook me like a rag doll. As much as I wanted to claw his eyes and tear his heart out with my bare hands, then feed it to him with a rusty spoon, the trip down the stairs and the last blow to my head had damaged me somehow, or I'd inhaled too much smoke.

I'd failed. It was so hard to breathe. My muscles were weakening, going slack, one by one.

'*Don't stop. Don't! Live, damn it, you fucking rookie, you have to live!*'

The heat was so intense that the tears on my cheeks were drying almost as quickly as they leaked from my eyes. My hair was getting singed; the smell was awful, even beyond the way the burning building already smelled. I couldn't see a thing anymore, but I kept trying to strike out any which way I could.

Of course, that's when my muscles seized on me. A strange lethargy was eating away at my energy, sapping what little was left until I could no longer move. Even the effort to take a breath was becoming impossible.

This was it. This was really it. I was dying.

Distantly, I felt Chaz picking me up, but I could no longer see or fight against that hated touch.

Wasn't sure if I cared enough to fight anymore. Even with all the belt had to offer, after all my hard work, after weeks of hunting and worrying and going insane with the need for revenge and closure, I'd failed.

'*No. NO. I will not accept defeat. Not this close. Get up.* Get up!'

My body gave out. The belt's angry tirade faded into whispers, then nothing as the ache of despair and failure followed me into the blackness.

Chapter 21

(Days left to full moon: 2)

When I opened my eyes, I was in Jack's loft apartment, sprawled on the couch I'd originally claimed as my bed. It wasn't hard to figure out where I was. I recognized the tacky painting of New York's skyline with the LED lights. Honestly, who decorated with those anymore?

Every part of my body ached abominably. A sharp twinge in my side that worsened every time I took a breath heralded another broken rib. My face felt like a sack of bricks had been dropped on it, and my muscles were so sore, even lifting an arm to cover my mouth when I coughed was almost too much effort to bear.

The pain from coughing nearly made me pass out again. I had no idea what time it was or how I'd gotten back here. The last thing I recalled was fighting with Chaz in that house.

That, and failing to beat him.

So what the hell had happened? How did I get back here?

"Ah, you're awake? Good."

Chaz's voice. If I hadn't been so busy coughing up a lung, I would've launched myself off the couch to attack the bastard again. What in God's name was *he* doing here? In the secret sanctuary of the White Hats, no less?

His hand pressed against my breastbone, shoving me down into the cushions. He brushed my fingers away from my mouth and placed a soft-rimmed cup there; I scrabbled at it to pull it away before I realized what he was giving me—and began taking painful gulps of the oxygen. It took a minute or two, but the coughing eased off, and it became relatively easier to breathe. I glared at him over the plastic as soon as I blinked the tears out of my eyes. He gave me a humorless grin, showing me very clearly the newly formed gap where I'd knocked one of his teeth out.

"I'm going to take my hand away. You're going to sit still. Got it?"

He took my wordless glare as an affirmative and withdrew, tossing the face mask aside and turning off a small cylinder I hadn't seen earlier at the foot of the couch.

I tried to sit up, but the pain in my back made the pain in my ribs feel like a minor twinge in comparison. Chaz gave a short, harsh laugh when I collapsed back, breathless and gasping.

"You finished?"

When I nodded, he called back over his shoulder. "She's up."

There was a shuffling sound coming from downstairs. People coming to join us. Judging by what I could smell of myself, though somebody had obviously used a washcloth to wipe off the worst of the ash and grime and changed me into a T-shirt and someone else's boxers after the fight, I wasn't in any condition to be dealing with whatever was coming. My hair hung lank and oily around my shoulders, and I didn't even want to *think* about who had undressed and then put new clothes on me.

Chaz didn't look at me or say anything else until Jack, Nikki, and a few Weres wandered in. One of them was new to me: a tall, slender woman with dark hair and hazel eyes. She'd linked arms with Nick, a Were I remembered from my trip to the Pine Cone Lodge. He looked the same, still covered in piercings and tattoos. Simon was there, too. He'd helped in the fight against Max Carlyle. There were a few more whose faces I recognized, but whose names I didn't know. Lower-ranking Weres. The room got pretty crowded very fast.

Kimberly was noticeably absent. I sorely hoped the bitch had died back in that house.

The White Hats looked uncomfortable, but weren't making any move to attack the werewolves. Either I was drugged up, or there was something really wrong with this picture. Maybe both.

"Jack," I said, my voice gravelly from what I assumed was smoke inhalation, "you feel like letting me in on what's going on here?"

He settled on the arm of the couch by my feet, his arctic irises scanning my body with the clinical gaze of a scientist studying a bug under a microscope. There was nothing comforting or human about it.

"You almost died when you decided to Lone Ranger into that house. Your boyfriend here—"

"*Ex*-boyfriend," Chaz and I both said at the same time. Then glared at each other.

"Fine. Ex-boyfriend. Whatever. He dragged you out and called for a truce. Long story short, he told us what's been happening behind the scenes, who betrayed me, and who's behind the murders. Looks like your boy wasn't the one responsible for the death of that reporter. Remember that fight in Carl Schurz Park? The guy in the hat and trench coat? You almost got him. It was someone from a rival pack, the Ravenwoods."

That gave me a nasty start. Some of the Ravenwoods were behind the Embassy Incident. The same altercation that had landed my name and face in the papers months ago and changed my life forever. If I hadn't been feeling exceptionally brave that day, I never would have become so well known by the Others. The Circle never would have decided to draw me into their affairs and hire me to fetch the *Dominari* Focus from Alec Royce. Though I hadn't known it at the time, it had also put the wife of the Ravenwoods' pack leader in my debt. Patricia Hutchinson had promised me I could call on her if I ever needed her help.

Chaz knew all about that. He didn't seem particularly upset or put out at the news. He'd had more time to come to grips with this strange twist than I had.

Nikki was watching Chaz with narrowed, distrustful eyes from her seat on the edge of a chair across the room. Smart girl. "The Sunstrikers are going to help us take the Ravenwoods out."

That prompted a few snorts of derision and wry chuckles from the Weres. Simon, once he managed to stop snickering, gave her a pointed look. "You mean the White Hats are going to help the Sunstrikers kick some Ravenwood ass."

"Semantics," Jack said, giving Nikki a shut-up-if-you-know-what's-good-for-you look I knew all too well. She said nothing, turning her face away. Good to know she still considered Jack to be in charge.

"We are willing to work with you," the woman who was arm in arm with Nick said. Her English had a slight French lilt to it. "You should be grateful. This woman nearly destroyed herself taking only a few of us down. The rest of your warriors could not bear to face us in open battle. How do you think you would fare against an entire pack that rivals the Sunstrikers in size? You require our aid, and we could use yours. I fail to see the difficulty here."

Chaz ran a hand over his face, as though this was an argument he'd already heard one too many times. He turned his attention to me, his expression so hangdog, I couldn't help but feel a twinge of regret. If only I could have stayed ignorant of what he was, never known anything about the supernatural side of his life. We might not have stayed together, but now that I wasn't in the middle of fighting for my life, I could appreciate that he had done his best to incapacitate me while I'd killed his friends and been out for his blood.

He'd certainly succeeded at beating my ass to a pulp. I wasn't sure I was going to be able to eat other than through a straw for the next couple weeks, let alone try for round two.

That prompted another worry, one that should have hit me based on how weak and badly in need of a shower I was. I was so jolted by the thought, it prompted another coughing fit. I had to wave off the oxygen when Chaz tried to administer it again.

As soon as I could speak, I choked out a few words. "When . . . how long . . ."

Jack knew what I was asking. "A few days."

Chaz glanced back and forth between us, understanding dawning. "You weren't kidding back at that house, were you? You think you're turning Were."

I flinched at hearing it put so bluntly, then nodded. He reached for me, and I shrank back as Jack and Nikki got to their feet, alarmed. Chaz took hold of my arm, waving the hunters off with his other hand and lifting my wrist to his face to take a sniff. He frowned and leaned closer, sniffing again before releasing me. I tucked my hand under my chin so he couldn't grab me again.

"Funny," he said, touching his thumb under his nose and making a face like he'd smelled something rotten. Great. Nice to reaffirm that I reeked as badly as I thought. "You're . . . different. I can't tell what you are. Not quite Were. Not quite vampire. There's—you smell like both."

Oh, that was reassuring. His brows lowered, and he looked me over anew, like he was seeing me for the first time.

Nikki, on the other hand, was unimpressed. "Why am I not surprised? We should kill her, then. Get it out of the way before she turns. There are only a couple days left 'til the full moon. If she managed to destroy half as many of your wolves as you claimed, we can't afford to let her loose once the wolf in her comes out."

Chaz growled, a deep, threatening sound, as Jack came to my defense. "No. She might be turning, but that doesn't mean we can't still use her."

"I don't want her in the pack if she turns." Nick, who had once saved my life by protecting me from Dillon, sounded more bored than anything else. "She was never really one of us. Plus she killed Alana, Cameron, and Dillon."

"Don't forget Vic Thomasian," Nikki added helpfully.

Everyone turned to stare at me. I'm pretty sure my face was now the color of faded brick.

Nick ran his fingers through his short-cropped hair and continued as though Nikki hadn't interrupted him. "I don't know why we're letting her live—something must be done about the losses she's caused us. If her life is unacceptable, I know she's supposed to join us and take their place, but I don't think it's right. She's unstable."

That was a laugh, coming from a Sunstriker. Of

course, some of the other Weres in the back made soft sounds of agreement. Chaz was scanning the crowd with a tight expression, but he didn't counter anything being said. This wasn't looking good for me.

The girl who'd linked arms with Nick regarded me curiously. "Is this true? Would you continue to cause trouble for this pack after joining it?"

I gave her a flat stare. She didn't flinch away, and the silence stretched so long that I felt obligated to fill it. "You must be new."

"Yes. My name is Cindy. Cindy Bacon. I was part of the Timberpaws in Montreal, Quebec, but moved to join with the Sunstrikers a few weeks ago. I had no idea New York would be this exciting." Her cheerful expression was at odds with the hint of fang I could see in her smile. Nick didn't appear quite so pleased with her anymore. "It seems most of what I have heard about you on the supernatural grapevine was correct. They said you were a monster in human skin. Born to fight."

The way she said it made it sound like a compliment.

"That doesn't change anything," one of the wolves in the back said. "She's killed pack members. Something has to be done about that. We can't just let it slide. It's an insult. Makes us look weak to the other packs."

Cindy shrugged and spoke up above the others, her eyes briefly flaring with a green luminescence in their depths. "She can fight. For now, that is all we need to know. You can decide what to do with her after she helps us deal with the Ravenwoods. They must pay." Chaz gave the girl a look that had her cowering back. "I mean no disrespect, pack leader. Only that she could be a valuable asset in the fight to come."

I gathered from Cindy's words that the Ravenwoods were connected to whoever Chaz had been referring to when he said he knew who was behind the murders. Or had something to do with all of the people who had been infected outside of contracts, and that this somehow affected the Sunstrikers. Whatever the Ravenwoods had to do with it, they weren't my problem, and there was no way I was going to get involved in the Sunstrikers' mess.

"Hey, I'm right here, you know. No offense, but I would rather slit my wrists than be a Sunstriker. I'll be sitting this fight out."

Chaz turned that withering look on me. "The hell you say."

"Yes, the hell I say," I retorted, returning his look in kind. "I would have killed you if I could have. Still might, once I'm back on my feet. You might not have killed Jim Pradiz, but how about all those other people who were infected? How about what was done to me? To my family? You still have to answer for that."

Simon cleared his throat. "Not saying what he did was right, but I think murder is a little extreme for a bit of infidelity."

Chaz and I both glared him into silence. He raised his hands and took a step back, averting his gaze.

When Chaz turned back to me, he had plastered on a chagrined expression that might have been believable if I hadn't already known he was so artful at lying and deceit. "Shia, really, I'm sorry about that. I didn't want you to find out that way."

"Don't start this now," I warned, the growl in my throat hitching on the dry, sore spots. "I'm still ready to tear your balls off and feed them to you, so don't act like we're friends again just because you pulled me out of that fire."

"It's lovely that you two want to talk things over, but we're diverting off topic. We need manpower," Jack said.

Nick smiled, the golden hoop on his lip glinting in the light. "You've got it, hombre. The Sunstrikers have almost fifty more pack members than the Ravenwoods. Most of us are of fighting age. We'll mow them down."

Cindy ruffled his hair. The two of them smiled at each other, like they were talking about going to dinner and a movie instead of a battle to the death.

"Shia, my offer still stands," Jack said, drawing my attention back to him. "You can sit this one out if you want to. You're too hurt to be much use, anyway."

Well. At least he was being honest about it.

"Thank you."

Chaz looked back and forth between us. "Offer? What offer?"

I gave him as hostile a look as I could muster. "That's none of your business."

Jack shook his head and rose to his feet with a soft groan. For the first time since I had woken up, I noticed how tired he looked. There were dark circles under his eyes, and he looked like he'd lost weight over the last few days. That was somewhat alarming, considering he didn't have much weight to lose to begin with. His illness was accelerating. This battle would probably be his last.

Then again, I'd thought the same when I had walked into that house a few days ago. If anything, that just went to show how little I knew. It was possible he'd prove me wrong and continue soldiering on for another decade or two.

Nikki gave him some support as he shuffled out of the room. The Sunstrikers all regarded me with expressions that ranged from ambivalence to curiosity. Save for Chaz. I couldn't quite tell what he was thinking. His eyes were hooded, his brows knitted, and he had a slight twist to his lips as though he was stuck somewhere between angry and amused.

"Would you excuse us?"

Chaz didn't word it as a request. Nick, Simon, Cindy, and the other Weres followed in Jack and Nikki's tracks without a word of protest.

He didn't speak right away. Just looked down at me, arms folded across his broad chest, a muscle in his cheek twitching. He'd healed most of the silver burns on his face already, save for where I'd broken his skin. Those would leave behind telling, minor scars. One eye was a little swollen, and there was a bit of discoloration around his jaw, but that was all. Aside from that, and the missing tooth, you would never have known I'd smashed his face in just a few days ago.

"I know you don't believe me, but I am sorry. For everything."

I stared up at him, not replying.

"You were right. Going behind your back with Kimberly was a shitty thing to do. I shouldn't have lied to you. Assuming you had slept with the vampire was . . . Well, I didn't know what to think at the time. I'm sorry for jumping to conclusions, and for using it against you. You were right to try to kick my ass. I know it will never be enough, but . . . I'm sorry."

"Chaz," I said, then paused, not sure what to say. He looked at me expectantly, like he half hoped that I would say everything was okay now, and we could go back to the way we had been. I looked into his puppy dog eyes, that tentative ray of hope in his gaze, and hated that he still had the power to move me. I'd thought my heart had been shredded into so many pieces that nothing was left to feel.

Instead of burning hatred, all I felt was exhaustion.

"Chaz," I repeated, gathering up what remained of my good sense and clutching the memories of his betrayals like a security blanket, "don't bother. Just . . . don't."

When it became clear I wasn't about to say

anything else, that hopefulness in his expression faded behind a thundercloud of anger. He gave me a wounded look before spinning on a heel and stalking out.

Why did I feel like the asshole in this conversation?

Chapter 22

Left to my own devices, I lay back on the couch and just hurt for a while. It wasn't particularly productive, but without the others there to distract me, there was too much pain for me to do much more than work on breathing. Nikki came by with a bowl of something that she pushed into my hands, but I wasn't hungry and didn't bother eating it.

After a while, long after sunlight had stopped streaming in through the windows to be replaced by moonlight and reflections of city lights, I figured out why my stomach was doing its own protesting version of the Macarena. It wasn't hunger. I couldn't stand the smell of myself. Or the ache in my joints. I needed a shower or bath like nobody's business.

Getting up to take one seemed completely out of the question, but the desperate need to get the stink of the battle with Chaz off of me was my number one priority. I couldn't think with the smell of him on me. It was there, particularly where he'd touched me when he pushed me down. Right between my breasts.

I couldn't get clean fast enough.

Though the pain was phenomenal, I carefully rolled on the couch, legs first, so I wouldn't have to bend my back too much. Experience from the last time I'd busted a few ribs had unfortunately made me expert at figuring out how to get around despite that type of injury. It took a long time, and a few breathless curses, but I made it to my feet without adding any new injuries.

Walking and breathing were pushing me to the limits of my endurance, but I still managed to make my way to the shower. This felt far too close to how badly I'd been beaten after the fight with David Borowsky. Similar to how I had felt after the belt had used up all my reserves and I'd gone looking for the White Hats earlier this month. Perhaps some of this was just a holdover from the belt's using me up like a battery during the battle with Chaz, draining me to the point of no return.

Lying down in a bath would have been amazing if I could have bent at the waist. Instead I gave the tub a longing look before making do with a shower, peeling the borrowed clothes off and stepping into a spray that was almost too hot to stand. It washed away the dirt and the ash, but no matter how much soap I used, Chaz's musky scent clung to me.

There was something dark and earthy there, underneath it, like the simple act of touching me had woken something dormant under my skin. It took a while for me to realize that it didn't matter how many times I washed or scrubbed—it wasn't coming off.

Was this another sign of me turning? Was I marked by the pack somehow? Turning into a Sunstriker?

Feeling queasy, I stayed under the spray until my skin wrinkled. I couldn't keep my arms above my head long enough to work shampoo or conditioner into my hair, so I had to make do with a few quick swipes of liquid-covered fingers and hope for the best.

When the water was off, I attempted to wring my hair out, but by then lifting my arms that high was unbearable. I couldn't even wrap the heavy mass in a towel. The clothes I'd been wearing were too soiled for me to wear again, so I'd have to find something to change into outside the bathroom.

Resuming my zombie-shuffle, I went to the room down the hall that had the dresser with my clothes in it that Keith had brought from the house on City Island, and shut the door behind me. The belt was on top of the dresser, left there for me in a neat coil. There were signs that other people had dropped their things off in here as well. Bags and backpacks, mostly. The smell of Were was overpowering in the enclosed space. I wondered where they were all sleeping.

One thing I hadn't considered was how hard it was to pull clothing on without help. It had been many months since I'd had to try that after having been beaten to crap. I had the added pain of my spine injury to go along with it this time, too. The more I thought about it, the more I was surprised Dr. Morrow wasn't hovering over me, and that I was on my feet at all.

The doc hadn't been around for a while, actually. Maybe he had something to do with whatever that other project was the White Hats had been working on concurrent with dealing with my problems. The project nobody had yet seen fit to tell me about. I had the feeling they never would.

Placing the towel on top of the dresser, I selected another T-shirt, some underwear, and a pair of jeans. The bitch of it was, I couldn't bend over or put my arms up high enough to put any of it on. Wherever I'd found the strength to get my clothes off before the shower, it had deserted me now.

Tears of frustration pricked behind my eyelids as I leaned against the dresser, balling up the clothing in my fists.

There was a click, and the door opened behind me. I barely had time to grab the towel to cover my nakedness before Chaz walked in.

He shut the door behind him. I snarled at him, clutching the towel closer. "What the fuck do you think you're doing in here? Get out!"

Expression set, he approached me, reaching out. I grabbed for the belt, yanking out a stake and holding it before me in warning, though every muscle in my body protested at the sudden movements.

He stopped. Closed his eyes and took a breath. Exhaled and opened them again, some of the harsh lines easing out of his features. "Relax. I heard the shower." Spreading his hands, he nodded at the pile of clothes at my feet. "You're in no shape to handle that yourself. I knew you'd need help. So here I am."

I lifted the stake a bit higher, protecting my modesty with the towel as best I could one-handed. Energy of some kind buzzed against my fingertips through the leather. The belt was awake, and it wanted to be used—but Chaz would be able to stop me long before I managed to put it on.

"Don't you fucking touch me," I hissed. "You haven't got the right."

"No? Who do you think changed you? Cleaned you up after the fight?"

Heat suffused my cheeks. I hadn't wanted to think about it before. Having him throw that in my face was enough to prompt a wish for the floor to open up and swallow me—but I didn't give any ground.

"Would you prefer I get Nikki? Or maybe Jack—"

"No!" I practically shrieked it. He didn't seem overly impressed by my outburst. I repeated myself, quieter this time, but no less emphatic. "No. Nikki hates me, and I don't ever want Jack touching me. Just leave me alone. I'll deal with it."

The one raised brow was answer enough.

"I'll handle it. Just fuck off. Find some other girl to feel up."

"Christ, what do you take me for? I'm not here to feel you up. I know you need help. Stop acting like a brat and let's get this over with."

God, I hated him. Hated this whole situation.

As badly as I wanted to use the stake on him, I couldn't handle getting dressed by myself. Chaz had helped me with that mundane task, along with a million others, when I'd been recuperating from the fight against the mad sorcerer. He'd managed to keep his hands to himself all those times, waiting patiently until I was ready to do more.

This would be no different. I kept telling myself that as I reached out with a shaking hand to drop the stake on the dresser next to the belt.

He took the towel away—tugging a little, since I'd gripped it with both hands so hard that my knuckles went white—and set it aside. As I stood there, naked, I looked anywhere but at him while he arranged the clothing I'd selected. He helped me balance, not saying anything when I was forced to grab his shoulder as he knelt to lift my feet so I could step into the panties. His grip on my ankles was hot enough that it burned against my skin, even through the heat of my embarrassment.

His fingertips skimmed against the outside of my calves, then my thighs, tracing a scalding trail. The scent of him was thick enough to choke on and only made me feel sicker than I had been in the shower.

He repeated the process with the jeans and then stood, carefully doing up the zipper and button for me. His voice, when he spoke, was cold and unmoved, though there was something under the surface that I wished I couldn't smell on him.

"Is there a bra? There's only the shirt here."

Desperately avoiding his eyes, I swallowed. Hard. "No. I don't think . . . no."

With a detached nod, he reached for the shirt. As gentle as he'd been dealing with the rest, he helped tug it on over my head and maneuver my arms until I was able to tug it down myself over my breasts and stomach. Only then was I able to look at him. He was staring at my chest as though he was still seeing what was under the cloth.

He said something, but I was too rattled to get it right off. "Excuse me?"

"You need socks? Or are we done here?"

"We're done." I'd scream if he touched me again.

Without another word, he turned and walked back to the door. As much as it hurt to think the thought, let alone say it aloud, I opened my mouth.

"Wait."

Hand on the knob, he looked over his shoulder at me. There was no warmth there. No desire in the way he looked at me, though I could smell it as strongly as the apple-scented shampoo I'd dumped in my hair.

"Chaz, I—thank you."

That forbidding expression remained, his blue eyes gleaming with whatever plans were roiling through that head of his. With a nod, he turned away and continued out the door, leaving me alone with my own thoughts and regrets.

He hadn't touched me inappropriately, but the memory of his skin on mine was going to haunt me for days to come. If I survived for days, that was.

Warmth trickled down my upper lip. I pressed my fingertips under my nose and was unsurprised when they came away bloody.

I glanced at the belt, lying inert on top of the dresser. Spreading my fingers, I held my hand out, red-speckled digits splayed a few inches above the coiled leather. Energy buzzed in a prickle over my skin, marching along my palm until it reached my wrist. A throbbing sensation built in my bloodstream, pounding along in time with my heartbeat, felt strongest in that hand.

Curious, I closed my fist around the leather, right over one of the runes branded behind the buckle.

'*I thought you were dead.*' The belt's voice was a faint whisper, much like it had been the first time I'd worn it. Barely penetrating my consciousness, but still there, a reassuring and familiar presence. '*You were gravely injured. I'm surprised the beast dragged you out.*'

"Me too, Isaac," I said, keeping my voice low. No telling what the Weres might overhear.

'*It will speed the healing process if you wear me. You still can. There are changes going on in your body, but it's not yet to the point where you can no longer use me.*'

"Tempting as the idea is, I don't think the Weres in the house would take kindly to that," I replied.

I filled the belt in on what had happened since I had woken. About the Sunstrikers in the apartment and the deal they had made with the White

Hats. How I was going to be sitting out on the fight against the Ravenwoods and spending the night of the full moon locked up in a cage in case I turned.

The belt mulled that over, not responding for a while. I didn't do anything to rush it, leaning my hip against the dresser and resting my hand on the leather while I waited.

'*Take me with you tomorrow.*'

That response surprised me. "Why?"

'*This could go one of two ways. You will either turn, in which case you no longer wish to survive, yes?*'

I didn't answer.

'*You can use one of the stakes to end it if you must. It would be preferable to being at the mercy of the White Hats. They will prolong your death.*'

My tongue felt thick in my mouth, making it hard to speak. "You can't be sure of that."

'*I've seen enough through your eyes to know that you would not be treated with mercy by the White Hats. Bo is your ally, yes, but he will wish you dead as badly as the others already do if he sees you turn into a monster. And Jack only sees you as a tool to use to achieve his own ends. If, by some chance, you do not turn, you will need me.*'

"Not that I see that happening, but why?"

'*To destroy the vampire.*'

I stilled. A sudden, intense desire to hunt Royce burned in my blood, seared in my mind like a brand.

'*He must be stopped. Before he hurts you again. Hurts your friend. You must rescue her.*'

Sara. Oh, my God, *Sara.*

She'd been in the hands of the vampires for

too long. They could have done anything to her. Anything at all. She had no legal recourse. No way to go to the cops if something went wrong. And I'd left her with them.

They could be feeding on her. Using her. Manipulating her, the way Royce had manipulated me.

'*Yes,*' the belt whispered. '*Yes. You will stop it.*'

"I will," I said. My voice shook, but new purpose gave me strength. I had to make things right. "I'll stop him. For good."

Chapter 23

(Days left to full moon: 1)

I spent most of the night following and the next day trying desperately to avoid Chaz. Every time I turned around, there he was.

Nikki seemed to delight in my discomfort. She followed me around, too, though at a more discreet distance, watching how I jumped and swore and flinched every time I ran into him. Every time I caught her watching, her crystalline irises were sparkling with pleasure and malice. If I hadn't respected her brother so much, and hadn't still been in so much pain, I might have called her on it.

As it was, there wasn't a chance I was about to come to blows with her over something so stupid.

It wasn't like Chaz or I had much choice in the matter, either. The apartment just wasn't that big. Everyone was feeling a bit cooped up and restless, particularly the Weres. Tomorrow was the first day the moon would wax full enough to start the werewolves' cycle of forced shifts that came three days out of every month. Every one of them would have to change into their half-man, half-wolf form.

The suppressed energy of a half dozen Weres close to their change combined with the fear of the White Hats was a recipe for disaster in the making. Frankly, it seemed a miracle no one had tried to shoot or beat the crap out of anyone yet.

The White Hats really didn't like the proximity of the Weres. Though they'd never bothered before, now every one of them, except for Jack, was armed at all times. The White Hats stayed grouped by Jack's cot, standing as an unnecessary honor guard. Avoiding crossing paths with anyone who wasn't human enough for their tastes, including me.

As for the Weres, they prowled around, exploring every inch of the apartment until the whole damned place smelled like a kennel. They didn't make any overtly threatening moves toward the White Hats, but I think that was mostly because Chaz beat the snot out of Simon when he started getting too confrontational with Bo.

Their behavior made me wonder—in truth, a bit snidely—whether some of the males might not start marking their territory if the pressure contained in this place didn't let up soon.

What really surprised me was that *nobody* made any effort to come near me. Jack spent a lot of time studying maps and stuff on the computers with Keith. Chaz studiously avoided me, save for when our paths crossing was unavoidable. I hadn't been able to bring myself to try changing my clothes or showering again since last night. Even Bo didn't come by to wish me well or see how I was doing.

Nikki brought me food at mealtimes, but she didn't stick around, and no one came to visit me while I lounged on the couch.

I got up now and then to stretch, walking despite how much it hurt to get up and move around. With every hour, the pain became less. However, I'd noticed a low-grade fever. Yet another sign of the impending change. My appetite roared to life within hours of Chaz's dressing me last night, and hadn't abated since, no matter how much I ate. Even with the fever and the queasy reaction my stomach was having at the smell of the Sunstrikers, I was always hungry. Oddly, I craved sweets and carbohydrates instead of meat, as I had that morning I'd woken up from my bender at the other hideout a few weeks ago.

Chaz was in the kitchen sipping at a cup of water when I went to scrounge in the fridge. I ignored him as much as I had every other time I'd come across him in the house. With a few savage moves, shifting things around, I found a tub of cream cheese and set it on the counter, digging around in the cabinets for some crackers or bagels to spread it on.

He watched the whole time, his butt propped against the counter, and a calculating gleam in his eye. I knew the look. He was planning something that involved me. Not that I cared overmuch. His thoughts had always been fairly transparent and straightforward—other than the lies, that was. And I wasn't interested in playing his games anymore.

He set the glass aside as I found a box of Ritz crackers and grabbed the cream cheese, intending to hightail it back to my couch.

"Shia?"

I stopped, not looking at him.

"There's a place for you in our pack. Whether you turn or not. You have a place to go."

That sounded way too much like Royce for my peace of mind. With a snarl, I rushed out of there, not wanting to face him or have to consider that too closely.

Simon was sitting on the couch when I finally reached the top of Mount Stairwell. I nearly wept. Exhausted from the effort it had taken to get back up the stairs by myself without collapsing or toppling backwards, all I'd wanted was to sprawl on what passed for my bed.

He'd settled right in the middle, his arms over the back, and gave me a smirk when I came to a swaying halt in front of him.

"You mind?"

He arched his brows, giving me a faux-innocent look. "Not at all. Why?"

Simon always had been an asshole. His dark, slanted eyes watched me with a mischievous glitter; he knew he was being a dick and that there was nothing I could do about it.

It was a very Were thing to do. He was challenging me.

Dredging up the nerve from somewhere deep down, I dropped the containers on either side of him and circled behind the couch. He turned his head to follow my movements. Though my gait was unsteady, I didn't falter.

I braced my hands on the back of the couch, on either side of his narrow shoulders. He started to twist around, his expression suddenly shifting from cocksure to wary, regarding me with suspicion. This was really going to hurt.

I bent at the waist and pecked a kiss on his cheek.

With an explosive growl, he practically leapt to the ceiling, vacating the couch and plastering himself against the opposite wall. His hair, a lovely sable color, had been combed flat moments ago, but was now standing on end, and his eyes were a bright amber color similar to my own.

I grinned, maintaining the pose, though it was making my eyes water. "Thanks. Appreciate your keeping the couch warm for me."

He loosed another thunderous growl and stalked off, highly offended.

With a groan and a crack, I straightened my back, pressing the small of it with the heels of both palms. Though I couldn't maintain the position for long, I couldn't have done that at all last night. Whatever was going on in my body was healing me much faster than was normal.

Tired and sore, I moved around to sink into the cushions, no longer interested in the food.

The doubts about whether I'd be turning Were were almost nil at this point. There was no other explanation for the healing, the heightened senses, the way my stomach had been rebelling, or the fever. I'd been putting off deciding how I'd deal with the moment when it came. All month, I'd been doing my best to deny it. Now that the time was at hand, and I was no longer distracted by my need to hunt Chaz to the ends of the earth, there was plenty of time to consider my options and make a decision.

Yet it was the last thing I wanted to do.

My nose felt sore. I rubbed at it absently, then glanced at my hand. It came away streaked with red. Another nosebleed.

"Need a tissue?"

Jack was at the top of the stairs, watching me with those flat, dead eyes.

"Sure, if you've got one on you."

He wandered closer to sit on the end of the couch by my feet, leaning over to hand me a cloth handkerchief from his back pocket. I pressed the dark blue fabric to my nose, closing my eyes as I tilted my head back.

Jack and I sat together in relatively companionable silence for a while. I'm sure he had better things to do, but maybe the reason he came to sit with me was because he knew no one would bother him while he was here.

Usually I was the one who got nervous and broke the quiet. He surprised me by speaking first.

"Tomorrow's the day."

Like he needed to tell me that.

"We'll be facing down the Ravenwoods. It's probably better if you don't know where."

Yes. God forbid I should turn and decide to

follow the scent of the hunters for my first meal as a mindless beast.

"The cage I told you about. It's in the lowest basement of this building. I'll take you down there before we go. Lock you in."

That sent a chill through me. What kind of building needed more than one basement? What did they do in the other ones? "Should I bring anything with me?"

He shrugged, patting my leg lightly. It was an awkward move, as if he wasn't quite sure how to be comforting and it was the best he could come up with. "A book, maybe. You'll be down there a while. The lock is silver, so if you turn, you won't be able to open it or touch the bars. If you don't turn, you can come out after moonrise and wait for us here. Doc Morrow will be by. He'll probably need some extra hands to deal with the injuries after the battle."

It seemed a bit naïve of him to think after all the signs I was showing that I wouldn't turn. I appreciated the thought, even if I had no faith that I was still human. Too many signs pointed otherwise. I'd had my skin broken multiple times by shifted Weres. If Dillon's scratch hadn't infected me, no doubt one of the others had. Even Chaz thought I smelled like an Other—though the mentions of the scent of vampire clinging to me did make me wonder if maybe there was something about this process I was missing.

Maybe my agitation over these thoughts was making things worse. The blood trickling out of my nose suddenly became a steady flow. Cursing,

I sat up, balling up the handkerchief and pinching the bridge of my nose.

Jack's brows knitted as he watched me attempt to stem the tide. "Are you all right?"

My nose was clogged up, making it difficult to speak. "Yeah. It doesn't hurt."

He gave my leg another awkward pat, then leaned back into one of the cushions with one arm propping himself up, making himself comfortable. I had the feeling he was going to hide up here with me as long as he could.

Right at that moment, I didn't mind the company.

"So," he said, with deceptive casualness, "what will you do if you turn?"

Of course he had to ask the same question I'd been beating my head against the wall about.

"I don't know. It scares me, Jack."

"I know how you feel."

My brows lifted, and I gave him a sardonic look that went right over his head. Though I understood why before long. He spoke very quietly, almost in a whisper.

"The last time I talked to Royce, he said I can't wait more than a month to decide if I want to let him turn me. My body is becoming too weak."

My eyes widened, and I sat up straighter.

"If I wait much longer, even with so much of his blood in me, I wouldn't survive the transition."

"What did you tell him?" I asked.

"The same thing I've been telling him. I'm not ready to decide yet. I will. Soon."

There was a question I was on the verge of

asking, but it didn't seem appropriate. Biting my lower lip—then making a face as I tasted my own blood—I reached out to place a hand over his. He looked at where my fingers rested over his, then back to my face, meeting my eyes. The raw fear there was undisguised in that moment, and I knew that no matter how hard his outer shell, inside he was just as frightened and human as I was.

It gave me the courage to ask.

"Jack, is that why you've been so easy on me? Has thinking about becoming one of them changed how you look at Others?"

He jerked, pulling his hand out from under mine. The look he gave me was positively venomous, all of the anger and frustration coming across as crystal clear as if he had chosen to shout his response.

Without a word, he got up, leaving me there on the couch wondering if I'd just ruined any chance of ever calling Jack my friend.

Chapter 24

(Days left to full moon: 0)

"You're sure you want to stay behind? You don't want someone to stay with you?"

I ignored the pain that shot up my legs and spine as I paced, not looking at Jack as he hovered in the doorway of the cell lined with silver bars. "I'm sure. You need your people for the fight more than I need someone to stick around to hold my hand. Have fun hunting the Ravenwoods."

He gave me a look that I had no trouble returning. He was still pissed at me for asking him about his thoughts on Others. Chaz, Bo, and Nikki waited by the stairwell, watching, but not interfering as Jack flipped the latches on the outside of my cell.

It was pretty bare down here. The ceiling was set intermittently with shaded bulbs. There was no furniture except for a couple of folding chairs against a wall and a shelf with a digital clock so I had some way of measuring the time. It was early yet, not quite 3 PM.

Dominating the center of the room, four stories below ground, was a large cage made of thick, silver bars. It put me in mind of Hannibal Lecter's jail cell toward the end of that movie, *The Silence of the Lambs*, except that this one had an enclosed top. The entire cage was made of silver so a Were couldn't claw its way out. The thing must have cost a fortune to make—but it would hold a Were captive more effectively than anything else I'd ever seen.

This far underground, no one would hear a werewolf howling for release.

There was something altogether chilling about knowing that this was here, and that the White Hats had probably used it before.

Actually, after getting a whiff of the place, never mind probably—had *definitely* used it before. Cripes.l

Bo and Chaz lingered after Jack walked away, Nikki hot on his heels. Both of the men obviously wanted to say something to me without the other around. Rolling my eyes at their distrustful posturing, I settled into the chair Jack had left me and went through the small bag I'd packed with sweets and a few other necessities, withdrawing a paperback and a candy bar as I settled in to wait.

The hunter came to me first. He crouched, one hand clutching a silver bar for balance. "Shia . . . Shia, if you change—no matter what happens—

I'm still your friend. I just wanted you to know that. I'd stay here with you if you'd let me."

I glanced over the top of my book, giving him a wan smile. "Thank you—but no. The other hunters need you tonight. Don't worry about it, Bo. I never doubted you."

He grimaced. "Yeah, but I have been avoiding you these last couple days. Since the fight at the house. I'm sorry."

With a sigh, I put the book and sweet down in my lap, facing him squarely. "Bo?"

"Yeah?"

"You're still my friend. You always have been. Don't think for a second that I blame you for anything. This has been a rough month. We'll give movie night a try when all this business is behind us."

He knew as well as I did that those were probably empty words. There was almost as much of a chance he would be killed while fighting the Ravenwoods tonight as there was for me to shift into a werewolf. The smile he gave me was a shadow of his usual, cheerful grin. "Yeah. When this is all behind us."

With a heavy sigh, he turned and trudged to the stairs. Chaz waited there in the shadows for a time, only his eyes glimmering unnaturally in the dark. He didn't approach until I went back to my book. It didn't take him very long, which I was glad for since I was getting sick and tired of waiting for him to man up and talk to me. Not that I was particularly interested in anything he might have to say, but I doubted he was going to leave without giving me one last mental hurdle to deal with.

"If you change, you will be a Sunstriker, Shiarra. I know you don't want to hear it, but you'll be the pack's responsibility. My responsibility, thanks to Dillon."

I set the open book and candy on my knee, then pressed the tips of my fingers to the bridge of my nose. There was another bleed coming. I could feel the pressure of it building in my sinuses, bordering on painful this time.

"Nice of you to offer, but the Moonwalkers have already pledged to show me the ropes and teach me how to make it on my own." That promise had been made before I went on the warpath. I only hoped that it was still true considering how my little escapades in Central Park must have pissed off the pack. "Thanks, but no thanks."

A rumble sounded in his throat, and he bared his teeth. Upper and lower fangs were peeking out. Uh-oh. That wasn't a good sign.

"You belong to me. Not Rohrik."

Oh, now the claws came out. I tossed the paperback aside and stared at him, knowing full well what that meant to a werewolf. He held my gaze with a snarl, his eyes glowing with a fierce inner light.

"You," I said softly, my calm reply getting under his skin better than any shouting or screams ever would, "lost any chance of having me in your pack when you lied and cheated on me. You made your choice. Live with it."

He came closer, one hand closing around a silver bar. Even from where I sat, I could see the redness of his skin, the blisters and boils forming at the contact. Smoke drifted up from his fingers, and the smell of burning meat soon filled the enclosed space, mixing with the heady scent of musk. What the hell was he doing?

"You can't deny your bloodline. When I call, you'll come."

He stayed that way a few seconds longer, holding my gaze, maybe proving something to himself by holding onto that bar despite the pain that it must have caused him. That he still felt this strongly about me was more worrisome than flattering. Combined with his words, it was more terrifying than impressive.

He turned and melted away into the shadows, disappearing up the stairs and leaving me to my thoughts.

The idea that he might have some hold on me as the pack leader of the Were who had infected me was more disturbing than anything else I'd dealt with these last few days, even taking into account when he'd had to help me dress.

Did that mean my choices were even more limited than I had previously suspected? If he wanted me to come to his side, would I be forced to go by some instinct? Driven by need rather than conscious choice?

Werewolves were pack creatures by nature. There were some who roamed alone. Few and far between, Chaz had once explained that the loners were often hunted by the packs so they could be assimilated or driven away, forced into the fringes of society. The lone wolves could not live in cities, as they were too likely to give in to their baser nature and hurt someone if they didn't have a wild, untamed land to roam and hunt.

Was that what would happen to me? Would I be driven away? Or forced to be by his side, unable to make my own choice in the matter, and hunt beside people I'd much rather *be* hunting?

God, he was a bastard to leave me like this.

I got up from the chair, pacing, absently gnawing on the chocolate bar, hardly even noticing that my nose was gushing again. There was warmth on my face, trickling over my lips and onto the candy wrapper, but it wasn't important.

I looked at the clock. 3:04 PM.

This couldn't be. Hours to go, and I was nowhere near ready to know. I couldn't turn. Not without having some answers first.

What if Chaz commanded me to come to his side like Max Carlyle once had? Would he be able to control me the way the vampires once did?

I should have spent more time this month educating myself. I didn't know nearly as much as I needed to about Weres. All that time spent on the OtherNet, and I couldn't even bring myself to look up the basics. Other than the symptoms of infection and a pending change, none of it had held my interest. Nothing about packs or the pack dynamic. What powers the alpha held over the lesser wolves who answered to him. I'd assumed I'd learn all those things from Rohrik Donovan and the Moonwalkers.

On the verge of panic, I tossed the now empty wrapper aside and reached for the closest lock, needing to get out of here and put as much distance between myself and the Sunstrikers as possible before moonrise.

My fingers tingled when I touched the silver. Real or imagined? Whichever it was, I couldn't stand it, withdrawing and resuming pacing.

It didn't matter anyway. Better sense, now rearing its ugly head, dictated that I couldn't go. If I left, and I did change, I might hurt someone. At least in here, I wouldn't do any irreparable damage to anyone but myself.

Also, distance might not matter when it came to the hold the pack leader had on his wolves.

Fuck me *sideways*. Why did it always occur to me too late what questions I should have asked?

I looked at the clock again. 3:10 PM. For the love of all that was holy, I'd almost swear time was going backwards, it was so slow. The wait, the not knowing, the anticipation of the pain of the change was killing me.

The bag. The belt was in my bag. I dived for it, forgetting the pain of my injuries and impending change, not even noticing it anymore. The front of my shirt was becoming soaked with blood that was . . . strange. Streaked with both black and clear mucus, all threaded through the normal red stuff. Nothing I'd read about online said anything about that.

Disgusting, whatever it was. The fever was creeping back on me, too. A chill traced along my spine as I closed my hand on the belt.

There was no response. Oh, God.

Then I remembered. Daylight. No wonder it was inert. The spirit was dormant until the sun went down. I thrust it back in the bag with a curse. Good God, I was far too shaky to think straight. Light-headed from blood loss or something. Nothing was coming together right. My thoughts were too scattered, too much fear racing through me to make sense of anything.

I hugged the leather to my chest and sat down on the ground, rocking back and forth on cold cement while I watched the clock. 3:12 PM.

Who was I kidding? I was a fucking wreck. It was pointless to try to focus on anything other than the clock while I was like this. To do anything to pass the time other than cling to the remaining shreds of my sanity and pray.

It had been a while since I'd done that. Somehow I doubted I had been one of God's favorite people, considering how I lived my life and the mistakes I'd made. My vision blurred with tears as I bowed my head over the belt, clutching it close, and mouthed the words while blood spilled over my lips and dripped on the floor.

There are some things best kept private. What was said between God and me is one of them.

By the end of it, I felt a little better. Calmer. Maybe He was on my side, maybe He wasn't, but it made me feel better to know I'd made my peace. No matter which road I walked, I was damned— but at least I felt like I had made an effort to repent.

Royce. Damn him. Had he known this would

happen to me? Was that why he'd suggested making me a vampire, way back when, before I'd run from him? He was so fond of hiding things from me "for my own good" and playing things close to the chest. From our meeting by the park, I was positive he knew more than what he'd been saying.

If he'd bothered to take a few minutes to tell me what was happening, maybe I wouldn't have made so many mistakes. That, too, was another thing to blame the vampire for. Even so, I would have found it preferable to be under his thumb than Chaz's.

No matter what happened tonight, I was going to find Sara and set her free. She was only in this mess because of me. My penance would be to see to her safety, taking her out of the world of monsters—away from me.

That hurt. Knowing I'd probably never see her again after this. More than knowing what a monster I'd become, whether or not I changed, and all the death and misery I'd caused. She was more than my business partner—she was my best friend. The only person who had continued to believe in me, even after my life had gone to shit.

And where had it gotten her? Hiding in the shadow of a vampire. Because of me. If not for my mistakes, she would be safe and sound at home with her dogs, going out on dates with her boyfriend, Arnold the mage. Our business wouldn't have gone under—without the two of us there to pay bills and field clients, no doubt we were too deep in the hole to ever dig H&W Investigations back out again. Her life wouldn't have been ruined.

She might have been happy if she hadn't had me riding along her coattails for so long. She and her relatives were rich. Far richer than mine. Yeah, she always said she liked to hang with my family, but I knew some part of her pitied us for how much poorer we were.

Well, no more. I would use the change to advantage. That boundless strength could be directed. I might be a monster, but I wouldn't be mindless.

After tonight, Sara would be free of Royce—and free of me.

Chapter 25

It felt like a millennia before the clock read 5:50 PM. Per the almanac I'd looked at online, sunset was technically in three minutes. My skin was *crawling* with sensation, but I was going so crazy, I wasn't sure if it was all in my head or not.

I'd been alternately pacing the cell, chewing on my nails when I wasn't nervously nibbling at the candy I'd packed in my bag, and curled up in a ball on the floor. Sitting was worse. Nothing but rocking back and forth, arms wrapped around my legs to hold my shivering frame together so I wouldn't fall apart into a million pieces. The wait was killing me.

Would I turn as soon as the sun set? The almanac said the moon had risen earlier in the day, so it was already somewhere above me, high in the sky. Every time I'd seen Chaz or one of the other wolves turn, it was always right after nightfall. Did it have something to do with the position of the moon, or the position of the sun?

Too many questions. I'd been thinking about these things, along with what Chaz had said, for hours. I was no closer to figuring out what was going to happen to me than I'd been when I started out on my hunt at the beginning of the month. Now that I was on the verge of knowing, despite that the hours had been crawling by like days until only minutes ago, all I wanted was more time.

I was back to pacing, occasionally kicking aside empty candy bar wrappers, my eyes closed. Hours ago, I had memorized the number of steps I could take, one end of the thing to the other. Five paces to one side. Turn around. Five more paces. Turn. Rinse. Repeat. All the while rubbing my hands up and down my arms to ward off the sensation of the hairs on my body rising like the place was full of static electricity.

The nosebleed had trickled off some time back, but the fever had worsened, and my nose and sinuses remained stuffed. I'd thought ahead and packed a handkerchief and a box of tissues, but they were long since used up. As if thinking about it summoned the blood again, more wet warmth seeped over my lips and chin. Damn it. I ran a hand under my nose and glanced at it, frowning at the dark color of the liquid on my knuckle. Black, not red.

A sudden, shooting pain pierced my temples, and I fell to a knee, clutching my head. The dribble of blood became a flood, and I coughed and gagged as some of it went down my throat. The lower half of my face felt covered, turning tacky and hot to the touch. There was so much that it was dripping onto my shirt faster than I could wipe it away. Violent shivers wracked me.

My eyes started burning and watering. When I touched the corner of my eye, it took a second for me to focus, but I choked out a curse when I saw that fluid was black, too.

I'd never seen any werewolves bleed when they shifted. Or exhibit symptoms like this. Was it because this was my first time shifting? The pain was tolerable in comparison to what I'd had to deal with after the fight with Chaz, but it was still hard to breathe, and whatever that black stuff was scared me.

I stayed that way for what felt like forever, but nothing else happened. Other than a few excruciating coughs, my eyes stinging like a mother, and a lot more blood, my body stayed the same.

By the time I blinked the black crud out of my eyes, the clock read 6:40 PM. My hands were still white and pale, the nails blunt and showing signs of having been bitten to the quick during some of my more nervous moments.

I hadn't changed.

Holy shit.

I sat back on my butt, stunned, too shocked to process it right away.

Nothing had happened. No fur, no claws, no nothing.

Holy. Shit.

Laughter bubbled up from somewhere in my chest. I laughed until the tears came—real tears, not more of that black goop—and sat there, head in my hands, coming to grips with the sudden release of all that tension and terror that had held me in a choke hold until now.

Once the hysterical laughter eased off, and it didn't hurt quite so much to breathe anymore, I took better stock of how I was doing. Though I still felt hot, and I'm sure I looked like some zombie horror-movie extra with all of that gunk on my face and shirt, it was clear nothing else was going to happen.

Well. That was a relief.

I scrubbed my eyes with my palms and then used my shirt to wipe off the worst of the crud on my face. I couldn't stay down here like this—covered in filth and blood—and I wanted out of the cage, *now*. With a huge sigh and a groan, I levered to my feet, gripping one of the bars to steady myself.

An uncomfortable pins-and-needles sensation worked its way from my fingertips all the way up to my elbow.

That was something I didn't want to think about too closely.

Collecting my things and trash, I tucked them into the bag I'd brought with me and then flipped the latches on the locks, walking out of the cage, not looking back. Funny, I felt more clear-headed than I had in a long while—and my sweet tooth, finally assuaged, had earned me one hell of a stomachache. Painful, but it was far more bearable than becoming a furry beast hunting for fresh meat and howling at the moon.

This development brought a lot of my actions this month into a much darker light than I'd considered at the time I was carrying them out. I'd never taken into account that Dillon might not have illegally turned me. Nor had I ever considered that Chaz and the other Sunstrikers might not have been the ones infecting unwilling, uncontracted people and committing murder to hush up any witnesses. I'd assumed that the Sunstrikers had been the ones who were killing all of those people mentioned in Jim Pradiz's article. Maybe—just maybe—Chaz had told the truth, that the Ravenwoods were the ones who were doing all of the killing.

I'd believed the worst of everyone since this mess had started. At this point, even if the Ravenwoods really were behind it all, I wasn't sure it mattered.

As hard as it was to consider, I owed Chaz an apology. There really was no reason I should have flown off the handle like I had. Something dark and vicious had opened inside me along with the fear of being turned Other. That I would even think about killing Vic and the other Sunstrikers without having solid proof of their involvement was so unlike me, I couldn't figure it out. Where the hell had all of that hunger for violence come from?

Dillon, now. I wasn't sorry for what I had done to him. But with the worry of what I was becoming now moot, reflection on my actions was showing a much uglier picture than I was prepared to deal with.

I took the stairs slowly, my head aching and my heart heavy with the realization that I'd made some incredibly stupid mistakes while under the pressure of thinking I was no longer human. That didn't put me above the law, or make me the one responsible for seeking revenge for Jim Pradiz or the other victims. I'd made that assumption even though I knew there was a chance I wasn't going to be changing. Why had I done something so reckless and stupid?

Luckily, I didn't see anyone on my way up the stairs. When I stepped into the hallway on Jack's floor, some guys passed me. They didn't say anything right away, but I heard a quiet *what the fuck* as I dug in my bag for the keys. Hopefully, they'd think I was dressing up for an early Halloween party or something.

I was glad they weren't sticking around to see if I needed help.

The apartment was empty. I wasn't expecting anyone to be here, but it still worried me that Jack had chosen to go with them instead of sitting the fight out.

I wondered if my hunting gear would still be waiting for me where I'd left it, tucked in a drawer in the room where Chaz had helped me dress. I'd put it out of sight of the other hunters, but someone could still have taken it while I was downstairs to use during the fight against the Ravenwoods.

The only piece of gear I'd taken with me was the belt. It had as good as told me that I could use it to end my own life if I turned. Pausing with my hand on the knob, I had to fight down a touch of sickness at the thought.

I felt palpable relief on seeing the neatly folded armor in the drawer next to my last vial of Amber

Kiss. Another worry put to rest. Nobody had found my things.

I set down my bag, pulling it open so I could touch the belt. Now that night had fallen, it was alive. Or, well, as alive as an inanimate object could be. I ran a finger along the edge of the leather. It was exuding impatience to be used and no small measure of surprise at my touch.

"Don't worry, Isaac. Soon."

I had to get ready first. With a grim smile, I rose, taking the armor and perfume with me.

It didn't take me long to handle the basics. I washed my face, hands, and chest—seriously, I was straight out of a Halloween nightmare—and tossed my clothes in the trash. They were beyond saving.

Next came the Amber Kiss perfume. I hadn't used it much lately as I hadn't felt the need for stealth. I dabbed a few drops on all of my pulse points. Neck, throat, even a little on my inner thighs. Couldn't hurt. The stuff was supposed to hide my scent from Others and help suppress their appetites. It might be the edge I needed to help me get inside enemy lines undetected.

Getting the armor on was a bit more difficult than usual. Painful, but nothing I couldn't handle. A few curse- and grunt-filled minutes later, I was dressed. Knotting my hair in a bun to keep it out of my face and then tugging on my combat boots, I went to the makeshift armory Jack had set up next to his cot to see what weapons were left.

The pickings were slim in the weapons chests since everyone had stocked up for the fight tonight. All that was left were a few derringers and a couple of other bits and pieces. Lord knew what the hunters were doing with pansy guns like that. All the Desert Eagles, Colts, and Glocks were gone. So were the rifles. My guns were gone too, though the custom chest holster was still hanging where I'd left it when Jack had instructed me to store my weapons here.

The only suitable weapon I could find was a Smith & Wesson 500. The revolver was large for my hand, but it would leave a hole big enough to drive a truck through. As much as I didn't want to use them, I took one of the derringers, too. Better to have two guns than none, I figured.

There wasn't much ammo left, either. I scrounged what I could, but it looked like most of my fighting was going to be done up close and personal. Five bullets for the derringer and three for the S&W. That didn't leave much room for error, and neither weapon was going to do me much good against something as tough as a vampire unless I was close enough that there was no chance I would miss.

The derringers would probably just piss the vamps off. They were more of a last ditch weapon. And there weren't enough bullets for the S&W that I could rely on using it as a primary weapon.

Well. That should make the belt happy.

There was a small silver-edged boot knife that might come in handy, so I took that as well. Tucking the guns into the holsters and grabbing a small clip-on to keep the ammo in, I headed back upstairs to fetch the belt.

One thing I vowed as I made my way up the stairs was that I was not going to be responsible for any more deaths. I would save Sara, yes, and I would probably hurt some of the vampires very badly in the process, but I wasn't going in there to kill anyone. Not even Royce. No matter how badly the belt wanted me to hunt vampires, this was a rescue mission—that was all.

And after tonight, I was done with the Others. Done with hunting. I'd turn myself in to the cops and come clean about everything.

It was entirely possible I would face prison—or death, if the murderer survived tonight's battle and continued carrying out their mission to eliminate people attacked by Weres—but it would also mean my family and Sara would be safe. No more running. No more Lone Rangering my way through the mess my life had become.

I reached the landing, feeling pounds lighter than I had for a long time. The heavy load of guilt was a lot lighter when you decided to take responsibility for your actions.

The energy of the belt was so pronounced, I could feel it all the way from the doorway. With that in mind, I pulled the length of leather out of my bag and settled it around my waist. If I hadn't known better, I'd have said it was vibrating with anticipation.

'*About time,*' it said, anger radiating from the thing. Mental fingers worked through my thoughts, taking stock of the weapons I'd armed myself with and getting a feel for how it would need to compensate for my injuries. '*Are you ready to kill that vampire or what?*'

I took a deep breath, paying no mind to the twinge in my ribs, steeling myself against the inevitable outrage.

"No. No more death. Tonight or ever again."

There was a long silence.

'*I see. Time to change that.*'

There wasn't enough time for me to start saying "What?" before something . . . was different.

'*Let's try this again. Are you ready to kill the vampire?*'

I lifted a hand to my temple, feeling an echo of pressure there. Felt like I was developing a headache. And maybe was forgetting something? "I . . . I think so. Do I have enough weapons?"

I didn't understand the satisfaction behind its next words.

'*There was another knife in the armory downstairs. Go get it, and then we'll be on our way.*'

Chapter 26

Outside the vampire's apartment building, it was cold and miserable, with heavy clouds and a light rain that I had little protection against. The armor was built to stave off vampire and werewolf attacks, not ward off the cold, and I hadn't thought to bring an umbrella or rain jacket with me. Even if I had thought of it, I might have left them behind. Umbrellas weren't exactly chic stealth agent material.

Shivering, I remained crouched behind a car across the street for a time. The wait gave the belt a chance to help speed up my healing process so I wouldn't be hurting too much to be effective during the battle to come. It also gave me the opportunity to see if anyone moved in or out as I waited for the right time to launch my attack.

Not that I was expecting to see much movement there, really. I had no plans to waltz in through the front door, and I wanted to wait until it was closer to sunrise before I made my way inside. The timing had to be perfect—when most of the vampires who worked in Royce's other businesses would be gone, but it was close enough to daylight that they wouldn't be able to follow Sara once I got her out of there.

Sunrise would be a little after 7 AM. If I waited too long, any remaining vampires wouldn't be able to follow me, but I might lose the advantage of the use of the belt if the sun rose and find myself trapped. On the other hand, if I didn't wait long enough, they might give chase. It was bad enough that my mode of transportation for rescuing Sara was a stolen car. Well, borrowed from one of the White Hats or werewolves who had left it behind in favor of carpooling to the fight against the Ravenwoods. I didn't need cops *and* vampires looking for Sara tonight once I got her out of there.

Thus far, and hardly to my surprise, I hadn't seen any sign of the vampires or donors using the front door. Most likely Royce had restricted them to using the underground tunnels when they wanted to travel, as he had after the battle with Max Carlyle. It kept their movements free of any scrutiny by the police, paparazzi, or rival Others.

It also meant I couldn't be sure how many of the vampires were present.

There used to be thirteen leeches living in there. After the fight with Max, there were only nine left, unless Royce had pulled others from his various holdings to replace them. After spending a couple of hours strategizing with the belt out in the cold, I'd gone over what I could recall of each one who might be present. Mostly the oldest and most dangerous had survived. The belt liked that.

I didn't.

Angus, Royce's security specialist, was usually one of the last to return, so I wasn't worried about running into the beefy Highland warrior. Clarisse hadn't been around much either, to my recollection. They were two of the oldest and most dangerous. Ken and Reece were also most likely working the club set. Those two weren't fighters, so I wasn't worried about what would happen if I ran into them anyway.

As for Royce, there was a slight chance I'd see him in there. From what I'd observed in my brief stay with him, he worked from home now and then, using the home office he had set up next to his bedroom on the top floor. If he was inside, he would be the real challenge, and the first I should meet. If I could defeat him—a pretty big if, though the belt didn't seem to think so—I could handle anything else that might be thrown my way.

Most likely, he was at his corporate office, still picking up the pieces of his empire that his traitorous second in command, John, had torn apart while working for Max.

That didn't mean this was going to be a cake-walk.

That still left Mouse, Wesley, and Sebastian, at a bare minimum. The odds of walking away from a fight with Mouse were very slim. Like Royce, the only way I could possibly defeat her would be through guile.

Sebastian was handy with a sword, but not old enough to move with Mouse's speed or to have comparable strength. He'd be dangerous, but a lower-level threat.

As for Wesley, I'd never seen him fight, but Royce didn't employ weaklings to guard his home. Handsome and flawless as his features were, he'd always moved with the kind of prowling gait I associated with a predator. He would never have been trusted with something as important as the position of house guard if he wasn't skilled and capable of defending the place.

They had human security guards, too. I wasn't worried about them. They handled the outside, kept an eye on the security cameras, that sort of thing. No, it was the inside of the house that I was interested in.

The belt agreed when I suggested going in through the roof. There seemed no better alternative. If I went through the front door, the security cameras would catch it, and I'd find myself picked up by the cops in no time. But if I went in through an entrance that wasn't so well guarded, it would give me enough time to scope the place out, find a decent place to hold my ground, and might fool the vampires into relaxing their guard. None of them knew I was after their blood. Hell, even Royce probably thought I wanted to jump his bones after that last meeting of ours.

Just thinking about it made my lip curl, the desire to retch only barely restrained.

There were a few hours left before dawn. The clubs would be winding down for the night right about now. Some of the vampires and donors would be coming home within the hour. Others would be "stuck at the office" far longer, working on all of the mundane tasks required to keep the businesses afloat. If I spent an hour cleaning house, fighting the house guards, and then maybe another half hour to search the place and find Sara, it would give me enough lead time to send her on her way to safety. I could stay behind and ambush any other vampires who trickled in through the tunnels.

If Royce showed up too close to dawn, the belt would lose its power and I'd be stuck at the vampire's mercy again. I'd flee if necessary and find someplace to hide during the day, get some rest, then return the next night to fight him. And the next, and the one after that, however long it took to get the job done.

Something told me that was more the belt's idea than my own.

That didn't matter to me, though. What did matter was to ensure Sara was safe. I had to get her out of that place. She meant everything to me. If the vampires had hurt her, I would take Jack up on his offer to let me assume the mantle of leader of the hunters and use every resource available to destroy whatever was left of Royce and his people. After all, there were still hundreds—

maybe thousands—of the leeches in this state, and they all answered to him. Something needed to be done about that.

With that in mind, I rose, knees popping, to make my way across the street. Cutting between parked cars, I rubbed my cold hands against my legs, every exhalation coming out like a burst of fog in the chill night air. The only illumination, thanks to the heavy clouds above, came from streetlights limned by a fine mist that dampened their radiance to a muted glow. The air was clammy, and many of the branches of the trees lining the street were now bare, scratching against each other like the clawed limbs of the dead.

Fittingly creepy, considering the monsters that lived on this street and how very close it was to Halloween.

I hopped up on the cement wall dividing Royce's apartment building from the one next to it. A good ten feet off the ground, it afforded privacy on both sides, and was most likely too high for most humans to try to scale. There was too much space on either side for it to be used by anyone normal as a way of breaking in through a window. Though it was narrow, not much wider than one of my feet, it was child's play for me to navigate. The dark was no deterrent either.

I worked my way about halfway down the side of the building before I found what I was looking for. A drainage pipe—thicker than the usual aluminum crap that most buildings had these days—was bolted to the brick. It looked just strong enough for me to use to climb to the roof.

Light as a cat, I landed in a crouch on the walkway between the wall and the building—and froze as an exterior light turned on.

There was no sound of an alarm or any change in movement inside the building that I could detect, even when straining my senses to the utmost. I waited for a few minutes to see if someone would come out to investigate, but all that happened was the light's flicking off again after a time. When I stood up, it went on again. A simple motion detector security light. Cheap, and occasionally effective, but nothing I needed to worry about. If there were security cameras set up out here, they'd already caught me, and there wasn't much I could do about that.

Putting any worries about the light and what it might herald out of my mind, I proceeded to climb up the pipe. Grainy rust or dirt ground under my fingers and palms, and the damp metal was bitterly cold from the rain. The grimy stuff helped my grip, and I moved as swiftly as I dared without risking slipping.

It never failed to creep me out that Royce had somehow gotten permits to hide the windows on the first two floors behind a curtain of bricks. You couldn't tell from the inside, but out here, I couldn't help but notice as I climbed past the blocky silhouettes.

His was the only floor that had windows, and they were lovely. Huge, ornate French doors set at intervals, fitted with an automated system of sunlight-blocking shutters, both inside and out. Some of those doors were open, and filmy curtains twitched in the breeze, sucked out into the cool night air. From memory, I knew that priceless works of art were set between those doors, each with its own soft spotlight so you could admire them individually as you made your way across the huge, open expanse leading from the stairwell to his private chambers. Right now there were no lights on inside, which only added to the creepy factor.

I kept going until I reached the roof, hauling myself over the edge and crouching there, listening.

Aside from the usual city sounds—wind rustling the trees, the soft coo of roosting pigeons, the swish of tires on concrete from passing cars somewhere nearby, and the occasional honk or distant siren—there wasn't anything to be heard. The house slept.

Though I wanted to move silently, the roof must have been fairly recently tarred. My boots made faint crackling noises with every step, and the smell of the stuff burned the insides of my nostrils. My tread was light, but if any of the vampires were alert to intruders, they'd hear me moving around. The smell of tar might also stick to my shoes, making my work with the Amber Kiss moot.

There was a raised structure with a service door to reach the air-conditioning and filtering units a few yards away. I crept along, taking care not to make noise, keeping an eye out for any security cameras I might have to disable. The overhang with the light above the security door could have held any number of traps or security devices.

At first glance, as far as I could tell, there were none. It surprised me, considering how much effort Royce made to protect the entrances below. Surely I couldn't have been the first person to try coming in this way.

I crouched and leaned forward, tilting my head to examine the overhang above the door more closely. That's when I spotted what I was looking for. A tiny, shining dot to one side. A pen-like security camera, angled to catch the profile of anyone who might come in or out. The light would help make for a cleaner identification. As I hadn't stepped under the thing, it hadn't picked me up.

Simple enough to deal with. Standing on tiptoe, I used one of the stakes to change the angle so it was looking straight ahead—at the other side of the overhang instead of down at me. That type of camera often went overlooked, but it was also laughably easy to change the angle if it was within reach. Then again, maybe Royce was more worried about those who might try to escape through this door rather than attack through it?

Unsurprisingly, the door, when I tried it, was locked. I had no equipment with me to pick it.

I could either kick it in, as it didn't look to be thick enough to present much of a problem, or shoot out the lock. Either way, it was going to make a lot of noise, and most likely draw every vampire in the building, and perhaps some of the donors and security guards, too. Resigned, I took a step back, and prepared to kick it.

And stumbled when my foot met empty air, the door opening inward just as I lashed out.

Chapter 27

Christoph stood there, holding the door with one hand, a cookie in the other. His shirt was tucked into the pocket of his jeans, his broad, hairy chest gleaming with sweat, and his curly brown hair just as unruly as ever. That weird fetish collar I remembered from last time was still around his neck, too.

Though I'd spoken to him maybe two or three times when I'd stayed here, all I knew about him was that he was Mouse's plaything and he wasn't from around here.

He looked me over with minimal interest while I tried to straighten myself, and my clothes, to achieve a semblance of dignity. Stumbling in the door hadn't exactly been my idea of a grand entrance.

"Hey. Wesley said you were trying to come in this way. There are some fresh cookies in Mouse's kitchen if you want some. Analie just made them this afternoon."

I stood there, staring, not quite absorbing what he had said at first. Wesley knowing I was here wasn't good. Not good at all. Did he also know I was here to fight for Sara's freedom, and that I planned on killing him if I could?

"Hey, you okay? Come on, get in here. It's starting to rain again."

With a start, I did as he said, scooting past him and into the stairwell. They must still think I was allied with Royce. He shut the door behind us and flipped a latch, following me down. My heightened senses were positively *prickling* with the smell and proximity of Were. The belt was stirring, wanting something to kill.

'*It's not possible. That man can't be one. Perhaps another is near?*'

Inside Royce's home? You've got to be kidding.

'*There must be. It makes no sense.*'

That Christoph was the source of the scent threw me almost as badly as having him open the door to let me inside. The moon was full. But . . . he was . . . ". . . how?"

He paused on the stairs, glancing at me. "Huh?"

"You're . . . are you . . . ?"

"What?" He lifted an arm to sniff his pits. Made a face. "Oh, sorry. Didn't have time to shower before I came up here. Wes caught me in the hallway on my way down from the gym and asked me to come get you."

I snorted laughter, though I put a stop to it as soon as I got ahold of myself. "No, that's not—I mean—are you a Were?"

I hadn't quite meant to blurt out such a blunt question, but the belt was prodding at me incessantly, spoiling for a fight.

His expression clouded, and he hooked a finger around the collar, tugging at it. "You didn't know?"

Shaking my head, I put a hand over where the charm under my shirt made a tiny lump. That funky-looking collar must be magic, like my charm. My necklace was supposed to protect me against the mind games vampires and magi liked to play, though there were some limits and exceptions to its powers. I could see through a mage's illusions, and lesser vampires couldn't beguile me with their gazes. Only the most ancient, like Royce, could toy with my mind, and then only with a great deal of effort.

Christoph's collar must have been enchanted to prevent him from shifting. I'd never known such a thing was possible.

That it was a spiked fetish collar only made it that much more surreal.

'That's unfortunate. He won't be much of a challenge as he is. Maybe we can put him out of his misery later, after we deal with the vampires.'

I wasn't sure that was how I wanted to deal with him. For some reason, the belt's bloody-mindedness was getting under my skin. *We'll discuss it after the vampires are taken care of.*

'Whatever. Prude.'

Meanwhile, Christoph rubbed the back of his neck, scratching at the edge of the collar. He was reddening under his tan. "Yeah. I made some stupid mistakes. Royce could have killed me for what I did. It's not so bad, I guess. Mouse is good to me, and I still have a couple of pack-mates here."

Analie and Ashi. Some things about him and the other people in the house were starting to click into place. I'd seen the three together while I was stuck here, waiting for the blood bond Max and then Royce had submitted me to to wear off. I'd never understood until just now why Analie, Ashi and Christoph, all so different in ages, backgrounds and personalities, stuck to-gether like glue.

'*Maybe we'll get to fight some Weres after all!*'

Inwardly, I cringed. *I do* not *need to deal with Weres on top of vampires tonight. Cover's been blown; this is already going to be hard enough to handle.*

Aloud, I said, "That's good that you have Mouse. She's nice."

Nice and deadly.

Christoph brightened, nodding. "Yeah. She's taken good care of me." I could only imagine. The thought of what that might mean gave me the heebie-jeebies. "Ashi wasn't so lucky. He's with Clarisse now, but nobody wanted to go near him after John bit him. He was kind of an asshole when he first got here, but he's mellowed out some now that he's used to the place."

We were nearing the first floor stairwell by now. He took the lead, holding the door so I could go first.

Royce's home was just as busy and just as over-

whelming as I remembered. I moved forward in
a bit of a daze, taking it all in.

Thad and Sebastian were sitting on the bottom
steps. Thad was eating one of Analie's cookies, his
elbows propped on his knees, and his arms covered with tattoos. His twin brother—the vampire
with the seawater eyes—said something that made
both of them laugh. Very nearly in unison, the
two noticed I was behind them and waved hello,
then scooted aside to give me and Christoph
room to get by.

Mouse was standing in the doorway of her
apartment, her free hand moving as she signed
something. Clarisse, whose Easter basket grass-
green eyes were alight with mischief, was chatting
animatedly with her. The Irish vampiress turned
from Mouse to regard me curiously, sweeping her
hip-length, black curls out of her face and giving
me a fangy smile.

"Oi, lovey, where've you been? We've missed
you!"

Mouse gave me an enthusiastic wave and a
brilliant smile. She mouthed "hello," then lifted
the plate of cookies she was holding in her other
hand and tilted her head in question.

I was torn between the desire to pull a stake
and wanting to run screaming into the night. The
warm welcome, as if I was some close friend or
family member just returned after a long absence,
was not what I wanted or expected.

Christoph elbowed past me and eagerly grabbed
another cookie off the plate Mouse was holding.
She beamed up at him and accepted his quick

kiss as he leaned down to catch her lips before biting into his cookie, then held the plate out to me. Her thick brown hair, streaked in a few places with gray, was pulled back from her deceptively youthful face in a ponytail. I shook my head, not wanting to take anything from the mute vampire's hands.

Wesley peered in from the foyer, his pale blue eyes glittering unnaturally. Leah, his donor, was hanging on his arm and whispering something urgently to him. The two of them had always struck me as somewhat incongruous together. He was tall and muscled, his hair short and blond, with a neatly trimmed goatee giving his handsome, angular features a roguish cast. She was short and rather plain, soft-spoken, and almost as much of a nervous wreck as Sara's sister, Janine.

Wesley hushed Leah and gestured me closer, calling out to Mouse. "Hey, it's your turn. Take over, will you?"

Mouse shrugged, passing Christoph the plate of cookies (much to his delight), and headed up to take Wesley's place guarding the front door. I stayed where I was, indecisive, as Wes and Leah approached. Now that they were closer, I could hear what she was saying, her whisper-soft voice stuttering around her request.

"Oh, come on. Please say it, Wes? Just once, for me? Please?"

He gave a long-suffering sigh and cupped her cheeks, looking down into her eyes. "As you wish."

The girl nearly swooned, I swear. Though after he said that, I could see why. The dread pirate resemblance was positively uncanny. With a giggle, she gave him a hug and a kiss on the cheek, then rushed off, barely giving me a glance as she passed. He watched her go with a look of bemused tolerance, shaking his head.

Shoving his hands into his pockets, he wandered closer to me, no doubt to find out what had finally prompted me to return.

I might as well start somewhere. Facing him, Mouse, and Clarisse all at one time would be suicide—they were all ancient vampires, hundreds of years old, though you couldn't tell it from their current antics—but it didn't look like I had much choice. Perhaps if I could take him out first, I'd be in a better position to handle dealing with Mouse and Clarisse.

I was not looking forward to fighting with Mouse. I'd seen her move. She was more proficient with a blade than anyone else I'd ever seen, her soccer mom figure and looks notwithstanding. Outside the movies, I hadn't thought swordplay like hers was possible. With her inhuman speed added to her skill with a blade, she was like a hellish cross between a whirling dervish and a blender set to purée.

The belt was positively *itching* to get started.

"Did Mr. Royce know you were coming tonight? Why didn't you just come in through the front door?"

My fingers twitched as I fought the urge to grab a stake. "No, he didn't. And I didn't want to be seen." I literally had to force myself to clasp my hands in front of me to keep from grabbing a weapon. "Is Sara in the apartment?"

He shook his head, frowning. "No, she's not here."

My heart did a flip-flop at that. Wes didn't seem to notice.

"Where is she?" I asked, doing my best to keep my voice low and level so it wouldn't come out as a demanding scream.

"I don't know. Mr. Royce didn't say."

It felt like my stomach plummeted all the way to the basement. If I'd been walking, I might have fallen over. As it was, I stiffened, losing all sense of balance at his words.

"What?" The word hardly made it out as a whisper. "What did you say?"

Conversation in the hallway died down, the others looking our way, curious. Sensing something was wrong. The silence was so profound, I could hear the sound of a TV coming from somewhere on the second floor, previously unheard over all of the chatter.

They'd done it. They'd done what Royce had promised would never happen. The vampires had hurt Sara. Taken her away. Used her as Royce had intended to use me.

My muscles began to go into spasms of their own accord. Though my first reaction had been sickness and fear for Sara, a righteous anger was quickly burning those lesser emotions away. Wesley stiffened, gauging my reaction with mixed wariness and confusion. Everyone in the hall had fallen silent, watching as I fought and lost an inner battle over whether or not to draw a stake.

The belt won. Wesley's eyes widened, and he took a single step back as I drew a stake, throwing my head back and arching as I howled a mix of loss, fury, and a righteous need for the hunt.

Much like my battle cry when I had faced Dillon, this sound was never meant to come from a human throat. It rent the air like a physical blade, cutting through the silence and driving the vampires back as if I were chasing them off with crosses and holy water.

It didn't stop until I ran out of air. And I only waited a moment, getting into position to attack Wesley, who was holding his ears and looking just as stunned as the rest of the vampires in the hallway.

"Jesus, lady," said Thad from somewhere behind me, "chill the fuck out."

With a snarl, I launched myself at Wesley, driving the stake forward—directly toward his heart.

Chapter 28

Wesley moved like he'd been expecting the attack. His arm came up to block me, shoving the stake off course and making a play to seize my exposed throat.

If I'd been any slower, any less jittery, I might not have been capable of countering his grab to dance back just outside his reach. He was holding back, or I would have been against the wall or on the floor already. That blow to my arm felt like smacking into a steel cable, and I'd dropped the stake, but the belt stepped in and muted the pain until it was nothing more than a faint ache on the edge of my consciousness.

Though most of my concentration was on the fight at hand, dimly I was aware of the details of my surroundings. Mouse and Clarisse were both watching me with wide eyes. Thad and Sebastian had risen from their seats on the stairs. Christoph poked his head out of Mouse's door, his mouth full of crumbs.

"Wha' th' fu—"

Clarisse got on tiptoe and slapped a hand over his mouth, her gaze locked on Wes and I as we darted and feinted in efforts to gain an advantage. "Oi, lovey, language."

Wes moved in a blur. Again, without the belt's help, I would have had no hope of escaping him—but I ducked under his grasping hands and swept a leg out to trip him, sending him stumbling into Sebastian. The two vampires went down in a tumble of flailing arms and legs.

I took advantage of the moment to run to the apartment I'd shared with Sara. I wouldn't have time to do a thorough search, but maybe there was some clue left behind, something that might tell me what had happened to her or where she was now.

Clarisse's voice followed me inside. "Looks like betting material, lads. Anyone up for a wager? Usual rules apply."

If things hadn't been so serious, I would have been rolling my eyes, particularly as I overheard Thad put fifty bucks on Wes.

The apartment looked the same as it had the day I'd left it. Same furniture, all in the same places as before. No, someone had picked the phone off the kitchen floor and put it back on the counter. My Rolodex was still there.

I went to Sara's room first.

There was nothing to see. Her things were gone, and there was no sign she'd ever been here.

'*Don't be a dolt. Use your other senses. What does your nose tell you?*'

Irritated, I took a sniff—then realized the belt wasn't saying this just to play the part of smart-ass sensei. Though I could vaguely detect the scent of her dogs, Roxie and Buster, clinging to the rug, and a whiff of her subtle jasmine-and-vanilla perfume, it was hard to say how long it had been since she'd last been here. More than a few days. The sheets had been washed since then. Somehow I could tell by how much the chemical tang of the laundry detergent had dissipated that it had been longer than a week.

My attention was so fixed on trying to figure out by smell what the hell had happened, I didn't notice Wesley sneaking up behind me until he took me down in a flying tackle onto the bed.

We bounced a couple times on the mattress. I managed to roll before he got a good grip, landing with a jolt on my hands and knees on the floor on the other side.

"Come back here!" He moved to follow me, but I kicked him in the face when he leaned over the edge, reaching for me.

With a vicious snarl, his head snapped back, and he clutched at his jaw. I caught a glimpse of fang before I turned away. While he was distracted, I stumbled to my feet and made another run for it.

Clarisse smoothly stepped out of my way. The bookie vampiress, who had been watching from the bedroom door, held her hands up and gave me a wry smile. "Just watching. Go on, now."

"Damn it, Clarisse, you could help me here,"

Wesley griped. She made no move to stop me as I fled past.

"Wouldn't be fair odds if I interfered. You know the rules."

Wes cursed, and I heard the slight thump of his feet hitting the ground. No doubt he was after me again.

'*Of course he is.* Run.'

My hair was coming loose of the tight bun I'd put it in. I reached up to tear it free, the long red strands flaring out behind me as I dashed out of the apartment, past a gaping Christoph, Sebastian, and Thad, and straight for Mouse.

This night was not going as planned and required some reevaluation. I had to get out of here so I could think it through and see if I could dig up any leads on where Royce might have hidden Sara. If Mouse kept out of it like Clarisse so obviously was, I could slip out the front door and be gone in seconds.

She didn't.

I yelped when she grabbed my arm as I passed, using my own momentum against me to spin me around and hurl me back the way I had come. Damn her for smiling at me while she did it, like this was all some stupid game. The men flattened against the walls so I wouldn't plow into them as I flew by. Once I touched down, my boots left streaks on the hardwood, and I slid on my butt right into Wesley's legs. He stared down at me with narrowed eyes, rubbing his jaw.

"Come on, Shia!" Christoph called. I was grateful until he added, "I've got twenty bucks riding on this thing. Get up!"

So much for moral support.

Wes wasn't impressed, either. "You finished yet?"

"Not yet," I huffed, going into another roll so I could crouch a few feet away from him. I started to reach for a stake, but he'd already closed the distance and grabbed my arms, not giving me a chance to draw a weapon. Christoph and Sebastian's cheers were more distracting than helpful, and for a second I wished mightily they'd just shut the hell up.

I hooked one leg around Wes's and yanked, then shoved when the unexpected move put him off-balance. Though I'd hoped he'd let me go, he clung tight, dragging me with him to the floor. We grappled, me panting for every breath, him grinning up at me like this was his idea of a good time.

"My kind of woman."

The bastard had the gall to wink at me.

Even though I knew he was using the same tactic I'd used on Simon the other evening to make him vacate my couch, it still infuriated me beyond reason. With a hiss, I managed to slide one of my arms up Wes's torso. I couldn't quite reach far enough to claw his face, but I did dig my nails into his skin just above his shirt collar hard enough to draw blood. His chest vibrated with a rumble of laughter under my hand.

"Mr. Royce never mentioned you were so feisty. Two ways to do this, sugar. Either way, I'll have a time of it."

It surprised me when he pushed me up by my upper arms, lifting me off his chest. He only did it to fit a foot under my stomach and send me sailing over him to land in a painful sprawl on my back a few feet away.

Gasping for air, I watched upside down as he kipped to his feet. Though my back had started up an ominous ache, and my head was killing me, I rolled over onto my stomach and managed to get my feet under me. My sense of balance was MIA, so I scooted backwards until my back hit the wall behind me, and I got to one knee. The belt was too busy trying to handle the injuries and restore my balance to make any smart remarks.

Wes stalked closer, moving like the predator he was, not stopping until he was standing over me.

"Falling head over heels for me, baby?" I flipped him off with a scowl. He laughed again. "Come on, tell me you've had enough. You can take a breather on my couch while we wait for Mr. Royce."

'*Don't do it. You're ready. Go!*'

My response at the belt's urging was to dart forward, using the tip of a stake to slash a line through Wes's shirt and skin, sending him stumbling back. He regarded me with shock, his fingertips brushing over the dark streak of blood like he couldn't believe I'd cut him. Even with the magical properties imbued in the silver, the shallow wound was already visibly closing. Freaky.

Still, it gave me the warm fuzzies to know I had the power to surprise him like that. And everyone else, too, apparently. No one else in the hall had said a word.

"Don't get too torn up about it," I said, winking at Wes. He gaped at me.

Then I took off for the stairwell.

Footsteps pounded behind me. Several of them. I imagined my audience was following on Wes's heels as he pursued me.

I wondered why he wasn't putting that supernatural speed of his to better use. As fast as I was with the belt, he was old enough to run rings around me while I hastened up the stairs.

I had my answer once I reached the third floor. Clarisse was leaning in the doorway leading to the roof. Not wanting to risk a repeat of the show with Mouse, I gestured frantically for her to move—Wes was hot on my heels.

"Get out of the way!"

She ignored my demand, that sly smile of hers widening until her fangs were showing. "Now, now, *ma mhuirnín*. 'Tisn't a fair fight if ye run off 'afore the game is through."

Cursing under my breath, I took the only other option open to me—I ran into Royce's quarters, slamming the door open and rushing for the nearest window. They were locked tight, the shutters down. Fuck, that left me trapped in the building with not one but *two* ancient elders guarding the only ways out.

Clarisse re-stationed herself at the door after Wes stalked inside. She shut it behind her and folded her arms, assuming a bodyguard stance that would have been impressive on someone a little taller.

As for Wes, he slowed once he saw I had stopped running, and he padded toward me on light feet. Ready to cut me off if I tried to escape again.

"Come on, now. Stop playing these games. I don't want to have to hurt you." The bright, excited gleam to his eye spoke otherwise. "Mr. Royce won't be happy if we destroy his artwork. Let's just find a place to have a seat and wait, hmm?"

I darted to the closest window, scooting around some spotlighted statuary to throw my weight against the shutters in hopes of breaking them and escaping outside. The metal shuddered at the impact, but didn't give.

Wes didn't give me the opportunity to regain my balance. Before I knew it, my face was plastered against the cold metal, his fingers digging into the back of my neck.

"Last chance, sugar."

I kicked backwards, landing a blow to his solar plexus. He fell back with a grunt, and I whirled with a follow-up kick that sent him in a sprawling slide to crash against a nearby chaise. Clarisse laughed, her lilting voice echoing in the enclosed space.

He was soon on his feet, and I was a few yards away, seeking a weak link in one of the shutters that I could slide my fingers into so I could tear the metal sheets off. He didn't get too close to me yet, though he did follow in my footsteps, watching my futile attempts. Toying with me, I suppose.

Letting me figure out for myself that there was no way out.

"Pretty spry," he said. "Just remember, you're the one who chose to do this the hard way."

In the next few moments, I completely lost sight of him—he moved that fast—but he struck me a number of times, hard enough that I would have fallen if he hadn't kept catching me and hitting me again. Most of the strikes were to my stomach, lower back, arms, and shoulders. Not a single one was hard enough to break any bones or do much more than bruise, but it was disorienting and painful. I knew I was jerking around like a marionette, but I couldn't keep my balance, and couldn't focus past the pain long enough to see where he was.

I'm not sure how long he kept it up. It felt like an eternity. He forced me in a circuit around the room at least twice, but it was too disorienting for me to tell much more beyond that. My body was turning into one giant bruise.

Once he stopped, it took me a few seconds to figure out that I was on my knees, and he was standing in front of me.

Gasping and clutching at my aching stomach, I glared up at him, too hurt to force out any harsh words. He had a cocky smile quirking one corner of his lips, his blue eyes glowing with an ember of red deep down in the irises.

I flinched back as he reached down, taking me by the arm. He hauled me to my feet and held on, maybe making sure I was steady. "I'm sure this has been more fun for me than it's been for you.

You're going to sit your ass down and wait for Mr. Royce over there." He pointed to the chaise I'd earlier kicked him into. "If you don't, the beatings will continue until sense returns. Yes?"

Closing my eyes, I nodded. He gave me a little shove in the direction of the furniture.

I pretended to stumble. He fell for it, bending down to help me—and I landed another solid punch to his jaw, right where I'd kicked him earlier, sending him flying backwards.

Looking mightily bored by now, Clarisse was slumped against the door, still watching. There was no other way out of here. I whirled just in time to keep Wesley's hands from closing on my arms again, skittering back out of his reach.

If I was going to escape, I'd have to fight my way past Clarisse.

Chapter 29

Getting to the door meant getting past Wesley first. I feinted left, then right, but he had been around for centuries before the belt. He knew what I was doing and didn't fall for the trick. Instead, I found myself pressed against the wall, stars shining in my vision as my skull reverberated from the impact. He had my wrists firmly in his grip, his usual roguish smile nowhere in evidence.

"Are you ready to stop this foolishness?"

As soon as I got my bearings, I tugged against his hold, squirming against him in hopes that the belt might have augmented my strength enough to shove him away. The position was too awkward, and he was far too strong.

'Stay still. I have an idea.'

Though I was uncomfortably aware of the contours of Wes's body, I went limp, hanging my head and waiting for him to make the next move.

After a few moments of suspicious silence, he drew back, pulling me with him.

I took the opportunity to knee him in the crotch.

He gasped, a red tint infusing his eyes as he tightened his grasp on my wrists. Before I could follow up with another kick, I found myself on my knees, my arms wrested behind my back as he held me down. Damn it. That had been a stroke of brilliance on the belt's part.

"*Skreyja tik!* Fucking *meyla*," he spat, shoving me down until I was flat on the floor, straddling my back. "That *hurt*, damn it! Don't do that again."

"Let me go!"

"Not on your life. You're lucky Mr. Royce wants you alive."

I lay still, panting, the belt going curiously quiescent around my waist. When pain flared up, putting stars back in my vision, I knew why. Shit— the sun had risen. Had we been fighting that long? I'd completely lost track of the time.

"Hey," he said, shaking me out of my pained reverie. "Stop that twitching. What's the matter with you, huh?"

"It hurts, you asshole," I muttered, grimacing at the way my shoulder was wrenched when he tugged my arms up higher along my back. "Ow! I'll stop, I'll stop!"

"Well, well. Ms. Waynest has returned, hmm?"

I cringed at the sound of the vampire's voice, cold and dispassionate as ever. I couldn't keep the sheepish note out of my reply.

"Hi, Royce."

He spoke again, closer this time, not bothering

to step into my field of view. "Wesley, do you mind explaining this to me?"

Wesley didn't mind. "She broke in while you were out, sir. Fought her way around the building looking for Sar—err, Ms. Halloway. She wouldn't listen when I told her the girl wasn't here."

It's not like Royce wouldn't have known I was here. Not if he could "feel me" like he mentioned back at the park. The thought made me want to punch him, but even if I'd been free to do so, he'd probably laugh at my efforts. Without the belt supplementing my strength, I wasn't going to be effective against him *or* Wesley until nightfall. Damn it.

"I see. Stand her up, if you would."

Wesley lifted me to my feet as though I weighed no more than a feather. The pressure on my arms was unbearable, and I couldn't bite back a pained wince. Once on my feet, I glared defiantly at Royce's chin and tugged to get free, but Wesley wouldn't let go. Clarisse must have left when Royce had arrived, because she wasn't hovering in the doorway anymore.

As for Royce, he moved as though he had all the time in the world as he approached. All I could do was watch. His suit jacket, made of some sleek black material that probably cost more than my car, was left unbuttoned. His tie, made of the same dark material, was held in place by a ruby tie tack matching the red shirt underneath. The contrasting colors and that tiny, glittering gem kept catching my eye. I fought the urge to stare at the contours of his chest outlined in the creases of that tailored shirt as he leaned in to check if I had anything hidden at the small of my back or under my hair. His touch gave me the shivers, even if he was swift and impersonal about his inspection.

He never once looked into my face, his focus all for the weapons I was carrying. He checked the small container clipped to my belt for the extra ammo, but the bullets had fallen out somewhere along the way and all I was carrying in that container right now was pocket lint. I sucked in my breath when his hands slid over my stomach, only to work the clasps on my shoulder holster, loosening it. With a couple sharp jerks, yanking painfully against my straining shoulder muscles, he broke the straps and tossed the guns aside.

He followed that up with a few tugs to the belt. A sudden desperation had me crying out and wrenching to the side, kicking out to keep him from taking Isaac away from me. All that did was hurt my shoulder sockets and upper arms as Wes's grip tightened. Royce didn't even seem to notice the blows when I kicked him, and despite my struggles, he removed the belt within moments. A wave of despair and aching loss washed over me, tears stinging my eyes as it was taken away.

As for Royce, he barely paid the stakes a glance once they joined the guns on the floor. His hands briskly swept over the rest of my body, checking for any weapons hidden under my armor, too quick for me to be terribly indignant about it. I cursed under my breath when he found my last remaining weapon, the small knife tucked into my boot.

My heart was beating fast, too fast. Being pressed between the two men was eerily reminiscent of when Royce and Max had had me pinned between them, bargaining for my freedom.

"Give her to me."

Wesley nudged me so hard I stumbled. Before I knew it, I was over Royce's shoulder, my hair dangling in my face and his collarbone digging into my stomach. Off-balance and gasping for air, I flailed briefly, then clutched at his jacket, wrinkling the expensive suit. Then moved my hand when I realized I was grabbing his butt. Eek!

"Take those with you and put them somewhere safe." There was a rustle of leather and jangle of metal as Royce toed my discarded weapons. "I don't wish to be disturbed during the day. Field anything that requires immediate attention to Angus or Jessica."

"Yes, sir," Wesley said.

I gave a breathy yelp of protest as Royce turned around, with me still slung over his shoulder, and stomped toward his bedroom, leaving me to stare longingly after the weapons the other vampire was gathering from the floor. Royce soon cut off my view by kicking his bedroom door shut behind him. The only illumination came from tiny, twinkling lights in the ceiling. They bathed the room in gentle light, but made for deeper, more threatening shadows in the recesses. There were no windows or other means of escape, either, unless I could barricade myself in his (from my recollection, windowless) bathroom until he died for the day, or whatever it was vampires did when they weren't stalking the night.

It was clear there was nowhere to run. The only way out was the way we'd just come in.

Before long I was back on my feet, nearly spilling to my knees at the wave of dizziness that washed over me. Royce barely paid any mind, his fingers quick and sure as they closed on the hem of my shirt. I gave him a bit of trouble once he pulled at it, yelping in fear and protest as he yanked the body armor up. He did it so swiftly that I didn't have time to tense against it. He ignored my squirming and my muffled curses, though he laughed when my rapid retreat backward as my head and arms popped out ended with me sprawled on my ass on his futon. The hardwood floors might have provided a softer landing. Yeowch!

Blushing furiously, I covered my chest with both arms, mortified at this treatment. Thank God I'd thought to put on a sports bra under the armor, the stretchy fabric covering more than the lacy numbers I used to wear for Chaz's benefit. It did nothing to hide the myriad scars on my stomach, though.

Still chuckling, he shucked off his own jacket, letting it pool on the floor behind him, and stepped out of his shoes.

"What the hell are you doing?"

He gave me a look I didn't like at all. "Something I should have done a long time ago."

I gasped and kicked at him when he knelt down in front of me, only to have one hand latch firmly around my ankle, the other working the laces to my boot.

"Royce, stop it!"

"Not yet."

"Stop!"

He ignored my command, tugging off my shoe and dropping it with a heavy clunk to the side. Though I fought to pull out of his grasp, he made little work of divesting me of the other boot, then hooked his fingers in the waistband of my armored pants. My struggling only made it easier for him to tug those down. My underwear would've gone with them if I hadn't made a grab for the elastic band at the last second. I took advantage of the few sparse seconds I was free of his hold to scramble back on the futon, intending to make a run for it.

Before I got very far, his hand shot out, circling my ankle again like a cold vise. He pulled me to him as he crept up on the sheets, the smooth, predatory way he moved reminding me of a panther.

Gone was any sense of stupid bravery and invincibility. In its place was nothing short of raw panic as the realization set in that, this time, he wasn't stopping. This went far above and beyond any scare tactics he'd used with me before. I had no weapons, no armor, and no hope of escape. He'd dragged me into his *bedroom*. I was nearly naked *on his bed*. And he was well on his way to having me pinned beneath him.

That could only lead to one thing.

Though I knew it was useless, I cried out in

terror, forgetting about modesty as I threw my hands up to shield my neck and face as he settled over me. For a moment, I had an irreverent thought that the least the bastard could have done was remove that freaking tie tack that was now digging into my stomach before putting his weight on me.

Though he was gentle about it, he ignored my tears and my breathless pleas for him to stop as he tugged my hands away from my throat.

"Don't—" he ordered, gently taking my wrists and pulling my hands from their protective position to pin them over my head. "Don't hide yourself from me."

"Please," I cried, tugging fruitlessly at his iron-clad grip. "Please, Royce, I don't want to do this—"

"Hush. I'm not letting you out of my sight until I'm certain you won't do something more to hurt yourself. Gods, just look at you . . . You and I are going to have a long overdue talk."

I quieted, but turned my face away, hating the blushes and bruising that I knew reddened every inch of my normally ghost-pale skin from hairline to navel. He was staring down at me, but had stilled, watching me as I fought not to have a breakdown, still squirming and tugging at his hold in hopes of getting free.

A deep sigh escaped him, and he released my wrists. I pressed my hands to his chest, pushing at him, but he didn't give, remaining a stolid wall of cold marble trapping me beneath him. He leaned in, his cheek brushing against mine, satin-soft strands of coal black hair drifting across my skin as he whispered oh-so-sweetly in my ear.

"Your struggling makes it more tempting to bite you, not less. Relax."

I withdrew my hands from his chest with a gasp, and satisfied myself with shivering uncontrollably as I clutched the bedding at my sides as though it could protect or hide me from this blood-drinking predator looming over me.

Though it was a marginal improvement when he withdrew from my ear, I flinched when his jaw brushed against mine. He kissed away the tears staining my cheeks, the touch of his tongue like the gentle flicker of an ice cube pressed to my skin. It only made the tears fall faster.

"Shiarra, I've told you before. I'll never hurt you. I don't give my word lightly; you know that. What are you so afraid of?"

"Please don't bite me," I whispered.

He paused, unmoving, not speaking. I didn't dare open my eyes to look at him, to see what thoughts might be passing through those black eyes. It took a moment for him to reply, a thoughtful "*hmm*" that vibrated against my hypersensitive skin.

"Shiarra, look at me. No tricks, no games. On my honor."

I was slow to comply, but he waited patiently until I was squinting up at him through tear-soaked lashes. I could see plainly he was now quite serious and thoughtful. His trademark smirk was nowhere in evidence, and I felt no sense of compulsion behind his words, despite the unwise eye contact we were making.

"Your tears are sweet, and under other circumstances, I might well have enjoyed them—but you and your partner are under my protection. Do you understand what that means? I've pledged to keep you safe. I won't allow you to run off on your own again until I am assured you are no danger to yourself or others. And while I would like nothing more than to taste your warmth, sink inside you, and make you mine in every way you deny me, I'm not about to hurt you or claim you against your will. It would be a poor way to repay you for saving my life only to take yours from you."

"Then let me go," I screeched, squirming to escape him. "Let me go, Royce! Don't do this to me!"

He held me fast, his hands suddenly holding my cheeks, though I hadn't seen him move. Trapped, I stared helplessly up at him, rage and fear warring for dominance as he arched above me and stared down.

"Is that why you fight me now? You think I intend to rape you, feed from you, make you my slave . . . ? Gods, but you are a foolish, irritating girl!"

"What did you do with Sara, you son of a bitch?" I hated that the question sounded so weak, that I couldn't push him away.

He glared down at me, expression hardening for the first time. "You think I harmed her, do you? Did it ever occur to you that the police might come to me in search of you?"

I glared back, saying nothing.

"She is safe, as she always was while in my care. Dawn agreed to let Sara stay at her home until I could make other arrangements." He pressed closer to me, those dark eyes sucking me in like quicksand, giving me no way to escape the weight of his presence or look away. "As for you—what have I ever done to make you think so ill of me, Shiarra? I'm tired of being seen as no more than a monster. This misguided attempt at removing me from your life doesn't change that we are bound. My blood flows in your veins, like it or not. Many have killed for that privilege; you have no concept of what an honor it is. It's unfair to me and to yourself to continuously deny that we have an unbreakable connection.

"Yes, it is true, my kind survives on blood. I've taken it by force when I needed to—but the current circumstances hardly warrant such behavior. I have no intention of forcing you to give any part of yourself to me."

"Then why won't you let me go?" I whispered.

A thrill of shock ran through me when he sat back on his heels, his hands briefly brushing over the sides of my breasts and my ribs as he pulled away. He didn't reach for me when I scooted across the bed until my back hit the headboard, nor make any move to stop me as I tucked my knees under my chin and wrapped my arms around my legs.

"I didn't let you go immediately because you might have run or made some foolish attempt at attacking me and mine again. You wouldn't have listened to reason. Now that you are listening,

I have no need to use force." That's when he smiled, the familiar wicked grin showing a hint of fang, sending a shiver through me.

"Stop doing that!" I demanded, hating the shrill waver to my voice, but unable to do anything about it.

"Doing what?"

I pointed a shaking, accusatory finger at the one visible fang. His smile widened, revealing both extended canines. "That! Put those away!"

He laughed. "Would that I had the control . . . Until you calm yourself, it's unlikely I'll manage. Now, to business. You are not to wear that belt again—ever."

I latched onto the anger that flared up at that statement, liking it more than the quivering terror I'd been subjected to only a moment ago. "You don't own me!"

"No, but whatever is inside that artifact would have if I hadn't intervened. It wasn't until tonight that I realized just how much it was altering you. I won't have that."

That gave me pause. It had a ring of truth to it that I didn't like at all. "What are you talking about?"

"As I mentioned the last time we met, I have been quite aware of your emotional state these last few weeks. When you finally calmed, I knew you hadn't turned Were, and that something had changed. Yet, hours later, you were back in a murderous mindset. And where did you go? Back here, to me. I gave Wesley instructions to detain you so I could see for myself what was causing the problem. Most of that rage has faded with the dawn, leaving the logical conclusion that the belt has been responsible for your inability to think rationally or control your need to hunt. I had put it down to the unfortunate events you'd had to deal with during your little vacation, but it seems there was far more to it than either of us had guessed."

That was a very terrible thing to consider. Had my actions really been mine this month? How much of what I'd thought and done had been the result of Isaac's manipulations?

Chapter 30

Royce said nothing while I sat there, second-guessing everything I had said and done for the last several weeks. His words seemed to have shed some light on memories and feelings that had been hidden behind the blindness of rage and hatred that had driven me for so long.

Though I was still frightened of and angry at the vampire, he was right. When I concentrated on it, I could recall moments of doubt and a desire to stop that had faded away like smoke on the wind once I put the belt on. The need to hurt and kill had grown stronger over time, fueled by my fear of change.

"Isaac," I said, my voice a faint whisper, then paused. "The belt. What will you do with it?"

"I trust Wesley will find some convenient place to bury it. You are not to go looking for it under any circumstances. Once I am assured it has lost its hold on you, if you wish, you may have your guns back."

I didn't say anything, breath hitching in my throat. Seeing my expression, his softened.

"I understand you want to right the wrongs done to you, and that you want nothing but safety for your friends. However, I won't let you do it at the expense of your own life, or at the risk of my people. Not if I can prevent it. Did you know that the belt was infecting you? That it would have taken you over completely if you had continued to wear it?"

Dull horror pierced through my shock, and I choked out a few words. "I knew it was doing something to me. Changing me. I didn't think it was that bad."

"No. No, you wouldn't have. I do hope you don't mind . . ." He waved a hand at me, and I blushed anew at my lack of clothes. He shifted on the bed, and I pressed harder against the headboard—but all he was doing was settling on his side, knuckles tucked under his cheek as he regarded me. His expression was bland and his mannerisms were casual, but the sparkle in his eye and the way he watched me made it clear he was getting quite a kick out of my current state of undress. "Putting you at a disadvantage seemed the most expedient way to shock some sense back into you."

"Oh, gee, thanks a lot," I muttered.

"You don't have to keep fighting me, you know. We could consummate this twisted relationship of ours, put an end to all of the difficulties between us." He smiled again, one fingertip tracing down my bare leg, making goose bumps rise on my flesh. I jerked back, slapping at his hand. "I would not be averse to using baser methods to prove to you how foolish these notions of yours about me are. That wasn't my intention when I started, but I know you're curious." He closed his eyes and inhaled, deeply, so there was no mistaking what he was doing. Creepy bastard. "I can smell it on you, taste it in the air. There's nothing quite like the scent of a woman's desire. It suits you—far better than that rubbish from The Circle you're using to hide your emotions."

I scowled at him, flushing all the way to my toes. "You—you sick—"

"Now, now—no false accusations. Am I wrong?"

I didn't answer, glaring at that shiny ruby on his tie again, my hands clenching into impotent fists.

"Fight it all you want, but you know you're attracted to me. We're contracted, yes, but I won't do anything to harm you. I find it difficult to believe that you have not realized this by now, particularly as this is not the first time I've had to reassure you that I do not now, nor have I ever, meant you any harm. You no longer have the moral dilemma of your boyfriend in the way. So, what is it that is stopping you? What are you so afraid of?"

It took a moment for me to find the words. When I met his eyes, I did nothing to dampen or hide my rage and frustration and fear of the situation. "You. I'm afraid of you. You're—sort of—nice to me now, but what will you do with me after you get what you want? What do I do when

I'm left with nothing but need for you, a slave like . . ."

I stopped, thinking. Who in this household would match that description? Who did I know who was like those kids screaming and crying for their lost, dead master in the police station some—what was it? Three years ago, now? It bothered me that, though I knew that some of the people in this household had to be bound and that all of the humans in this building were donors, not a one truly fit that mold.

It hung me up long enough that Royce finished my sentence for me. "A slave like the unfortunate Renfield in Mr. Stoker's fairytale? Like you were when Max and I bound you to us by blood?"

I said nothing.

"Shiarra, I could have forced you to remain by my side when I bound you the first time. Use your head. You must think very little of me if you think I have pursued you only to make you some mindless puppet. I'm not Max Carlyle; I don't intentionally set out to hurt those weaker than I am. What value would you be to me, broken and without that vital spark that makes you so precious to me? Just because you're afraid you couldn't stop me doesn't mean I'm about to take advantage."

"I'm sorry," I said, though I wasn't entirely sure what for. Since when had I been precious to him? And hadn't he been on the verge of "taking advantage" of me only a minute or so ago? "I don't trust you. I don't know how. You're"—*a monster.* I left the rest unsaid.

He sighed. "I'm not about to make you do something you don't want to. What I don't understand is why you keep denying yourself. You know as well as I do that I won't force the bond or anything else on you. Really, what are you afraid I'll do to you?"

"You'll bite me," I said, small voiced.

His brows arched, and he sat up, leaning toward me. "Is that all it is? You don't want to feel that again?"

"No!" I cried, the admonishing finger I waved at him trembling, even as anger rose up to quash any lingering sense of desire or curiosity I might have been harboring. "I won't go through it again, Royce. Not with you, not with anybody. It's bad enough I wonder sometimes what it would be like, what you could make me feel—I've already lost everything else. If you touch me, I won't be *me* anymore. Don't you understand? I don't want to lose what little is left. It's all I have."

He studied the tears tracing down my cheeks, the way my other hand rubbed at the ghost of bite marks on my throat—which I stopped as soon as I realized what I was doing—and his unruffled visage shattered into a deep frown of concern. I hated so much that he could look so calm and sincere, when all I could think about was that night when I had been trapped under the weight of a vampire who had only waited long enough to hear me scream in terror before stealing the life from my veins.

When Royce spoke, his composure grated on

my nerves far more than it should have. How could he be so collected when I was falling apart right in front of him?

"The sharing of blood isn't a horrible, monstrous thing when it's done between two people who care for each other. What we have may not be love or lust, but there is desire and the potential for friendship between us. All I wish to do is explore and perhaps even solidify that connection. You've not done so much as given me the courtesy of a moment's consideration to my wants or needs."

"You haven't exactly done the same," I accused.

"Not true. I respected your wishes in the situation with Max. I provided you and your friend shelter when I had nothing to gain. I have spent time, money, and other resources to preserve your life even when you seemed bent on destroying yourself. I don't think I need to explain to you how unusual it is for one of my kind to be so selfless—I've not felt so compelled to be so for anyone in centuries. And yet you spurn me at every turn, as though you see me as some terrible, wicked creature."

"Maybe I do," I countered, bristling at the accuracy of his statements. "Why do you keep trying to foist yourself on me, then? You're no saint, Royce. Not even close, and don't try to pretend that you've only done what you have out of the goodness of your heart. What do you have to gain?"

"Must I have an ulterior motive for everything that I do?"

"Answer the question," I snapped.

He regarded me steadily, saying nothing for a long moment. I was beginning to think he was going to ignore my demand before he spoke again.

"As I have told you before, you underestimate your worth. While there are many who answer to me, I value those of great will and strength and courage over the many who only work for me and mine because of some perceived chance at immortality or power. You have no idea what a rarity it is to find a person who will speak to me so plainly, particularly one who does not crave what I can do to or for them. It is not something I intend to let slip away. True, you are neither terribly wise nor clever—but your valor is what sets you apart. Your damnable stubbornness, or perhaps your prejudice, is all that stands in the way of what could be a mutually beneficial relationship. You so readily turn me away when I doubt you have any idea what it would really be like for you to allow me the liberties our contract grants me. I admit, your continuous efforts at rejecting anything and everything I have ever offered you—save when you had no other choice—both intrigues and irritates me. I'm not used to being thwarted, Ms. Waynest."

"Oh, we're back to 'Ms. Waynest' now? Well, Mr. Royce, I didn't take you up on your offer because I don't *want* to be bitten. Unlike some people I could mention, I *want* my freedom. Did you ever consider that?"

He didn't rise to my bait, remaining calm in the face of my anger. "Your safety and your freedom are hardly at stake with me, and I have no intentions of involving myself in the minutiae of your every waking move. Answering to me would be much like answering to your business partner—if a bit more intimate." The slight twitch at the corner of his lips and the way his eyes glittered were the only things that betrayed his amusement with my horrified gasp. "Now. Have you ever honestly considered letting me touch you, or have you only said 'no' out of reflex? Or to spite me?"

That shut me up. We stared at each other across the vast chasm of different worlds; he was trying to build a bridge over that nothingness to make me see vampirism in a different light. Knowing it didn't make it any easier to pause and take an honest look at the situation. He didn't give me time to come up with an argument or justification.

"Max and his people had no consideration for your feelings or safety. I do. I promise you that you are in safe hands with me. It's not the same experience when it's done with someone who cares about their donor. Give me a chance to prove that to you, Shiarra. Give me the opportunity to prove to you that it is not as bad as you fear."

I shifted my gaze down to my knees, fighting the urge to let the cold fingers of terror creeping up my spine translate into a shudder. My hands tightened in the sheets at the mention of Max. Being bitten by him and Peter were harsh memories I'd sooner leave to rot in the back of my mind. Having them brought up here, now, did nothing to soothe my fears.

Yet he did have a point. I'd never given him a chance before. Not by any stretch of the imagination. My phobia of being bitten had grown stronger after the two vampires forced themselves on me—vampires who didn't care overmuch whether I survived the experience.

The only times Royce had ever hurt me had been when he was under compulsion by the *Dominari* Focus. Outside of that, he'd been physically forceful at times, but had never actually forced himself upon me.

His behavior was a far cry from that of Peter or Max. Could I trust him? Could I really put my life in his hands?

I couldn't honestly say no, but just the thought of saying yes made my stomach give a sick lurch.

Perhaps sensing my weakening resolve, he slowly edged closer to me until he could wrap an arm around my shoulder, cradling me to his chest. I started to resist, but then shame at realizing that made me guilty of doing just as he had said—resisting out of reflex—soon had me relaxing against him. I breathed in the scent of mint and some spicy cologne with only the faintest undertone of copper as he lightly stroked my hair, then urged me to rest my cheek against his shoulder.

His touch, though cool, was not unpleasant or unwelcome. He didn't speak again, waiting with the patience of an immortal for me to give him my answer.

I couldn't deny that a tiny part of me wanted

to know. I wanted to know what he could do, what made him different. Why he had pursued me so heavily despite my adamant refusals.

As I pressed my hand to his chest, feeling for a heartbeat that wasn't there, he held me as he had when I had wept for the loss of my livelihood and my friends and my family last month—what felt like a lifetime ago. I had the feeling he would respect my decision if I said no; that this might be the last time he would ever ask so much from me. He gave no sign of eagerness or anger, only patience. When I tilted my head up to look at him again, he met my gaze evenly with those black, inhuman eyes, letting his hand come to rest on my shoulder.

Whatever my choice, it was one I could never change or take back. This would alter everything between us.

I leaned up to press a brief, chaste kiss against his cheek. "Okay, Royce. Alec. Okay. You can have your chance."

Chapter 31

Oh, God, why did I say that? It was too late to take it back—but I wasn't about to take the coward's way out and tell him I'd made a mistake.

Even if that's exactly what it felt like.

He didn't wait long to take me up on it, either. Despite having given him permission, I trembled uncontrollably as he settled those cold, effortlessly strong fingers under my jaw to tilt my head back. Braced to feel pain, I closed my eyes, not wanting to watch as he bent to feed, nor to see that beastly hunger that wanted to swallow me whole form in his eyes.

Thus I was not prepared for it when he kissed me instead.

Shocked, I jerked back at the brush of his lips against my own, lids flying open. He smiled slightly, that amused look at odds with the sure, proprietary way he slid his arms around me and drew me against him once more. The chills that wracked me weren't entirely from his cool body temperature, but I couldn't seem to stop the stupid trembling.

"You are terribly flighty, Ms. Waynest. Tell me, do you flee from any man who touches you, or is this something special reserved for me? Either way, I'll delight in breaking you of the habit."

I glared at him, putting my hands against his chest in a clear message—*stop*. "I—I just . . . I wasn't expecting it, that's all."

"I do so love watching you squirm," he murmured, leaning in to press another quick, playful kiss against my cheek that made me stiffen, then redden. My skin felt positively afire as his dark eyes examined me, calculating, measuring my frightened reactions against some unknown scale.

"That," I said, voice shaking, "that is what I can't stand about you."

"Hmm?" His response made me think he was only half listening. He seemed more interested in looking me over, searching for who knows what.

"When you act like a monster," I whispered, instantly wishing—again—that I could take it back.

That was sufficient to drag his attention off my body long enough for him to meet my eyes. There was a touch of red deep down in his irises, only a hint, but it soon died away. A sly smile curved his lips as I straightened and pointedly stared him down. Too bad he was more pleased than intimidated. I got another glimpse of those fangs I hated so much as he spoke in a slow, amused drawl.

"Ah. I see, now," he said. He leaned in, just a little, and I couldn't help but jerk back and press a hand to my throat. "Tell me, Ms. Waynest, did you think that I would lunge upon and ravage you like you were some helpless maiden in a fairytale?"

My embarrassed flush was answer enough. He had the sheer gall to laugh at me.

"Oh, you *are* precious. I see I have my work cut out for me."

Despite my indignation, my attempt to pull away from him was halted too easily by his fingers twining with my own, drawing me out of my protective crouch by the headboard.

He urged me to lay back and, in spite of my misgivings (and irritation at his teasing), I did so without protest. Now wasn't the time for that.

Once I was prone, his fingers stroked my bare skin, leaving behind an electric tingle and desire for more that somehow managed to frighten me more than his fangs. He didn't seem to care about the new bumps and contusions and scars, other than to take care not to put much pressure on any of the myriad bruises scattered over my frame.

Doubts and worries about the consequences of my actions assailed me, and I had to bite my lip to keep from telling him to stop, to wait, that I wasn't ready. That I'd never be ready. My fingers knotted in the silken sheets, my body practically vibrating with the involuntary shudders that threaded through me as I fought to remain still under his touch.

"Be at ease, my little hunter. I won't harm you."

Every instinct within me screamed to run, to hide, to fight and claw my way free if necessary. Instead of giving in to those urges, I said nothing and closed my eyes, doing my very best to think of Royce as anything other than a monster who would gorge himself on the blood in my veins once he deemed me ready for his bite.

He didn't speak again for some time; instead he knelt at my side as he carefully traced the lines of my body, memorizing them with his hands. I'd never been so aware of someone's touch before. Having my eyes closed had nothing to do with it. Those cold, powerful fingers could have easily crushed my bones into powder, but instead stroked me with the same delicacy as that with which one might handle a small, frightened animal. Barely brushing my skin, but leaving no doubt as to the enormity of strength behind that touch.

To both my consternation and relief, he did not lay a hand on my breasts or cop a feel between my thighs. His interest lay in other places, like the line of my jaw, the arch of my ribs, and even that horribly ticklish spot under my knees. He hesitated whenever I flinched—usually when he touched a scar, particularly those on my stomach—but would soon retrace his steps, repeating the motion until the tendon-creaking tension in my muscles relaxed.

It took quite some time for me to stop shaking and lose the immediate heat of embarrassment. My concentration gradually eased away from holding myself deathly still to focusing on what he was doing, along with a slowly growing sense of curiosity as to where he might touch next. Little by little, the gut-wrenching anxiety eased away, soothed by the gentle brush of his fingers.

Those hands came to know every scar and imperfection, every place on my body that responded without any thought on my part, whether it be from desire or shame. His touch was not judgmental, only probing, searching, learning where to caress to make me move with instead of against him.

At last he lingered on one of my arms, noting the way I shivered—not from fear, not at all—as he traced the fine lace of veins visible through my skin. He gathered up my right hand in both his own and, though I still refused to open my eyes to watch, pressed chill lips to my fingertips as he kissed each digit in turn.

Though he hadn't quite urged me to do it, I laid my hand against his cheek as he bent over me, his own hand settling lightly on my stomach. He stilled, remaining motionless as I tentatively did as he had, memorizing the strong planes of his jaw by touch alone. As I learned the slope of his brow, the softness of his hair, the butterfly kiss of his lashes against my palm, he waited with infinite patience for my hesitance to fade before moving again.

I didn't tremble quite so badly when he eased himself on top of me this time. I was still too cowardly to open my eyes, even as that damned tie tack scraped between my ribs again. He kept one hand pressed over mine at his cheek so I would not pull away as he switched to using his lips and tongue to taste and lightly nip at all of the places he had learned elicited a response.

Much to my everlasting shame, I *did* respond.

Unwanted heat settled under my skin and a sheen of sweat broke out upon my brow, my body arching up unbidden to mold itself to his. Tiny jerks at his gentle ministrations became more, shifting my hand from his cheek so I could tangle my fingers in his hair when he sampled the fine hollow at my collarbone.

It was like he'd flipped a switch somewhere deep inside my body. The light scrape of fangs on my skin . . . right . . . *there* . . . sent a shocking jolt of pure, toe-curling pleasure down my spine. A sudden, fierce flame of desire lashed through me, and I didn't care that I was baring my throat to a vampire who could kill me with little effort, and that I'd be helpless to stop him if he tried. All I knew in that moment was that I wanted more.

He took my unspoken invitation to heart, his attention shifting to my jugular where he settled into a series of kisses that seared me with their chill. I made an impatient sound, though I wasn't quite sure why I was now more frustrated than frightened at his pace. Why couldn't he get it over with, end this slow torture he was putting me through? A low growl escaped me, reminiscent of the werewolf I'd almost become, as I dragged my nails down his back, drawing him closer.

The low vibration of his laughter against my skin only further inflamed me. I wanted to regain some control over this situation. He wasn't going to be the only one here who was unaffected by desire, damn it. I would make him lose his cool, if only so he would put a stop to these games. I hooked one leg around his hips, the fingers of both hands now curled in his hair, drawing him to my throat.

My urges meant nothing to him.

He pulled away. *Pulled away.*

My astonishment was all that saved me from immediately exploding into the fury of humiliation or rejection. My eyes flew open, a tiny sound of dismay escaping me as I tilted my head to watch him.

Instead of sinking his fangs into me, he continued his oral exploration of my sensitive spots, his tongue flickering over and putting just the right amount of pressure on the places that heated my skin and set my heart racing. That, added to the light and somehow pleasantly deliberate brush of his fingers over the scar tissue beneath my ribcage, tracing the patterns on my skin that usually brought me so much shame, was driving me to the edge of madness.

It really wasn't fair that he should be so in control when I was turning into a basket case. Mostly I was angry at myself for falling apart while he was so clearly unmoved by any of this in any way that I could see.

"What are you doing?" I cried the words. Maybe sobbed is a better way of putting it.

He glanced up, a devilish grin curving his lips at my alarm. "Ensuring you will never find solace in the arms of another. That you will burn for me, little hunter, and only me. I will know you—all of you—and brand you in a way that no contract or bond of blood could ever substitute."

I gaped at him. His grin widened—a purely

male expression, one mirrored in the heat simmering deep in his hooded eyes. A look of possession.

"Not to worry, Ms. Waynest. You'll still be you when I have finished."

He didn't bother waiting for my response, though I was a bit too busy spluttering and squirming for him to follow the same pattern he'd been a moment ago. That put a slightly different spin on this than I'd assumed. A part of me was horrified at his words, but a far larger portion was reveling in the glory of being so thoroughly explored, even knowing it meant he would conquer my mind and body in the end.

Though I was already hot, burning for more of his touch, he stoked the flame higher by busying himself with removing my bra and taking to a light suckling on one of my nipples, his hand ministering to the other. They tightened instantly under the chill—or maybe from the pleasure. I couldn't be sure, and was too confused by his easy acceptance of my ravaged skin and uneasy reactions to know what to expect or how to respond. At that point, all I could manage, aside from quiet pleas or involuntarily arching into his touch, was a dim thought to pray that I'd be too lost in this pleasure to feel it when he finally bit me.

His fangs occasionally raked over my skin but never pierced and, oddly, never frightened me quite as I expected them to. Though I arched against him, pleaded both with words and actions for him to hurry up and claim me, and even bit his shoulder at one point to show my frustration, he never gave in to my wants. Aside from letting me urge him on with light touches to his head or shoulders, he wouldn't allow me to reach lower, and balked at every attempt I made to shift our positions.

I knew he was aroused—now that he was pressed closer, I could feel the stiff length of him through the silken material rubbing against my thigh—but I couldn't figure out why he wouldn't let me touch him. When I got too persistent, he moved with all the sinuous grace of a snake to elude my grasping hands, distracting me with a sharp nip or by briefly pinning my wrist to keep me from reaching for his belt. The message was clear: it was his turn and, until he was done, I wasn't allowed to reciprocate what he was doing.

I voiced a wordless cry when he fitted his palm over my sex, the sudden pressure over my soaked panties urging me into bucking impatiently against his deft fingers. He toyed with me, shifting to take my other nipple into his mouth as his fingers teased me with a ghost of the friction I so desired. It wasn't enough to push me over, only enough to drive me crazy, wild, thrusting against him with a reckless abandon I'd never known with Chaz or any other lover.

No one else I'd ever shared a bed with had had this kind of patience or self-control, and it was blowing my mind that he was pushing me well past the point of readiness without taking his own pleasure. Not that I really minded now. Sort of. Playing the role of patient, passive bed partner was new to me, and I wasn't adjusting too well.

Eventually, he took pity on me, sliding his way down my body as he agonizingly slowly drew my panties off. He didn't let me help, one hand pressing against my stomach to hold me down as I moved to rise with him. That implacable hold was driving me crazy. All I could do was grip the sheets and writhe in the hopes of finding some form—any form—of release.

Once the flimsy scrap of material was discarded, I was left naked under his hungry gaze. A gasp was torn from my throat as he settled between my legs, his fangs scraping in harsh counterpoint to the brush of silken strands of hair against my inner thighs.

"Last chance to turn back, little hunter," he said, eyeing me as I so lewdly sprawled for him. "Do you really want this?"

What the hell did he think I'd been asking for? Fuck whatever it was I'd been worried about before. The itch I felt wasn't going to be scratched by itself.

"Please, Royce," I begged, then gasped, jerking at the hips as a single fingertip traced the apex between my legs. "Please, don't stop!"

The devilish glint to his eye wasn't lost on me, but that wasn't my concern. He settled into a painfully slow thrusting of first one, then two fingers, his cold, calculating gaze at odds with the gentle way he touched me. Getting to know what I liked, exactly where he needed to touch those secret places to send me spiraling down into mindless need. Playing my desires against me. Using me.

I didn't care.

I thrashed and cried for more, but he didn't give it to me right away. When I tried to help him along, he took both of my wrists in one hand so I couldn't touch him, or myself, pinning me in place so all I could do was twist and writhe against him, and cry out for more. Playing me like a fiddle, he wasn't satisfied until I was pleading for him to speed up, to move faster, harder, to *finish* what he had started, damn it.

He played me right to the very edge of the precipice, and then withdrew.

I could have screamed.

Instead I cried. I'd never been such an emotional wreck during sex before, but he didn't seem bothered by it in the least. He ignored my tears of frustration, my futile attempts to free my wrists, and the blind thrusting of my hips as I begged for him to fill that emptiness inside me. Still, he had that gleam in his eye, the one that spoke of things to come—and when his mouth settled over the nub hidden between the slickened folds of my sex, I came with such force, I couldn't move for what felt like hours.

He didn't wait for me to recover. Instead, his attentions were focused on lapping up the traces of my desire while the fingers of his free hand were soon exploring, prodding, stoking the flames back up from embers to a blind, needy conflagration, screaming for release into the wider world.

I'm pretty sure the second time I did scream. My throat felt raw, but I was so shocked by the heady rush, I wasn't totally sure what had happened. Only that there were stars in my vision, and that he'd moved away, leaving an empty ache behind. Bereft of his touch—and his punishing hold—I was too involved in moving with the rolling waves of ecstasy still pulsing in uneven tremors through my body to do anything so coherent as to pay any notice to where he'd gone.

It was a good thing he was giving me a breather. I wasn't sure I could handle much more. I didn't try to rise, left boneless and gasping for every breath as I squeezed my eyes shut and waited for whatever was to come next. My heart was racing, my skin hypersensitive, and only now did I realize that all of the places he had sucked and kissed on my body were still tingling with the ghost of sensation. As if he were still touching me—working his way inside me—and it heightened the sensitivity of my skin to every breath of air, every stroke of silk sheets, even the pulse of blood in my veins. It was the strangest thing; not at all unpleasant, just unexpected. Maybe a side effect from having been bound to him before.

It didn't take long for him to return. All of a sudden, he was there, his mouth on mine, and I could taste myself on his lips. His fingers curled around mine, pinning my hands at either side this time as he delved deep, his fangs occasionally pricking my lips and tongue in a shockingly pleasant way. It might have been the eroticism of the moment, but I couldn't recall ever feeling such a deep pang of longing or so needed as when his tongue plundered my mouth, like he was starved for the taste of me, sending renewed sparks of desire pulsing through my bloodstream.

He held himself over me, taking the time to ensure I was breathless before one questing hand drifted from mine and stole between our bodies again. As he rubbed between my legs in preparation for another assault, slickened fingers nudging my thighs apart, I reached up to embrace him—and very nearly recoiled at the feel of his cool, bare flesh.

That was soon forgotten; he eased his body against mine, settled between my legs so the tip of his arousal rubbed incessantly between the folds at the junction of my thighs. He finally released my mouth, but I'm pretty sure he only did that so he could listen to me cry out when a single finger briefly slid inside me. Christ, it felt glorious, particularly with this newfound sensitivity to his touch. His chuckle at the dismayed sound I made when he shifted his hand away might have pissed me off if I hadn't been so busy trying to get down to business. His arms around me were all the support I needed, but he wouldn't let me arch up and take him inside, withdrawing at the hips as soon as I attempted it.

"Please! Stop playing and fuck me already," I demanded, not caring how crude my request was, nor that he was laughing at my frantic attempts to seal us together, hip to hip.

"Ah, you still know enough to use words to beg. You're not ready."

And he taught me that there were whole new plateaus of frustration and pleasure to be reached before I was.

I'm not quite sure how long it took for me to grow mindless enough with desire that he felt it was the right time, only that once it was, I thought I might just explode from the intense need rushing through my veins. Orgasms shook me, one right after another as his thick length pressed inside, at first feeling like too much, far too much, before the friction between us brought me to new heights of gratification.

His hands always found the right place to touch, sometimes cupping my cheeks as his tongue delved into my mouth to match the thrusting of his hips, other times cradling me in his arms as though he was afraid I'd turn into smoke and drift away if he didn't hold me close. It was fierce and gentle and possessive all at once, overwhelmingly so.

I did my best to reciprocate, touching as much of him as I could while pinned under his weight by stroking rippling muscles that put me in mind of satin-covered steel. Some of that smooth, cool skin was marred with traces of scars like my own. Well, that might explain his ready acceptance of my physical imperfections.

A low, inhuman growl rumbling in his throat briefly sent a shock of terror through me. I withdrew with a gasp, panic and the claustrophobic sensation of being trapped settling in like old friends. Then, surprise, surprise, he grabbed my hands to put them back to where I'd found a death grip on his ass a moment before—and what a *fine* ass it was, solid as bedrock—because he was obviously enjoying my encouraging squeezes. That's when I figured out he wasn't growling so much as purring, and I met his questing mouth with renewed enthusiasm as I obliged his unspoken demand.

At one point, I was dimly aware of his fingers tangling in my hair, drawing my head back, followed by a sudden pressure at my neck. My nails scored his shoulders, digging deep furrows as that pressure turned into a pinprick—barely noticed considering what was happening between my legs—that exploded into synapse-frying fireworks against every nerve ending in my body, arching outward from my throat. It left me breathless and shaking as his churning hips sped up to the agonizingly pleasurable speed of a well-timed piston. It was every tingling ache under my skin from his earlier exploration magnified by a thousandfold, heightening the experience to the point where I was nearly certain my heart was ready to explode in my chest. It was a ferociously satisfying age before he slowed, his thrusts becoming uneven, but still sending shudders of fulfillment through me.

Sometime later, his tongue laved my throat, the simple motion radiating pleasant tingles that rocked me all the way to my toes. Sometime after he'd stopped sucking at that sweet spot on my neck, my heart had started again. The shivers that raced down my spine had me spasming around his length in an attempt to hold him there even as he drew away.

I couldn't speak. I could barely breathe, and tears leaked unbidden from the corners of my eyes. Though there was a measure of soreness, he had held that incredible strength of his in check and done exactly as he'd promised—left me unharmed. Sated, for all of that, and maybe a little bruised, definitely worn out, but not damaged.

He gathered me up in his arms, and I shook against him. Not from fear, but from an inability to keep still as aftershocks of bliss raced through my body. In exhaustion, I lay my head against his shoulder, tucking my hands under my cheek and focusing on steadying my breathing so I wouldn't pass out. He tilted my head up only long enough to kiss away my tears before letting me collapse in a sprawl against him.

At first, I couldn't figure out why he felt so much warmer—but the unspeakably pleasurable way my throat throbbed when I brushed my fingertips over the spot he'd latched onto during those last moments answered that question. Just touching it was enough to make me squirm, tingles of ecstasy radiating outward from the tiny bite marks when pressure was put on them. His soft laughter at my discovery was too genuinely pleased for me to take offense, and I was too worn out and felt too good to be upset about it.

Royce ran soothing fingers through my hair, calming my racing heart and making it clear that he didn't intend to leave my side. Whether this was a temporary reprieve or the end of today's lesson, the vampire was right. I'd never be able to match the intensity of his lovemaking with another. No one else had ever known me—even bothered to make the effort to know me—as well as he had.

Forevermore, I was ruined for anyone else. I was his.

Please turn the page for an exciting sneak peek of

FORSAKEN BY THE OTHERS,

coming soon from Zebra Books!

Every part of me ached. Though I was wrapped up in blankets, curled up on my side in bed, I was cold, too. Maybe it was my own shivering that stirred me out of sleep. Whatever it was, I didn't want to move right away.

Then something cool and spidery shifted under the covers, brushing over my stomach.

Startled, I screamed and twisted away, flailing at the sheets to bat it off. It only tightened against me, yanking me back against a hard, male body.

A clearly naked—*quite* hard—male body.

"Shush, now. You'll wake the whole building."

The initial rush of fright became a rush of a different sort. I wasn't being woken up by Chaz or Jack or one of the other White Hats. And I was all kinds of naked under these covers.

Momentary confusion became crystal clarity as memories of all the many ways Royce had explored my body the previous night came back to me. The surge of aggression and need that pulsed through my blood sang of a keen desire to leave my mark on the vampire the way he had left his own on my neck and other places last night. He didn't resist as I twisted around and bit his shoulder, my nails digging deep into his upper arm and tangling in his hair.

"Easy, now. We have all night." The rumble of his laughter vibrated through my body, my hot skin pressed to his cold. It was only when he took hold of the wrist I'd locked on his arm and rolled so he was on top that it struck me how easily he overpowered me.

Which served as another—this time unpleasant—reminder. The belt was gone. I wasn't turning Other.

I was human. I was nothing.

No. Not nothing. I was a legally bound and contracted vampire's toy.

I withdrew and shut my mouth with a snap, my initial rush of terror twisting into a different kind of fear. Wriggling uncomfortably, I pushed at Royce's chest with my free hand, wincing as the pressure of his body rubbing against mine revealed a whole slew of hurts from my battle with Wesley—and more than likely from the far more pleasurable activities that came thereafter.

Royce didn't let go, settling on his side to wrap both arms around me instead, one hand coming up to tweak one of my nipples. "Much as I enjoy that delightful squirming you're doing, you might try relaxing. You're safe here."

The sight of the bruises from last night's "festivities" had pushed me into a dark place filled with panic and despair, one that drove me to tears when I couldn't pry his hands off. I didn't mean to cry, but the sick, light-headed feeling combined with the undeniable weakness in my limbs brought on such a wave of shame, I couldn't help myself.

He pulled me around to face him, one hand cupping my cheek while the other kept me pinned against his side.

"What is it? I didn't hurt you, did I?"

I couldn't tell him I was crying for what I'd lost. Even if I wanted to, I wasn't sure I could explain it to him. My whole life had been defined by how I lived it, and that had not included being bound to, sleeping with, or becoming willing food for vampires. It was more than the blood he'd taken— it was a piece of me that I couldn't ever have back. It made me into the *thing* my father despised so much; no longer fit to be part of my own family.

Royce's brows lowered, eyes and hands searching my body for signs of damage. Aside from old scars and the plethora of bruises I'd acquired last night, he wasn't going to find anything. I was too choked up to tell him as much, and too freaked out to do anything more intelligent than frantically try to put some distance between us.

Though he was clearly puzzled by my behavior, Royce didn't push me for answers. Once satisfied that my distress hadn't been caused by something physical, he drew me even tighter against him, pinning me still. Though I strained away at first, he brushed his fingers through my hair and whispered half-heard endearments in my ear until my tears and uneasy squirming eased away. I buried my face against his chest and tried to get a hold of myself, to cling to the thought that my life wasn't over now, just changed—drastically, irrevocably changed.

I was his property now, and not just on paper.

He owned me, body and soul. Not only had I abandoned my morals and common sense last night, I'd *liked* it. Liked the feel of his lips and tongue and fingers and other parts so intimately pressed against mine, all over, inside me, all while he drank my blood. What the hell was wrong with me that I'd *liked* being wrapped in Death's arms and pounded into the mattress while my life was siphoned away a sip at a time?

Though I didn't want to be that twisted, ugly thing in my mind, I couldn't help myself. A shudder of longing crawled down my spine as his fingers swept over the place he'd bitten me last night. Desire bloomed, and I fought it, pushing his hand away before that need could fire up my blood enough for him to notice. Images of all of the ways he could take advantage of me while I was unable to defend myself whirled through my head like a maelstrom of horror-show terrors, a painful reminder that now I was just a blood whore, a plaything, and that I'd willingly put my life in his hands.

He pulled back, pinpoint sparks of red reflecting in his eyes as he studied me. Growing panic was pushing me in the direction of hyperventilating; I was too afraid to move again—he might realize why I wanted him to stop.

"Shiarra, don't make me drag answers out of you. What's wrong? Are you hurt?"

I squeezed my eyes shut and shook my head. My hurt wasn't of the physical variety.

"Tell me," he commanded, "what's wrong."

The words spilled out of my mouth before I could stop them. "My dad was right. I'm not a Waynest anymore. Not myself anymore. Just another vampire's puppet."

My eyes popped open and I slapped my hands over my mouth before I could say anything more damning. Royce's expression was unreadable, his gaze burning into mine.

"I'm sorry," I whispered from behind my hands.

I couldn't tell by his expression if he was angry with me for being honest with him, but it was far too late to take the words back, and I'd never been good at hiding my thoughts from him. Especially when he was staring at me so intently, like he could see right past my eyes to the darkest thoughts buried in the back of my mind. Like he knew all the horrible things I didn't want anybody to know. He might not judge me for them—but that didn't mean I wanted him to know every thought inside my head as intimately as he'd come to learn the secrets of my body last night.

Not wanting to meet his gaze, I buried my face against his chest, practically vibrating with tension. Maybe he got the picture that his actions were only making things worse. His voice, when he finally spoke, was strangely gentle, and made me feel like an even bigger fool for finding comfort in it.

"Even after last night? You still think that I was only using you, or would abandon you once I got what I wanted?"

I nodded, not trusting my voice. He kept running his fingers through my hair and down my back, not saying anything for a time. It took a while, but after the worst of my trembling tapered off, he slid a hand between us and nudged my chin up so he could peer into my eyes.

"What is it you fear has changed about you? What do you feel I have taken from you?"

Biting my lip, I looked away again before answering him. The tears made it a little hard to speak clearly, but I'm pretty sure he still heard me just fine. "My soul. My free will."

Shaking from a mix of stress and fatigue and a sickness more of mind than body, I jerked out of his grip and put some distance between us, turning my back on him as I drew the covers up to my chin. He might own me now, but that didn't mean I had to like it.

What hurt worst of all was knowing that my dad was right. I wasn't fit to be a Waynest. I wasn't even my own person anymore. Without the belt, I was just another helpless, hapless human, at the mercy of a monster who could feed on or kill me at any time with no cost to himself. No safety nets. No taking it back. I'd put myself here, and now I would have to suffer the consequences of my own choices.

The vampire's hand settled on my shoulder. The irony of that possessive gesture coinciding with my thoughts wasn't lost on me. If anything, it made it harder to get the tears under control. When I didn't turn around, he gripped my upper arm, not tight enough to hurt, but definitely enough to keep me from pulling away from him again.

"Shiarra, please look at me."

I wouldn't—couldn't do it. He made a soft, frustrated sound in his throat before speaking.

"I wish I had some way of expressing to you how much you mean to me in a way that you would accept. You saved my life, Shiarra, back when I meant nothing to you. You're brave when you have every reason to run scared, you've shown a remarkable ability to think on your feet, and you're resourceful. You've faced many of your fears, which is more than could be said for some of the most loyal of my number—but you hold to this idea that belonging to me makes you less than a person, and it's simply not true. You are no less the woman you were before you let me touch you last night, and I have no intentions of discarding you like some broken toy."

"This isn't something you can fix, Royce," I said. My voice might have been thick with tears, but I was proud of myself for being able to say what I was thinking for once instead of choking on my own angst like a brooding teenager. "You were just . . . you. It was my choice. I let it happen."

His voice was deadly cold and quiet. "Are you telling me you consider last night a mistake?"

I twisted to look at him, shocked.

He leaned in, using his grip on my arm to push

me to my back. Before I knew it, his fingers, icy and implacable, tightened around my wrists. The growl rumbling in his throat made my knees quiver, and I gasped as my hands were abruptly pinned above my head, his lips brushing over my throat with a teasing rake of fangs as he leaned into me. His usually smooth voice came out rough, ragged, and I could very nearly taste the anger and frustration radiating from him around the bitter flavor of fear on my tongue.

"You are the most aggravating woman I have ever encountered! I have fought everything that I am to be what I thought you would desire of me. I have left you to live your life as you wished it, rather than as I willed it. Do you know how difficult it was to wait idly by while you hemmed and hawed about whether you could trust me? Don't you know that the temptation to interfere with your choices was nearly unbearable? I have been as kind and generous and understanding as I know how to be, Shiarra. I waited for you to come to me of your own will—and now that you have, you think that what we did was a mistake? After all that I have done? Still you spurn me, fear me. Am I not generous enough? Have I not been merciful? What must I say or do to make you understand that I have leashed *everything* that I am so that you would choose me of your own will?"

Though my heart was still beating a million miles a minute and every breath was taken on a gasp thanks to the adrenaline rush, I didn't struggle. It took some effort to calm down, but his grip eased up as the tension in my body did. His lips were still but a hairsbreadth away from my jugular, but I didn't think he was about to bite me. Not yet, anyway. My reply came out small-voiced, not in the accusatory tone I was going for.

"You're taking away what makes me . . . *me*. You scare me, Royce. You scare me half to death, but I want you, too, and that just makes it worse. Am I even human anymore, or am I just a reflection of who you think I should be?"

My question gave him pause. He withdrew—though he didn't let me go—and I relaxed marginally as the harsh edge left his voice.

"You are every bit as human now as you were when you first entered my home last night. I have done nothing—*nothing*—to change that. Don't hate yourself for letting me make you feel good. Giving in to me isn't a crime. Liking the things I make you feel isn't a sin against your family or your God. There is no shame in it. I won't tolerate these misconceptions any longer, or see you destroy yourself, physically or emotionally, now that you're finally mine—do you understand? You mean too much to me for me to allow that to happen."

I shuddered at his pronouncement. Though a part of me was absurdly pleased with his words, the rest of me was screaming in horror at that *finally mine* part. It only validated the terror of losing my own identity, only to be overshadowed by a new "master" I couldn't live without.

"Damn it, Shiarra, look at me!"

I did. His normally black eyes were blazing red

with anger, shining like bright beads of precious stones set in a lake of tar. He lifted one of my hands and pressed it to his cheek, twining his fingers with mine, much like we had done last night.

"Why do you not believe me when I say you will remain your own person? Is it because you are frightened by what I made you feel? I still taste you, crave you, want to be inside of you again. Can you honestly tell me you don't want that, too? That you don't want me?"

I wanted it. I wanted it so badly, I could taste the remembered mint and copper of his mouth on my tongue.

But I wanted to stay *me*, too.

"Please," I croaked between shallow pants, my fingers against his cheek lightly stroking his skin and pressing the length of my body against his to ease the growing heat and need, even though I knew I should have drawn away. "Please, Royce, I can't do this again. Please don't make me lose myself. Please."

"No more tears. Not because of me." His hands cupped my cheeks as he tilted my head up so he could briefly press a kiss against each eyelid, his cool lips following the path of my tears as he whispered against my skin. "You don't need to be frightened anymore, my little hunter. You'll always be safe—and yourself—with me."

When he loosened his grip on my wrists and coaxed me to embrace him, I wrapped my arms around his neck and clutched at him. He stroked my hair while I battled an internal struggle between the dark corner of my mind telling me what a horrible idea it was to trust him and the hurting, lonely, emotional side that wanted to believe it all—heart and soul.

"You aren't a pet or some mindless puppet, Shiarra. I'll only take what you'll freely give me, never force anything from you. I might tease you now and again, but it will remain no more than the occasional attempt to fluster or coax you into trying something beyond your comfort zone." The fanged smile that curved his lips spoke of wicked things he already had in mind to talk me into. Even the dark, rational side admitted that might be some fun to go along with. "You have my word."

I believed him. He hadn't hurt me, hadn't driven me away, hadn't done anything other than reassure and comfort me. True, his methods were sometimes abhorrent, but his intentions, though not always clear, were good. I was the one with the hang-ups here, and felt no small measure of shame for constantly treating him as the bad guy or thinking him responsible for every evil that had befallen me since I'd been drawn into the doings of the Others in this city.

I pressed a kiss to his chest before ducking my head, mumbling a few words that might or might not have been coherent. Spitting out the truth hurt, but I meant everything I said. "Sorry . . . I'm sorry, too. Shouldn't have said—shouldn't think so little of you. I'm sorry, Royce."

He rested his cheek on the top of my head as his fingertips ran soothingly along my back, just holding me. It took a while, but eventually my tears tapered off.

I'd done some abhorrent things during that time I thought I might be turning into a werewolf, but maybe with Royce's help, picking up the shattered pieces of my life wouldn't be as hard as I feared. Tackling everything alone had been incredibly foolish—as had my decision to go to the White Hats for help—so why not accept that the vampire could assist me? Doing things alone and ignoring his offers before had only gotten me into more trouble. The idea of trusting him no longer seemed like the epically bad idea I'd once thought it to be.

When I tilted my head back to give him a speculative look, considering the possibilities, he leaned forward just enough to brush a kiss over my brow.

"It's been an intensely stressful month for you. I imagine there may be other times in the days ahead when you will need reassurance. There is no need to suffer in silence. You will come to me and allow me to help you instead of rushing off on your own now, yes?"

That hit a little too close to home. I gave him a sharp poke in the side, giving him a disgruntled snort. "Can we talk about anything other than that right now?"

"After you promise you will come to me if you need assistance."

I pulled back, tugging the sheets over my chest

as I sat up, and frowned at him. His pointed look as he curled his arm under his head and stared back gave me the courage to say exactly what I was thinking.

"Fine. I promise—" Royce's triumphant smirk faded when he realized I was tagging my own stipulation onto the deal. "—*if* you promise you'll stop trying to blackmail or manipulate me every time you want something."

His smile became more genuine. "Is that all?"

I thought about it. "You're also going to answer some questions. I'm tired of being scared and left in the dark. I hardly know anything about you. I want that to change."

"A reasonable request. Agreed."

"Good. Then I have something to ask right now." He nodded for me to continue. "What the hell is with the futon?"

He blinked. Then another slow smile spread, followed by a chuckle. "I suppose you were expecting some vast acreage of satin sheets and mounds of pillows, hmm?"

I knew I was turning red, could feel the heat blossoming in my cheeks, but I folded my arms, and gave him a raised eyebrow while waiting for him to answer. "Maybe I was. You're not some college frat boy who can't afford better, and every other piece of personal property of yours I've seen, from your clothes to your office—offices—whatever—practically screams 'look at me, I have more money than God!' So, explain it to me. Make me understand this piece of you."

He'd lived up to a number of vampire stereotypes in our previous encounters, being broody and dark and mysterious—but I knew there was more to him than that. The odd choice of furniture was one piece of the puzzle that didn't fit, and I thought it might be a safe place to start learning more about the real man hiding behind the mask of a monster. From the looks of things, he didn't mind my prying, either. He rolled onto his back and folded both hands under his head, giving me a boyish grin and an excellent view of the scars ranging across the toned muscles of his chest.

"Yes, I lived up to the cliché. Up until recently, I had the huge bed and all the necessary accessories to make this place a suitable haven to live out every imaginable debauched and depraved sexual fantasy that I desired." As hard as it was, I kept my gaze steady on his, even though I was pretty sure I was about to ignite from my own embarrassment. "Do you know, less than a year ago, a woman—a human woman—reminded me how very important it was to value my freedom and humanity?"

I was getting an inkling that he was referring to me, but I still didn't see what that had to do with his futon or the sexcapades he was referring to. I'm sure he gathered I was confused. As he continued speaking, he rolled onto his hands and knees and crept toward me. I laid back as he approached, a teensy bit apprehensive about the predatory nature of his movements; he didn't stop until he was positioned above me.

"A very brave and foolish girl saved me from the very fate I had subjected countless others to. She freed me from what could have been lifetimes of slavery to someone who cared nothing for who or what I was. And while she could have taken that artifact and used me for her own ends, she did not. Though I wished that she would let me do something to show her how thankful I was for showing me such mercy, she would not have me."

I bit my lip and pressed my palm to his cheek, not sure what to say to this strange confession of his. He was still smiling, so I knew he wasn't angry with me, but it was surreal to hear him talk about me like I was some brilliant savior. Considering how little I knew about his world, that could be taken as very flattering, or very alarming.

"When I saw how humbly she lived, it served as a reminder of who I really was and where I came from. A futon is not quite the same as the bedding from my home on the farm when I was human, but it serves as an adequate reminder. Every night—from the moment I wake, and again, before I take my day's rest—I am reminded that despite all of the luxuries available to me, they are not to come at the expense of another's freedom. That there is no shame in taking the weak and making them strong." He leaned in to kiss and nip at a spot that nearly had me come off the bed. ". . . and, perhaps now I can get that great big bed back and keep you close instead. What do you think? Will you remind me when I should show mercy?"

"If you keep doing that thing with your tongue." I tangled my fingers in his hair, gasping when he repeated the motion. "I'll . . . I'll . . ."

He paused, glancing up at me with a fangy grin and raised brows. "You'll what?"

I laughed and pushed him back. "I'll think of something. Don't stop!"

And after that, he didn't.

Books by Bestselling Author
Fern Michaels

___	**The Jury**	0-8217-7878-1	$6.99US/$9.99CAN
___	**Sweet Revenge**	0-8217-7879-X	$6.99US/$9.99CAN
___	**Lethal Justice**	0-8217-7880-3	$6.99US/$9.99CAN
___	**Free Fall**	0-8217-7881-1	$6.99US/$9.99CAN
___	**Fool Me Once**	0-8217-8071-9	$7.99US/$10.99CAN
___	**Vegas Rich**	0-8217-8112-X	$7.99US/$10.99CAN
___	**Hide and Seek**	1-4201-0184-6	$6.99US/$9.99CAN
___	**Hokus Pokus**	1-4201-0185-4	$6.99US/$9.99CAN
___	**Fast Track**	1-4201-0186-2	$6.99US/$9.99CAN
___	**Collateral Damage**	1-4201-0187-0	$6.99US/$9.99CAN
___	**Final Justice**	1-4201-0188-9	$6.99US/$9.99CAN
___	**Up Close and Personal**	0-8217-7956-7	$7.99US/$9.99CAN
___	**Under the Radar**	1-4201-0683-X	$6.99US/$9.99CAN
___	**Razor Sharp**	1-4201-0684-8	$7.99US/$10.99CAN
___	**Yesterday**	1-4201-1494-8	$5.99US/$6.99CAN
___	**Vanishing Act**	1-4201-0685-6	$7.99US/$10.99CAN
___	**Sara's Song**	1-4201-1493-X	$5.99US/$6.99CAN
___	**Deadly Deals**	1-4201-0686-4	$7.99US/$10.99CAN
___	**Game Over**	1-4201-0687-2	$7.99US/$10.99CAN
___	**Sins of Omission**	1-4201-1153-1	$7.99US/$10.99CAN
___	**Sins of the Flesh**	1-4201-1154-X	$7.99US/$10.99CAN
___	**Cross Roads**	1-4201-1192-2	$7.99US/$10.99CAN

Available Wherever Books Are Sold!
Check out our website at **www.kensingtonbooks.com**